LETHBRIDGE-STEWART

A MOST HAUNTED MAN

Sarah Groenewegen

CANDY JAR BOOKS · CARDIFF
2022

For all the school teachers and support staff
battling the odds to make a positive difference in people's lives.

The right of Sarah Groenewegen to be identified as the Author of the Work has been asserted by her in accordance with the Copyright, Designs and Patents Act 1988.

A Most Haunted Man © Sarah Groenewegen 2022

Characters from The Web of Fear
© Hannah Haisman & Henry Lincoln 1968, 2022
Lethbridge-Stewart: The Series
© Andy Frankham-Allen & Shaun Russell 2014, 2022

Brendon Public School first appeared in the
Doctor Who serial *Mawdryn Undead*

Doctor Who is © British Broadcasting Corporation, 1963, 2022

ISBN: 978-1-915439-05-5

Range Editor: Andy Frankham-Allen
Editor: Shaun Russell
Editorial: Keren Williams
Licensed by Hannah Haisman
Cover by Martin Baines & Will Brooks

Printed and bound in the UK by
Severn, Bristol Road, Gloucester, GL2 5EU

Published by
Candy Jar Books
Mackintosh House
136 Newport Road, Cardiff, CF24 1DJ
www.candyjarbooks.co.uk

PROLOGUE

THE SULPHUR burned up his nostrils, and his throat constricted to stop the poisons getting in any further. He doubled over and spasmed in a series of coughs, like his lungs demanded to escape.

His whole body burned as he stumbled about.

He squeezed his eyes shut against the fumes. Blinded by the toxic air, he couldn't get a sense of direction. He couldn't recall his location, how and why. Nothing made any sense except the drive to get out. He had to get away from the fire.

Cool air brushed his face. He gulped at it. A mistake. He gagged and spluttered. Tasted blood. Spat it out.

He staggered towards the cool air, his arms outstretched as though his hands could grip it. He clutched for any lifeline out of whatever hell he floundered in.

Hell. Fire. Brimstone.

Embers caught on his trousers. They burned through and bit his leg. He brushed them away and they stung his hands.

The cold fingers of fresh air caught his face again. They curled around his neck and pulled him forward.

He collapsed down to his knees, then sprawled down on the floor. He breathed in and filled his lungs with cooler, cleaner air. Coughed. Cleaner did not mean clean.

He scrabbled forward. Ghosts of men shouted at him to move. To get the hell out of... hell. Their voices fell into a rhythm, a cadence. His body moved to it. That and a drumbeat. His heart. A strange, discordant set of sounds. Wild. Frightening. Exhilarating. The sound of battle. Blood in his ears.

Ba-doom. Ba-doom.

It quickened with his pulse.

He scrambled through the dirt beneath him. Scrambled towards the cool air. Away from the fire. Under the blanket of the toxic smoke.

A crack and a roar rushed over him.

An alarm bell rang.

His heartbeat joined another. His raced, beat out its rhythm at double time. The other beat at exactly half the speed of his. Calm. At rest.

He wanted to pause, to puzzle over the sounds. To rest his limbs, to recover his breath, but the ghost men shouted. Old mentors.

'Get up, man. Get out.'

He grunted. Heaved himself up to his hands and knees and pushed himself forward. Everything glowed red. Everything rumbled or roared.

The two heartbeats merged.

He shivered as the cold fingers and hands caressed his head and back. Water drenched him. The noises deafened him. Roaring. Crashing. The alarm bells. The shouting. A terrible crack in slowed-down time. The heartbeats not quite aligned. The heartbeats he felt more than heard.

He bundled up all of his muscles for one more heave forward, but then the whole world crashed down around him.

CHAPTER ONE

Tower Block Inferno

JACQUIE ARMSTRONG woke with her alarm clock. She batted it off, then stretched and yawned. Sunlight glinted through a gap in her curtains and dappled on her ceiling.

Down in the kitchen below, the local BBC radio station burbled the news. The coffee grinder drowned out the serious voice of the newsreader. Not that it mattered. They would only be spouting rubbish about the Tories. Two weeks to the election and Jacquie wished it was all over already.

She got up and dressed in blue jeans and a black t-shirt with The Who's logo bold in red, white and blue. After visiting the bathroom, she clattered down the stairs and grabbed a slice of bread as it sprang from the toaster. She layered butter and strawberry jam on it, sliced it in half and bit into it.

Her father lowered his broadsheet and frowned. 'That was your mother's.'

Jacquie shrugged, but she turned and put another slice of bread into the machine. She cocked her head and heard no evidence her mother stirred. She didn't turn the machine on.

'Do you have your paper round today?'

Her eyebrows arched. 'Is the Pope Catholic?'

'No need for that insolence, young lady.' He rattled the paper he hid behind.

She heaved a sigh. 'Yes, Father. It's the hols, which is when I do the paper round each weekday as well as the usual Saturday.' She finished her toast. 'Can I have a coffee?'

'No, you may not. There's orange juice.' He turned the page of his newspaper. 'And it's "may I" not "can I".'

She mouthed what he said back to him, but she poured herself a glass of juice anyway. She drained it in one go. Upstairs, her mother shuffled to the bathroom. Jacquie lowered the bread in the toaster to start it cooking.

'Right. I'll be off. I'm seeing my friends at the park afterwards, and possibly going to Molly's in the afternoon. We've got a geography project to do.' She skittered down the hall, picked up her blue denim jacket and shrugged it on.

'Don't forget your coat.'

'I won't.' She checked her pocket for change and her keys, then left.

She grabbed her bicycle from the shed beside the garage and rode to Mr Patel's where she collected her sack of newspapers. She pedalled around her route through the suburban streets and delivered the papers to their respective homes. Done, she collected her wages for the week from Mrs Patel and scored an earful from the old woman about how wonderful everything would be if the Conservatives won the upcoming election. Jacquie nodded along, but as she pedalled away she fumed. 'They hate people like you, you daft old cow.'

Contrary to what she told her father earlier, she headed out of their suburban dullsville to the patch of countryside that clung on between them and a poverty-stricken housing estate. Specifically, she headed to a hill of green, crowned by a gleaming white obelisk. Contrary to their parents' wishes, she had an appointment with her brother, stuck boarding at the school that owned the hill, despite it being the Easter break.

Brigadier Alistair Lethbridge-Stewart woke with a start. His alarm clock rattled and shook on his bedside table behind a book he was struggling through. A whimsical thing, badly written, about a hyperspace bypass threatening the earth. He'd confiscated the advance copy from one of his students who had it from an uncle who worked at the publisher. He nearly knocked it flying when he thumped at the clock with a heavy arm.

The smell of sulphur hung for a few moments in the air, and he swore he heard his own heartbeat, doubled with another's, echoing in his ears. He sat up and glanced around his bachelor's quarters. With a heavy sigh, he stood up.

He shivered.

The dream he woke from lingered. In the dream, he couldn't see anything but a red glow. His other senses stepped up, and his waking versions all reacted as though he actually experienced it. The noises, the awful burning smells and tastes. The crash. The rawness in his nose and throat. He touched his forehead gingerly and ran his fingers to the back of his head and neck. He examined his fingers, wet with sweat. Not blood.

He rumbled a laugh. 'Just a dream.' But, he did need a haircut.

He shuffled through his normal morning routine, opting for a sports jacket to wear rather than his suit jacket. He also opted to have breakfast in the school dining hall. With most of the students and some of the teaching staff away, it would be tolerable.

On entering, he saw the boys had already abandoned the room to five teachers and the dinner lady, Alice. She saw him, smiled, and went to get him a cup of tea. She carried it to him as he settled with his plate laden with a cooked English next to Henry Grey, who taught History. Grey's copy of *The Echo* lay on the table between them, folded neatly to reveal the crossword puzzles. All but a few squares contained Grey's confident letters. The cryptic puzzle contained more blank spaces than completed.

Ms Peters bustled in and sat opposite the Brigadier. She made a show of opening her copy of *The Sentinel* over her bowl of cereal. He saw nothing of interest on the front or back pages.

'I say, Brigadier.'

He turned his attention to the History teacher. 'What? Sorry. Miles away.'

Grey grunted. Peters noisily turned a page of her paper.

'You should be able to guess this one.' Grey pushed his paper closer to the Brigadier and stabbed a finger at a clue for the cryptic puzzle. 'Dante's reformist. Seven letters.'

His lips dried, but the Brigadier managed to croak, 'Inferno.'

'What's the matter? You look like you've seen a ghost.' Grey leaned back in his seat, his eyebrows up.

Peters lowered her paper and peered over it at the Brigadier. Mrs Young, who taught English, blinked across at him.

He swallowed and shook his head. 'No, no. Fighting fit.' He pointed at the clue. 'Inferno is the answer.'

Alice arrived and took his empty plate and cup. 'Another tea, sir?'

He shook his head. 'No, thank you. I'd better go see what's what.'

*

Jacquie met her brother Jack at the obelisk on the hill that overlooked Brendon Public School. He wore the same outfit she did, and they sported the same hairstyle. Rare to have identical twins of different sexes, but not impossible. She and he embodied the near impossible.

Jack sat on the grass, his legs outstretched and his head back against the obelisk. As Jacquie neared, she saw his eyes were closed and he breathed as though asleep. She picked an early flower and flung it under his nose while she flopped down to sit beside him. He spluttered, coughed, and sneezed all at the same time.

'Hey, hey.'

'Whatcha.' He sneezed again.

'My holiday job is so dull.'

'At least you can get out and about. I hate being stuck here at the school.'

Jacquie snorted and waved her hands around. 'It's hardly Wormwood bloody Scrubs is it.'

'It's the principle of the thing.' Jack straightened up and turned to face her. 'It wasn't my fault, but they've got it in for me. I can't even go home for Easter Sunday for lunch, and we're within spitting distance. It's not like Alfie. I mean, he was the one who exchanged the chemicals that turned what should have been a good rocket show into a damp squib. I only noticed the switcheroo and complained.' He slumped back against the obelisk. He picked at the grass and threw the blades away. 'I hate this place. It's not even as though the rugger team is any good.'

Jacquie regarded her twin after his outburst. She scratched the back of her head. 'So, that was the excuse.'

'What?'

'I earwigged the olds talking about what to do over Easter to keep us apart. Father said his company didn't make as much money as they thought it would, which meant he got less pay, or something. I missed some of what they said because they were playing music.'

'What are you on about?'

She slapped his knee. 'Shh. I'm talking. Anyway, Father said it meant they had to cancel sending you away now so they could still send you away for the summer.'

'Summer? Seriously? The whole seven weeks?'

'I think so, yes.' Jacquie folded her arms. 'I'll be the one stuck at home with them, like always.'

Jack ripped up a clump of grass and tossed it. 'It's not fair.'

'Oi! You boys.' A man called out from halfway down the hill. Jacquie squinted at him. 'I think it's your maths teacher.'

Jack swore under his breath. 'The Brigadier. If he sees you...'

'He already has.'

As the Brigadier approached them, Jack leapt up to his feet and brushed himself down. Jacquie stayed sitting down. She'd seen the old soldier before at her brother's school on official visits with their parents. That was before their olds did their all to split the twins up.

'Ah. Mr Armstrong. Who's your friend?'

Jack squirmed and didn't answer.

Jacquie stood up, smiled, and held out her hand. 'I'm his sister, sir. I don't think we've had the pleasure. My name is Jacqueline, but everyone calls me Jacquie. How do you do?'

The Brigadier shook her hand with a pleasant grip. His eyebrows danced upwards in an endearing way for an older man. 'I have seen you before, though, haven't I?'

She shrugged, cocked her head, and kept her smile up.

'Even though it is the school holidays, this is private property.'

Jacquie scrunched her face up. 'Well, sir, technically the obelisk marks the boundary of the school and public right of way neighbouring the grounds.'

The Brigadier frowned.

'I don't have the relevant map with me, sir, but it is available for viewing at the public lending library.'

'That may be, young lady.' The Brigadier straightened up, puffed his chest out, and set his chin. 'However, your brother was denied permission to leave the school grounds by agreement between the headmaster and your parents. You both may well be obeying the letter of the law, but it's hardly observing the spirit. Mr Armstrong, come with me, please.'

Jacquie's mouth hung open.

Jack's head angled down to the grass, his shoulders hunched over, and his hands dug deeply into his jeans pockets. He kicked at a clump of grass.

Jacquie spluttered. 'It's not a law.'

The former soldier smiled a cat-eating-cream smile. 'Oh,

young lady, I think you'll find that the Education Act allows schools such as Brendon a degree of autonomy over its students who are under leaving age, especially when parents or guardians are in agreement. Come on, Mr Armstrong, unless you would like to spend the entirety of Easter confined to quarters.'

Jacquie stared at the teacher who turned around to march back down the hill again. She reached out to her brother and flashed a quick message on her fingers in their old sign language. He nodded, and signed back that they would meet up later.

'Armstrong.'

'Coming, sir.'

Jacquie watched the two figures as they trooped to the main clump of buildings that housed the school. She narrowed her eyes as she ran through a few options for revenge.

Sanctimonious so-and-so. He might have been a soldier once, but by the look of him his fighting days were a long time ago.

The Brigadier deposited Jack Armstrong with two other boys who remained at the school over the holidays. He told Armstrong it would be a productive use of his time to revise his maths before the next term began.

The boy's work intrigued him with its inconsistencies. Not quite enough to suspect cheating but, now he thought of it, that genie refused to return to her bottle.

He resumed his patrol of the grounds and found nothing else untoward. Returning to his quarters, he tidied up the obvious mess, and settled to read more of the novel he'd confiscated. He worked through a chapter and fell into a doze.

Jack waited half an hour after lights out before he got out of his bed. No one else slept in his dorm room during the holidays. He huffed at the unfairness of it all as he put the pillows under the blankets to fool anyone looking in.

The full moon and nearly cloudless night gave plenty of light, but he took his torch with him. He slid open the window and climbed out. Practice allowed him to find each foot and handhold without having to look, and no one patrolled the school grounds. As he trotted up the lane towards the estate, he kept an eye and ear out in case anyone pursued him.

Up ahead, lights blazed in the forecourt and playgrounds of

the tower blocks. Jacquie sat on one of the swings, lazily moving back and forth. Other kids, and a few adults, grouped around, but avoided getting too close. He grinned, picked up his pace, and whistled *Livin' Thing*. Jacquie joined in. One of the groups of kids backed away to give them both more space.

She stopped whistling. 'Hey, hey.'

He sat on the swing next to hers. 'Whatcha.'

'He didn't give you grief, did he?' Jacquie meant the strap, or birch, or whichever they chose to thwack them.

'Nah.'

'Detention?'

'I'm not to go beyond the school grounds. He only had me work through his maths classes from last term. He didn't check it, but. He condescended to tell me it was for my own good.'

'What would he know?'

Jack shrugged. He glanced at his sister and grinned. He launched himself on the swing to go as high as he could. Beside him, Jacquie howled like a wolf and joined him. He howled, too.

The kids and adults slunk off into the night. A breeze whipped up. Paper, cardboard boxes and cans rattled about. Jack slowed, in sync with his sister. They stopped. The clouds covered the full moon and rain drops fell in a fine mist. Jacquie jumped off her swing and raced to the locked-up community centre. Jack followed. She picked the locks and they both slipped inside.

They kept the main lights off. The light of the glass-fronted fridge and the snack machine glowed brightly enough for them to see by. Jacquie yanked two chairs from the table tops where they'd been put to help the cleaners. She placed the plastic seats in front of the snack machine and straddled one, her folded-up arms rested on the chair's back.

'I want to teach your maths teacher a lesson.'

'I want to know why our olds want to split us up.'

'That's easy. We scare them. Always have. They think we're like twin versions of Carrie.'

'Is that a guess, or for real?'

'For real. I've heard them say it when they didn't know I was there. I've even heard Mother tell people she regretted not splitting us up as babies and adopting out one or both of us. Only both them and the world were in shock because of JFK's assassination, and it all got complicated. It's been a source of consternation for the olds ever since.'

'So I'm in boarding school and you're stuck with them.'

'Stuck with them, yes, but luckily not too far from you. Our olds are stupid and slow, otherwise...'

'...we couldn't do this.'

They both howled, full-throated yowls with their heads thrown back. Finished, they laughed. Jack stopped when he doubled over, a stitch digging into his side.

'I am so bored.'

Jack glanced at his sister. He stood up and crossed to the cigarette vending machine that stood next to the snack machine. 'One of the lads said there's a trick to getting free packs out of these.'

'I'd rather some chocolate.'

'Different type of machine.'

Jack stood at the squat machine and racked his memory for what the Toad told them. Something about wiring and the power could trip and trick it into thinking money had been fed into it. All the electrics would be at the back of it. He squared his shoulders, squatted so his arms reached around the machine, and he heaved it around to an angle.

Sparks flew. He swore. Jacquie squealed and backed up. Jack fell over backwards and twisted away from the machine as it toppled over. He shook his head. Clambered up to his feet and leaned over the exposed back that fizzed and popped. He reached a hand out to move a loose panel, but Jacquie batted his hand away.

'It's live. You'll fry.'

'Someone else has tampered with it.'

'What do you expect in a dump like this?' She sighed, long and loud, righted her chair and sat back down.

'Shouldn't we put it back?'

She looked at him. 'Two things. You moved it, we didn't. Second, not on your life should we touch it, no. I want you to think of ways to get back at your maths teacher for disrespecting you. Or, are you okay with it?'

Jack sat back in his chair after he moved it opposite hers. He held up his hands in surrender. 'Okay. What are you thinking?'

They played their favourite hand-clapping game. Jacquie aired her suggestions, and they both riffed off them. They settled on one, and worked through the finer points.

Jacquie yawned. 'Better scarper.'

They bumped their fists together and left the community centre to return to where they lived. As Jack crawled back into his bed, he heard sirens in the distance. He sat up. Listened, but they remained distant. No fire at the school. He settled back and sighed.

The Brigadier tossed and turned in his bed, his unconscious mind gripped by the same nightmare from the night before. The heat, the smell, the noise – all squeezed around him as he desperately struggled to escape a veritable inferno.

Ringing in his ears woke him. He shook his head as though it would clear the effects of the nightmare. He groped for his telephone and answered it.

Mr Newton, the headmaster, squawked something about a fire in the estate nearby and could he check that all the boys who should be in the school were, in fact, in the school.

The Brigadier woke fully and affirmed his task. He pulled on his clothes and shoes in double-time. Outside his quarters he looked up and saw the terrible red-orange glow in the clouds. He raced to the dormitories and checked each one, entering each room and double-checking the shapes under the covers. He knew that trick well enough from when he slept at barracks and men went AWOL for a night out. A few of the boys woke and muttered. Armstrong's hair was damp, but the boy might have taken a late shower. He told them all to go back to sleep.

Downstairs, he assured Mr Newton that all the boys were present and correct.

'Good. It's a terrible thing. One of the tower blocks must be ablaze if we can see it from here.'

'Why did you think one of the boys might be there?'

'You know how they can be, but in this case the police called. One of the residents said they thought they saw one of our boys there earlier tonight.'

CHAPTER TWO
After-Image

WITH A bounce in his step, and Mr Newton's approval, the Brigadier left the school grounds and made his way to the nearby housing estate. He kept an eye on the awful orange-red glow in the clouds as it loomed large. As he rounded a bend, he stared at the flames and dark billowing clouds of smoke belching from one of the tower blocks. Blue and red lights strobed from multiple emergency vehicles. He found a place out of the way to park and abandoned the car to join a group of police officers. He introduced himself to a constable and asked to see his superior officer. He registered the doubt in the young man's expression, but the constable nodded and headed off.

'Terrible business,' the Brigadier addressed the other police officers.

'It is, but at least there's no reported casualties so far.'

'Really? That is a relief.'

'Aye. The building manager told us that block and the community centre were both closed for fumigation.'

Another officer shifted his feet. 'Of course, there might have been people ignoring the order, which is why we have to stick around. That and crowd control.'

All of the officers sniggered.

The constable returned, accompanied by a woman in a sharp suit and impeccable mac. In the flashing lights, her face fractured, but he saw no nonsense in the way she held herself. She offered her hand. They shook. Her grip was tight and didn't linger. 'I'm DI Hayes. What can I do for you?'

'Brigadier Lethbridge-Stewart, retired.' He indicated they should move away from the cluster of police. Other police, he corrected himself.

He followed the detective inspector as she strode a few yards away and found shelter in a doorway to another of the tower blocks.

'I'm now a teacher at Brendon Public School. The grounds run up against that of this estate.'

'I see. Aren't you on holidays?'

'We are, but some of our boys need to board with us even now. I understand someone reported one of our students here.'

She nodded.

'Maybe I can help.'

'Do you think your student was responsible for this?'

The Brigadier frowned. 'No, I don't. Everyone who's meant to be at the school is, but we have concerns about the one seen here earlier. They aren't supposed to leave the school grounds without permission.'

'I see.'

'Look, Inspector, I only came here to offer our help.'

A fireman called across to Hayes. She waved at the man before turning back to the Brigadier. 'Chances are your lad had nothing to do with this, but it does look like arson. If you want to help, stay out of our way and that of the fire brigade. You can see Mr Weller, the estate manager. He's up that way. He might be able to tell you more.' She gestured across to the remaining tower blocks.

The Brigadier thanked her with a curt nod and half-smile. She strode away from him towards the fireman. The Brigadier stood for a few moments to watch the streams of water pummel the fire roaring up the building. The smell of burning plastics stung his eyes and throat. He turned away and made for the place the police officer suggested he should try.

He found a man sitting on the low brick wall near an entrance to one of the tower blocks. He hunched into his cast-off army jacket and looked down at his boots that needed a good polish. The Brigadier cleared his throat and the man looked up at him. The Brigadier introduced himself.

'Are you Mr Weller?'

The man nodded. 'What can I do for you?'

'The Headmaster of Brendon School, Mr Newton, offers our help to tidy up, and whatever else might be needed.'

13

'That's kind.' Weller shrugged deeper into his jacket. 'I'll have to talk to the council about it.'

'Of course.' The Brigadier glanced behind him to the blaze. 'Do you know what happened?'

'Naw. The plod reckons it's arson, but there's no motive for that. Nothing credible, at any rate. The fire brigade reckons it started in the community centre, which is attached to the block. It's totally gone now.'

'I understand no one's been hurt.'

'Apparently so. Everyone was supposed to be out to avoid a bug spray, but it's still destroyed everything they owned that they didn't have with them. It's devastating.'

'Maybe we can help replace some of their things? Essentials, at least.'

A crash deafened them. Both looked over and saw part of the tower block collapse. The Brigadier shuddered. He glanced back at Weller.

'I'll be in touch with you next week. Is here best?'

Weller nodded. 'I live on the ground floor in C-block.' He shivered. 'It's marked *Caretaker*.'

Another crash spurred the Brigadier back to his car. As he dodged the police, a gust of wind blasted from the burning building. He reached his car, unlocked it, and the smells of ash hit him. He slumped forward on the steering wheel, his eyes closed against a rush of intense heat. He shook his head. Opened his eyes and saw the night lit up with emergency services lights. Damp ash spattered across his windscreen. He activated the wipers, which brushed the worst of it away. His heart raced and he gripped the steering wheel for a few moments to calm down.

The roar from the flames flared in his ears and he shook his head once more. 'Get a grip, man.'

The Easter bank holidays passed without incident, and while Jacquie enjoyed a further week off school, her olds returned to work. At one o'clock, by the church tower, Jacquie set off to the estate by the public pathway. The smell of dust and ash, and damp, teased a volley of sneezes from her as she emerged into the estate. The community centre no longer existed beyond the rectangle of burned-up rubble. Only a charred

14

skeleton of the tower block remained, like the pictures she'd seen of bombed-out London and Coventry. Soot blackened parts of the other tower blocks, and the asphalted playground. Broken glass lay scattered everywhere. Common sense would keep kids out of their play space, surely. Police signs tied to a ridiculous bit of fence reinforced the message for those who might need it. No kids played. No one else stood or sat about. She heard people noises through and up towards two of the other blocks.

Jack sauntered into view from the lane that led past his school. He whistled a tune she didn't recognise. He paused. Looked about. Wolf-whistled.

She waved. He approached. 'Hey, hey.'

'Whatcha.' Jack turned. 'Quite a scene.'

'Do you think we caused it?'

'How?'

'That machine.'

'Was damaged before we touched it.' Jack scowled. 'We all got the third degree because someone here is a grass.'

'But they haven't grassed you up.'

He shrugged. Turned to look at her. Grinned. She grinned back. They made fists and bounced them off each other.

Jacquie outlined her plans to him and smiled as he grinned at it.

Jack put his hands in his trouser pockets. 'Could you do it for a full day?'

She shook her head. 'There's the time either side, so I don't get missed at my school. We would have to synchronise timetables, too.' She pushed a bit of ashy broken glass with the toe of her trainer. 'Unless you want to be me for a day?'

'What, and wear a dress?'

'I have to.'

'Maybe a nice dress, but your uniform is horrid.'

Jacquie placed her hand on his arm. 'Welcome to the patriarchy, my son.'

The Brigadier saw Armstrong stroll past on his way to the dining hall. He picked up his own pace to catch up, but the boy hailed one of the other boys and they disappeared inside. The Brigadier turned towards his quarters to have his supper there to avoid the hall and its smells and noise. If duty didn't dictate his presence that evening, then he wouldn't be there. Pudding, on the other hand, might tempt him back.

Half an hour later, he strode to the hall where Alice served pudding. Apple pie, cream or custard. Or both, as some of the boys opted for. He chose custard.

He paused by the table where Armstrong sat. 'Mr Armstrong. I didn't see you about today. Everything all right?'

The boy twisted around in his seat, but he didn't stand up. The Brigadier quashed his irritation at the slight.

'I was in the library, sir.'

'I didn't see you there.' The smell of smoke teased at the Brigadier's nostrils.

'I also went for a run, sir.'

The Brigadier sniffed. The source of the smoky-scent eluded him. 'Right you are then. Good, good.' He left the boy to it, and purposefully didn't round on him and his friends when they sniggered.

He joined Mr Newton and Ms Peters. Peters lifted her head when Newton nodded.

'Everything okay with those boys, Brigadier?'

'I believe so, Mr Newton. I just hadn't seen young Armstrong all day. He said he was at the library and went for a run.'

'You sound sceptical.'

'He hasn't showered and smells of smoke.'

'Cigarettes?'

'No.'

'The estate.' Newton sighed.

'I suspect so.'

'Do you think he's the one who was seen up there?'

'I'm not sure, no. The description the police have is vague, and doesn't really fit the boy.'

Newton steepled his hands. 'He is a good lad from a decent family, although vulnerable to being led astray. At least here he's not mixing with a bad crowd.'

'His twin sister, you mean.' Ms Peters frowned.

The Brigadier raised his eyebrows. 'What's the story there? I understand from Miss Nugent they are to be kept apart.'

'She is the trouble-maker of the pair, by all accounts,' Mr Newton said. 'Too smart for her own good. The family wanted to board her at a prestigious and strict school in Scotland, I believe. Somewhere north, anyway. The economy put paid to that idea.'

'If she's so bright, what about a scholarship?'

'Well, that's the thing. She failed the exams. Deliberately. We therefore have to do our best to keep them separated from each other to limit the risk of trouble.' Newton huffed as the boys got up and left. 'I'll have a quiet word with young Mr Armstrong to see if he did leave the grounds at all.'

'Thank you.' The Brigadier ate his pudding and passed on his appreciation to Alice.

As he headed out to return to his digs, he caught a wave of the smell of smoke that made him stagger. He reached out to grab hold of a bannister to the grand staircase, missed, and toppled forward. Flames licked at him. Burned. Sweat drenched and boiled on his skin and through his clothes. The smell and toxic taste made him gag and retch. He clawed at the floor. Eyes shut tight against the burning and stinging. The roaring in his ears dulled the sounds of crashes and cracking.

'Get up! Get up! Be a man!'

One eye burned with a different sort of pain. Like it had been crushed, or stabbed, or shot out.

'Sir! Sir!' A boy called out. He stank of stale smoke.

Someone else grabbed his arm. Mr Newton. The Brigadier groaned and he struggled to sit up. He touched his sore eye and blinked.

Someone – Peters – pressed a glass of water to his mouth. He grabbed at it. Drank. Nodded his thanks.

'I'm all right. Really. I'm all right.' He stood and made a show of pointing out where a rug had gathered up. 'How many times have I told the boys to check the rugs and smooth them out if they've gathered like this?'

Armstrong and the other boys backed away. None of them dared to protest what the maths teacher said.

To Mr Newton, the Brigadier said, 'I'm fine.'

That night, the dream caught the Brigadier and refused to free

17

him. This time he got out of the cave and into the open air. Warm air pressed him down into mud and mulch. Helicopters thundered overhead. He coughed up mucus and each cough stripped his throat raw.

He woke, drenched in sweat, his heart pounding. He grabbed his bedside lamp and switched it on. The familiar faces of his family and friends smiled down from the walls. He sat up and cradled his head in his hands.

The dream haunted him. Clawed at him with hot, smoky talons that sank into his flesh. He couldn't shake the weird sensations. The double heartbeat. The burning smells. The roaring. The sweat and blood. The voices telling him to stay awake, to get up. The roar and shake of a helicopter.

He forced himself to open his eyes and look up. To look around. Echoes of his therapist from two years ago elbowed away the urgent voices.

'You've had a nasty shock, Brigadier. That's why you have amnesia. It's temporary memory loss. You will recover and it will pass.'

Poppycock, he thundered at the time. Only his memory *did* skip and jump over things. It took him a while to recall all those he knew in his life. Even the pictures in his digs included people he no longer knew.

The ghostly voice reminded him he'd been under pressure, switching from one job to another, neither easy. Letting his struggles fester without any release meant it built up inside him until it exploded. To prevent such a thing from happening again meant he needed to recognise the signs and take steps to release it.

'You'd do the same in a military situation, wouldn't you?'

He conceded the point. Took the card with the details of the clinic that would help if he needed it again. He put the card in a safe place.

He got up and crossed to his desk. He rooted through the drawers and finally found what he looked for. He placed the card near his telephone. He checked the time. A few minutes before four. He didn't think he would be able to sleep again, and his duty at the school took up most of the morning.

After lunch, the Brigadier wearily picked up the card and

debated if he should call. He yawned. Shuddered and touched his forehead above his eye. He dialled, spoke to a receptionist and booked an appointment for that afternoon. A cancellation. It would take him an hour to drive there, so he had time for a cup of strong tea.

He enjoyed the drive on the open roads. Even the motorway didn't faze him, but the outskirts of London's metropolis did. He avoided a few prangs and finally broke through the stop-start of a traffic jam. At the clinic, he found a place to park. He tapped his fingers on the steering wheel as he contemplated the wisdom of being in this place. A bunch of silly dreams. He'd faced worse. He had faced worse than talking to a therapist before, too.

With a final slap of his hands on the wheel, he got out and locked the car.

He strode towards the reception of the clinic that took both out and in patients. A private practice, but his insurance would cover it.

Inside, he expected the typical smells of a modern hospital to match the clinical decor. Instead, he smelled roses. A light scent. Sweet. He saw the bunch in a vase and he smiled.

'Can I help you, sir?'

The Brigadier crossed to the young woman at the reception desk. He introduced himself. 'I called for an appointment.'

'Oh, yes, of course, Mr Lethbridge-Stewart.'

'Brigadier.'

A look of horror flashed across her face. She apologised. 'Not everyone is forthright about their service, sir.' She checked her book. 'I'm sorry, sir, but the doctor you saw last time is unavailable. Dr Pelham-Rose is filling in.'

'Rose?' His eyebrow quirked upwards.

The receptionist smiled. 'Yes. She brings them in from her garden.'

'She?'

'Is that a problem?' Her tone hardened.

'No, it isn't.' He smiled.

'Take a seat. It shouldn't be too long to wait.'

The Brigadier thanked her and took a step towards the waiting area. Down the corridor to his right a door opened.

A man with great walrus sideburns shuffled with two walking sticks towards the reception area. Behind him fluttered a butterfly with diaphanous wings. A woman, smaller in stature than she looked from her kaftan and wild gestures. She hid her hair under a towering turban of the same pinks, oranges and browns as her clothes.

The Brigadier's eyes widened as he stepped back to allow the older man to hobble past to the door. The woman-butterfly wished the old man well, then she turned with a wide smile to the Brigadier and the receptionist. The receptionist confirmed what the Brigadier suspected. The woman was Dr Pelham-Rose. They shook hands.

'Come through, come through.' She waved him forward. She collected a folder from the receptionist and followed him. 'Door's open. Take a seat. Tea or coffee? Or water? Nothing stronger, I'm afraid. Not now, at any rate.'

She shut the door behind them and pressed the 'do not disturb' sign. She swept up her kaftan and sank into a plush armchair opposite an equally plush sofa. As the Brigadier sat down on the sofa in his habitually neat way, she opened the file and skim-read it. She lowered it. 'Thank you for your service.'

He raised both of his eyebrows.

'It's something they say in America. I quite like it, if it's meant sincerely. I meant it sincerely, by the way. How would you prefer me to address you?'

'I, um. Brigadier is what people usually use now.'

She nodded, and dropped the folder onto the coffee table between them. 'Tea, then? Real tea, not herbal.'

He smiled and nodded. She picked up a box on the table and pressed a switch. She spoke their order for a pot of tea.

'You've been here before?'

'Two years ago, yes.' He shifted in his seat. 'I was an in-patient for a few weeks or thereabouts. I don't remember much about it, to be honest.'

'The notes say trauma-induced amnesia. General trauma, built up over a long time.'

He cleared his throat.

She beamed a smile that lit her whole body. 'Our body's responses are not under our control. Anything might have triggered it, and the trigger may have very little to do with the cause. One thing I must reassure you about. This practice specialises in situations like yours where you've had a career in a highly sensitive area.' She tapped the side of her nose. 'I hold a security clearance, but more importantly I don't need to know details. It's all about your feelings and responses. Is that okay?'

His shoulders dropped and he nodded.

A young man brought in a tray of tea things, set them on the table, and left.

'Now, what did you want to talk to me about?'

The Brigadier took a breath, rested his hands on his knees, and told her about the dreams.

CHAPTER THREE
Child's Play

THE BRIGADIER attended a second session with Dr Pelham-Rose, which he left feeling like they achieved a few breakthroughs. She encouraged him to write, or record in some other way, his feelings and thoughts as they occurred. She stressed to him to call her at any time. 'If I am with another patient then the clinic's reception will answer. You can trust everyone here.'

The boarders returned to the school the day before the last term of the academic year began. The buildings and grounds rang with the shouts of boys and staff members alike. More nights than not, the Brigadier slumbered without dreams he could recall in the mornings. For the first time in a long time, the fog that drifted in his mind thinned enough that he could pretend it no longer existed.

That Saturday morning, the Brigadier woke from a vivid dream that threw him for its mundane content. He could only see indistinct white and blue shapes like a Cézanne painting. He heard singing – Calypso songs, mostly, or reggae. Closer, but softer, he heard rasping breaths and a regular beep of a heart monitor. He felt air-conditioning shield him from a jungle's heat. He smelled a hospital, the antiseptic scents overlaid with the spice of rum and cigars, and a hint of tropical fruit.

He wrote it all down, and tried to catch what he felt. In one word – unsettled. Like there should be more, but everything else stayed back.

He shuffled through his Saturday morning routine, glad to put his uniform on for the cadets. As he fastened the belt and tugged down the khaki-coloured jacket, he felt relief his

Cadet activity excused him from keeping an eye on the cross-country run.

He breakfasted in the dining hall and sat next to Mr Grey. Ms Peters bustled in and sat opposite him. He caught her glare of disapproval at his uniform. She rattled out her copy of *The Sentinel*, its front page covered by their take on the current state of British politics heading into the General Election. Only one article promised anything different. It described the ongoing eruptions of a volcano on an island in the Caribbean. It provoked a return of his burning nightmare. He shook his head.

Ridiculous.

Jack puffed and panted behind Alfie Granger as they ran up the hill towards the obelisk. A few lads passed them, and they passed a few others. The sun's rays beat down upon them and Jack wished for an English summer and not a repeat of the heat from three years ago.

The incline flattened at the summit and he and Alfie picked up their pace. Jack heard his sister holler out to him. He grinned, looked up and saw her perched up in a tree firmly outside the school's boundary. She waved at him and he waved back. Alfie reached the obelisk, followed closely by Jack. Both boys circled around it and got their names checked off. Jack looked up at Jacquie while he and Alfie took a moment to gulp down a cup of water and catch their breath. She signed that they should meet up afterwards in their usual place. He nodded at her and turned away.

Alfie punched his upper arm. 'It's unhealthy, you and her.'

Jack scowled at his friend. 'It's not.' He huffed and aimed himself to chase Alfie back down the hill.

They completed the course. Alfie came fifth and Jack a close sixth.

They showered and changed out of their running kit. Alfie dressed in his cadet uniform and Jack into his denims.

'Seriously, man, she's your sister.'

'We're twins separated by the patriarchy.' Jack examined his hair in the mirror and dragged the comb through it a few more times to tame a cowlick. 'Better than playing at soldiers.'

Alfie groaned. 'Not my choice, and you know it.'

Jack shrugged. 'What's the old boy got planned for you poor sods today?'

Alfie scrabbled about in his locker for his stable belt in Brendon's colours. 'You know. Volunteering to mend the community centre. Why the toe rags responsible for torching it can't do it I don't know. Have you seen my belt?'

Jack picked it up from Alfie's bed. 'This?' He waggled it.

'Don't you dare.' Alfie lunged for it, but Jack already twisted around and dangled it out the window.

'What's in it for me?'

'Please, don't.'

'Aw, you're no fun.' Jack flung the belt across the room. Alfie dove for it in case Jack could somehow magically grab it again. Jack laughed.

The two boys left their dorm and went outside. Alfie straightened his beret and rattled across to join the cadets who had already lined up. The Brigadier in his uniform bellowed at them.

Jack put his hands in his jeans pockets and leaned against the wall to watch the old soldier berate them for imagined slovenliness. Jack shook his head slowly. He checked his watch and sauntered off.

The Brigadier watched Armstrong slouch away from the school grounds. He knew the boy had obtained a pass for that day. Ill-advised, as he told Mr Newton. In return, Newton told him that Miss Nugent had received assurances about the sister's absence. The Brigadier accepted the assurance, but he still considered the lad needed discipline. Just as his chum, Alfie Granger, did. The cadets could provide that discipline.

He put his thoughts on those matters to one side.

The twenty-strong contingent lined up and stood to attention. Well, a semblance of that stance. Better than at the start of the school year, he conceded. At least they all now wore their uniforms to a decent standard.

'All right, you lot. We are going to spend the day helping a community in need to repair its social space, thoughtlessly destroyed by selfish no-hopers. We will march there and back. Lunch will be provided. At the site, you will obey the instructions of the men in charge there. Understood?'

'Yes, sir.'

He cupped his ear and sighed.

'*Yes, sir!*'

'About turn.'

He winced at the imperfect manoeuvre, but he held back from bawling them out. At least they all turned in the same direction, and all but three stood to attention, shoulders back and chests puffed out. He pointed out the main errors to the three boys and, satisfied when they altered their stance, he led the contingent at an easy march out of the school grounds.

He expected to see the Armstrong boy on his way, and breathed easier when he didn't. Stupid, really, to be worried about a fifteen-year-old boy given what he'd faced during his career in the army.

They reached the six tower blocks, one now a blackened skeleton, that loomed around a row of shops and an outdoor playing area. The burning smell, even after the two weeks, tickled the Brigadier's nose and he swallowed. Memory of the nightmares teased him and he blinked it away. His head itched above his eye and he strove to ignore the sensation of blood oozing from a wound that didn't exist.

He brought his cadet unit to a halt in front of what little remained of the community centre. He touched his forehead and glanced at his wet fingers. Sweat, not blood.

He looked around and found a group of men standing to one side. He told the boys to remain in formation, but at ease. He strode across to the men.

One, Mr Weller, turned to face him. 'Ah, Brigadier. Good to see you.' He looked past him. 'And the lads.'

'All ready to help.'

Weller introduced him to the other two men, Newman and Jones. Newman owned and ran a local lumber yard and joinery business. He volunteered to supply timber and expertise at near cost price. Jones wore a business suit and explained his role as a Council official who would look out for the boys' safety and health. The Brigadier groaned inwardly, but he plastered a smile on his face.

'What's first?'

Weller looked over at the wreckage. 'Clear the old community centre out. The tower is a no-go area. It needs to be taken down by a professional crew.'

They crossed over the asphalt to inspect the charred ruin. When Jones joined them, the Brigadier told him he would assign the job of clearing the rubble and smaller pieces of debris to the younger boys. The oldest could help the men in moving the larger beams and metal struts.

Jones nodded his approval, and rubbed his hands.

Jack met his sister outside the public library in a town a local bus ride away for them both. He arrived at the same time as she did, but from opposite directions.

'Hey, hey.'

'Whatcha.'

They wore the same clothes, their hair in the same style, and carried the same type of satchel slung over the same shoulder in the same manner. Despite their different sexes, anyone casually glancing in their direction would not be able to tell them apart. His Adam's apple and a shadow of facial hair started to mark their differences, as did Jacquie's changing body shape. He now edged taller than her, like she stopped growing and he hadn't.

Inside, they strolled to their usual table that might as well have their names on it. No one else dared to sit there in case one or the other, or both, twins would turn up to claim it.

They sat. He pulled his books out from his satchel and dropped them onto the table.

'Which first?' Jacquie asked.

'History.' Jack pushed that exercise book forward towards her. He flipped it open to the last filled page.

She read the questions and nodded to herself. She didn't look up at him, but she made a grabby hand movement that meant she wanted paper and a pencil. He obliged. She scribbled a list of six books and magazines – journals, he corrected himself – for him to collect. She told him to read the relevant passages so he could fill in the details of the answers she drafted for him.

'Maths or chemistry?'

He pushed both of those books towards her, chemistry on top. 'Revision.'

She shooed him away on his assignment. He found all of

the titles on the list, and two other books that looked like they might help. He got the wrong journal number, though, so he returned it and the right one proved elusive. He returned empty-handed from his second foray. Jacquie told him to read the set history questions and work through the books while she worked through his chemistry homework. After a while she looked up at him.

'I really do want to sneak into one of your maths lessons.'

'I know.' He bounced one foot against the other under his chair.

'Do you reckon he'll be around in the next school year?'

'Who?'

'Your maths teacher. The soldier.'

'Yes. Why?'

She flipped through his maths exercise book and stopped when she found something that produced a wide grin. She dropped the book down and slapped her hand on it. The nearest librarian cut short his admonishment when he saw who made the noise. He apologised and backed away. Jacquie ignored him.

'This is the second time your old soldier-teacher has set that particular series for you.'

'Revision?'

Her eyebrows shot upwards and disappeared under her fringe.

He frowned. 'He has been a bit distracted since Easter, I suppose.'

'Don't you think it would be fun, me sitting in. See if anyone would notice.'

'Our voices have changed.'

'Not that much.' She lowered her voice and smirked. They laughed.

Jack sobered first. 'How are the olds?'

'Same as.'

'I hate how they keep trying to keep us apart.' He pulled a face.

She scowled. 'I know. Buck up. They haven't succeeded.' She extended her arms out and up. 'And they won't be able to keep us apart over the entirety of the summer holidays.'

They high-fived each other, then returned to his school

work. It consumed their attention for the next half an hour, until Jacquie broke their concentration with a vocal yawn and theatrical stretch.

'I didn't see your maths teacher at the obelisk this morning. Doesn't he usually wave the flags, or whatever?'

'He doesn't always.'

'Isn't it compulsory for the teachers to teach something on Saturdays at your school?'

'He takes the cadets.'

'Oh, yeah. Where?'

Jack brightened up. 'The estate today. Granger's moaned all week about it. They've been press-ganged into helping rebuild the community centre.'

'Forced labour?'

'Voluntary.'

'Bet they're not being paid.'

'It'll be gubbins about teamwork and learning practical skills.' Jack shrugged.

'Want to go look later?'

'I'd rather go to the pictures.'

'What's on?'

'Dunno.'

'Go get a paper, then,' Jacquie said.

Jack scraped his chair back and slouched to the table where the library displayed the local newspapers and newsletters. He flicked through the one with the ads for local entertainments and scowled at the paltry list. The only film on at a nearby cinema that attracted his attention was *The Wiz* starring Michael Jackson and Diana Ross. Not to his sister's taste. Or his. The estate would just have to do.

The boys broke for lunch, driven across by Alice from the school. She made extra for any locals who might be about and hungry. The Brigadier asked her to stay and eat with them, which she did. He explained to her what the boys had achieved so far. Explaining it all to someone else allowed him to see the progress from the morning.

Labourers from Newman's yard swarmed all over the piles of rubble made by the boys and loaded up two of his trucks. They gladly took the rest of Alice's sandwiches before she packed up and returned to the school.

The dust and ash stirred up visions in the Brigadier's mind of an inferno – a full on audio-visual show to rival the best Hollywood spectacle. He blinked. Sweat stung his eyes and he mopped his brow with a handkerchief. His temple pounded and his heart beat in double time.

No.

Two heartbeats pounded, not quite in sync.

'I say, old man.'

The Brigadier shook his head. No one stood near enough to him to sound as close as the voice that spoke. No one around sounded like the voice he heard.

'Sir!' Alfie Granger trotted towards him.

The other students stood around. The last of Newman's trucks disappeared with its load of rubbish up the road. Mr Jones leaned next to his car and examined a clipboard. Mr Weller was nowhere to be seen.

The Brigadier turned his attention to Granger. 'Yes?'

'Shouldn't we head back now, sir?'

'What?' He looked about him. He found Weller and waved to him. He returned his attention to Granger. 'Yes, of course. Get the unit into formation.'

As the boy went to his fellow cadets, Weller approached the Brigadier. He rubbed his hands together. 'Excellent start, Brigadier. Thank you. We really would be struggling without your generosity.'

'And that of Mr Newman.'

'Oh yes, and Mr Newman and his men. Um, I don't really want to ask this of you, but might it be possible for the boys to be able to help once more?'

'I don't see why not. We signed up to help build a new community centre. It's good experience for them. To be honest, I thought it's what we would have been doing today.'

Weller looked down at his feet. 'Yes, well. I had hoped so, too, but we didn't get much help for the rubble clearing. The community feelings we try to foster here is taking its time to grow.'

The Brigadier nodded tightly. 'I see.'

'I will have to keep the Council bureaucrats happy, too, Brigadier.' He nodded over at Jones.

The Brigadier glanced over at Jones, too, and raised his eyebrow. He winced at the phantom pain that lanced into his head. He touched the sore place to make sure it didn't bleed, even though it felt like it did. It didn't. He frowned. Blasted dream, still niggling at him.

He shook hands with Weller and marched over to the boys. He nodded to Granger who stood at attention in his place. If the boy kept showing initiative like just now, he ought to be promoted. The Brigadier paused. Such helpful behaviour from a known troublemaker normally indicated he hid something. He put his idea of promoting the boy to one side.

'All right, Cadets. Well done today. Mr Weller is grateful for our assistance. You're all a credit to the school and I shall inform the headmaster as such. Forward march.'

Jacquie and Jack decided that Thursday afternoon would be the optimal time to play their prank. The stars aligned, or so it could be spun. A General Election before a long weekend, and maths class at Brendon up against sports at her comprehensive. At lunch, she feigned cramps – not for the first time – and bunked off to a deserted home. Both parents toiled in their respective offices. The school knew. For appearance's sake, she drew her curtains and prepared a hot water bottle. All going well, she would be home before their olds.

She changed out of her school uniform and into jeans and a plain white t-shirt. Despite the unusually warm sunshine, she pulled on her denim jacket. She cleared her pockets of extraneous rubbish, double-checked she had her keys in her pocket, and jogged to the hill with the obelisk.

Jack, alone, sauntered up. He carried a gym bag slung over his shoulder.

'Hey, hey.'

'Whatcha.'

They found a place in the trees where they swapped what they wore.

While Jacquie tied the shoelaces, she said, 'Do you think he's the full quid?'

'What you mean?'

'Soldiers are supposed to be super fit, aren't they?'

'Old Stewpot's retired from all that. The closest he gets

to his glory days is playing dress-ups with the cadets.'

She tied the other shoe lace. 'Do you know if he's killed anyone?'

'Don't know. He doesn't talk about all that during our lessons. Alfie says he sometimes mentions the army in cadets, but nothing exciting.'

She stood up and he told her once more where he normally sat in the classroom. 'I still think it would have been wicked fun if we did a full-on swap.'

'I refuse to wear a dress. Besides, your school is dull, dull, dull. Full of dull teachers and dull students, as you keep telling me.'

She humphed. 'How can you stand wearing this get-up all day? Especially on a lovely day like today. I thought boys wore more comfortable clothes.'

'Grass isn't always greener.' He stepped back.

'Well?'

'Like looking in a mirror.'

She tilted her head to one side. She grinned. 'Only in reverse.'

He screwed his face up. 'What?'

She sighed. 'Mirrors show a reflection, which is an image in reverse.'

In the distance, a bell rang. She swore. He checked his watch.

'First bell, but you'd better get moving. Oh, books.' He scrabbled in his gym bag and handed her a text book and an exercise book.

She made a gimme gesture towards it and they quickly swapped their watches, too. She set her shoulders and strolled down the hill in plain sight. She resisted glancing over to the trees where Jack kept pace. Their paths diverged when they reached the buildings. She saw Alfie Granger and made her brother's habitual greeting.

'I am so not looking forward to a double period of maths this afternoon.' Alfie slumped his shoulders as the second bell rang.

She shrugged, and turned away to hide her smirk.

They both entered the building and trudged up the steps to the classroom. Other boys jostled around going up, but not all of them trooped into the same room. She glanced up and found Jack's desk and mooched towards it. She sat in the seat, and read the scratched messages passed down from one bored student to the next. She followed her brother's rituals as he had explained them to her while they plotted for this momentous day.

The volume rose in the classroom, then hushed when the Brigadier walked through the door. He shut it behind him and he strode to the board. He grabbed a piece of chalk and wrote 'revision' and 'test'. He turned to face them.

'First half we will revise what I've taught you this year, and in the second half we will do a practise test under exam conditions.'

Those facts Jack had not made known during their planning. Jacquie nodded, picked up a pencil and twisted it through her fingers. Sneaky, but fair.

'Put that pencil down, Mr Armstrong.'

She started, but did as the older man bellowed. Tetchy sod. And how odd to be called 'mister'. She said nothing, even in the face of his waiting. She suppressed a snigger.

The Brigadier huffed. 'Given your erratic performance to date, Mr Armstrong, I strongly advise you to pay attention.'

'That's me told.' She spoke under her breath.

The class settled down while the Brigadier went through what they struggled with, according to his analysis. They worked through a variety of problems, which she completed for her brother.

The Brigadier opened up the session for questions, and dealt with a few serious ones. She leaned back, and languidly stuck her hand up. He called on her and she yawned.

'Sorry, sir. Was stretching.'

He narrowed his eyes at her, and called on one of the other boys who had his hand up. She repeated the stretch and yawn routine once more, which he fell for again. Third time and she prepared for a switch of tack.

'Armstrong, do you have a question or not?'

'Chill, man.' She spoke in a low tone. 'I have a question. What is a proof?'

'What?'

She shrugged as nonchalantly as she could and not

snigger. Man, the soldier was wound up so tight. 'You heard, sir. What is a proof?' She enunciated each syllable slowly.

'Mr Armstrong, as you should know full well by now, a proof is a series of stages in resolving a mathematical problem.'

'You sure, sir? I thought a proof was one-half per cent of alcohol.'

The Brigadier stared at her. A smile slowly formed and he nodded. 'I see. Yes. Very clever.'

She stuck her hand up again. His shoulders sagged.

'How many mathematicians does it take to change a lightbulb?'

He folded his arms. 'We are not doing jokes, Mr Armstrong.'

'Oh, go on, sir.' Other students in the class joined in the clamour.

'Quiet! All of you,' he thundered at them, his face flushed red. 'Right. I'll set your tests now.'

CHAPTER FOUR
Cars

IT HADN'T been his intention, but the Brigadier ended up watching the election results as they came in. While he watched, he marked the tests he set for all his classes the day before, and every so often he shook his head to concentrate.

He marked in order of the classes. The method he employed in setting the tests suited him for its simplicity. The certainty of it was one reason he enjoyed mathematics at school level. No matter which way a problem was put, and which method deployed to solve it, the natural laws meant the answer never changed.

When he moved, his mug tipped its contents into his lap. He swore under his breath at his own foolishness at putting it on the arm of the chair. At least the drink had cooled. Nonetheless, he stood up and stomped to the bedroom to change into his pyjamas. He considered turning the television off and getting some sleep, but instead he put on his dressing gown and returned to his armchair.

Duty called. He had one more class of tests to mark. The talking heads on the television nattered on about the results and speculated about the Cabinet, and what of the manifesto points would be prioritised. He listened to their conversation about the plans for schools. Brendon would most likely be safe from any major changes. In fact, Mr Newton believed a Conservative Party victory might inject new life into the school's fortunes.

Those maths tests from his Fourth Form class were not going to mark themselves. As the pundits pontificated about free school milk, he marked away. No surprises until he gave full marks to one paper. He double-checked the working out, which leaned eccentric. Robust, though, and the results shone through on each and every set question. He looked at the name of the student.

Armstrong.

'Impossible.'

He checked again. All of the workings were sound. The boy could not have cheated by sneaking in the answers and making up the working. He'd only set the test yesterday morning. He delivered it mid-morning to the administration office and been told off for his tardiness. The ladies ran off the required number of copies for the class on the Gestetner machine and he collected the papers at the start of lunch time. None of Armstrong's Form had free time at any point that morning. He locked the test papers in his desk drawer, and none of his little security measures had been triggered.

Armstrong's behaviour during that class had been odd. His joking unusual for him, until he and the others settled down to do the test.

'No, they can't have... The little blighters if they did.'

Identical twins. Rare in siblings of two sexes, but apparently possible in terms of all but the obvious. Adolescence would accentuate those differences in inevitable changes, but not in bone structure or skin, eye and hair colourings. He'd seen them together a few times, and their likeness was uncanny. They were meant to be kept separated, but they exhibited a wily disregard for those rules.

He shook his head, and despite himself, he chuckled at their boldness.

The Bank Holiday weather dampened everything. Three days of steady rain, forecast and delivered from the grey skies.

Jack convinced Miss Nugent of his need for a pass on Monday afternoon to join Granger and his family, who were visiting a museum of relevance to their history classes. Before she signed it on behalf of the headmaster, she quizzed him about his sister. He stuck to the script he and she devised. 'No, miss, I haven't seen her. Not for ages. I miss her.' Pout. Wobbly lip. Careful not to go overboard on the theatrics.

He caught the bus, met the Grangers and they found the stupid museum. He saw Jacquie, but they didn't meet there and then. They couldn't risk it. Alfie's old man was in thick with the school. Jack picked up the note she left, which told him in their code the who, when and how they would meet up for their debrief.

Operation Rendezvous worked like a dream. He cried off afternoon tea with the Grangers, blaming the rain's habit of playing havoc with the buses. He caught the bus and hopped off in a part of town few people he knew went. He could walk back to the school if need be. Jacquie knew a place under shelter. He followed her instructions and crept into the old office block of the abandoned and condemned factory. She sat on an office chair near a desk covered in dirt.

'Hey, hey.'

'Whatcha. What a place.' He crinkled up his nose.

She shrugged. 'Better than the charred remains of the community centre.'

He pulled out another seat and brushed off the dirt. 'Rozzers were at the school last week.'

'Rozzers. Really? You're not Scouse.'

He shrugged. 'Cops, then. The plod. They didn't talk to me or any of the boys. The Toad earwigged. It was about the fire. They confirmed it was an accident. Faulty wiring. They think that the person who said they saw one of the boys in the estate was a lying liar.'

'Idiots.'

'The Brigadier isn't. He knows about our swapsies.'

'Let me see your hands.'

He held them out. 'He's not got the proof, and I stuck to our story. It was me in class, and I haven't seen you in ages.' He dropped his hands back down into his lap. 'Nugent quizzed me, too, but gave me a pass for today anyway.' He shrugged again. 'I will say one thing for the old soldier. He is decent enough to want evidence before dishing out a thwacking.'

'Maybe. For what it's worth, I judge Thursday's mission a success. He's a weird bloke, but. I don't think he's all there.' She tapped the side of her head. 'I mean, you'd think an old soldier could keep a bunch of fifteen-year-olds in order. I rattled him just with a few stupid jokes.'

'And getting a hundred per cent for the test.' He brushed a strand of hair away from his eyes and grinned.

'I took a gamble on a few of his problems.'

'He gave me the third degree on "my" process on some of the questions. Can you tell me what you did?'

'Yeah, of course.'

The rest of May proved pleasantly dull. Arsenal's victory over Manchester United in the FA Cup lifted the spirits of the boys who enjoyed football, but not as much as the excitement generated from the opening of an amusement park in Surrey. The Brigadier and the other teachers spent time clamping down on the excitement and jealousy of boys whose parents got them tickets for the next half-term break and those who missed out.

The third tussle the Brigadier waded into, to separate a have and have-not, resulted in one of the combatants clipping him on his temple. The boy, in the Upper Sixth, had swung wide and not known his own strength. The Brigadier advised Mr Newton that the boys deserved punishment for their fight, but not the punch that landed on him. He was fine, being made of stern stuff that had survived far worse.

He kept to himself the fact that the punch seemed to knock his weird dreams free again. They were less frantic dreams, at least, but unsettling for all that. Bright. Hot. That blasted double heartbeat effect like he had two hearts, which echoed in his temple. The eye below clouded over, unfocused. Blind. Disorientated.

Awake, he was fine. The blow hadn't left much of a mark, and it cleared after a few days.

He and the cadets helped make good progress on the new community centre in the nearby estate. He reflected more than once on how every little contribution added up to significant changes. It was a good lesson to pass on to the boys. The school's contingent grew to a strength of twenty-two.

The Brigadier looked forward to the half-term break with almost as much eagerness as the students. Even though he would stay at the school, he booked a few days leave. He made vague plans to visit old friends. Maybe even his family.

The last week of classes dragged as though time itself opposed their longing for their break. Finally, the late Spring Bank Holiday arrived. Most of the boys departed. The few who remained looked out with jealousy at their chums. He smiled at the secret he kept. Mr Newton had organised for these boys to attend the new amusement park. Permissions granted by all parents and guardians. Best of all, the Brigadier's request to stay behind was granted.

That day dawned grey, but dry, with sunshine promised for later. The boys, excited, piled into the mini-bus and set off.

The Brigadier settled with his newspaper in the common room. He read a long article about a volcano erupting in the Caribbean in which no one had died. Hundreds had perished during its last eruption. Everyone praised the early warning system now in place for the dramatic difference.

A ghost whispered in his ear, but he didn't catch the words. He turned around. No one joined him. In the distance, a radio played popular music he failed to recognise.

He turned back to the paper. He read an opinion piece about the new government's education policy. It fleshed out their manifesto commitments, and he imagined it would rile up those who wanted to feel aggrieved.

He rustled the paper. Frowned. Sighed. Moved on to skim the rest. He put the paper down in its place with the others. Boredom stirred. The relative quiet accentuated a loneliness that lay under the surface of his demeanour. Dr Pelham-Rose had got him to admit his ache for company, and for action. She'd advised him to write about it, in whatever form he wanted. If that didn't work, she told him to call her. His work had distracted him, and now on his first day of freedom and peace, his mental demons threatened him.

'Ridiculous.'

Despite her flighty looks, Pelham-Rose impressed the Brigadier with her solid common sense. She'd been true to her word, too, in focusing on his feelings and not the facts of his past career and life. He huffed. He didn't need to call her, but it wouldn't hurt to try writing down how he felt. He carried a pencil and biro – school teaching made both mandatory to hold in his jacket pocket – but no paper. Blank paper and scrappy ends of notebooks tended to be left on the table with the newspapers and magazines. He scrabbled about in the pile, muttering that someone should tidy it all up.

A magazine for vintage car enthusiasts caught his

attention. He rested his fingertips on the picture of a 1920s open-top racer. He closed his eyes as a fragment of a memory played out. Him in the passenger seat. Wind roaring in his ears as they raced a car a bit like the one pictured. No. It was an older model, but the driver had improved the horse power so it ran faster.

He remembered the breathtaking exhilaration, but nothing else. He couldn't recall the driver, or where and when they raced.

He opened his eyes and picked up the magazine. He flicked through it, but nothing else dislodged more of that memory or anything else like it. Instead, his mind threw up generic Land Rovers, the odd jeep, and other dull green working vehicles. His own car, safe and sensible.

'I'm no James Bond. That's you, surely, good sir.'

The Brigadier dropped the magazine and spun around. No one. He stepped out of the common room and into the corridor.

'Anyone there?'

One of the ladies poked her head out from the administration office. 'Only me, Brigadier. Is the radio too loud?'

Radio.

'Er, no. No, it isn't.' He flashed her a smile and retreated.

The radio played a pop tune. He could hear it, but it didn't disturb him. The voice he'd heard sounded so clear and strong, like the man who spoke stood or sat close by. But, no one was there. He didn't recognise the voice. Maybe he should call Dr Pelham-Rose for an appointment.

His eye caught the picture of the car once more.

Sod it.

Sunlight broke through the clouds and through the windows like a spotlight on the car. He would go shopping.

Dr Rebecca Pelham-Rose ushered the retired Naval commander from her office, all smiles and reassurances. She followed him to the reception desk where he confirmed his next appointment. She waved as he waved back. Once he departed, she turned to the receptionist.

'Dear old pet thinks he's twenty years younger than he is. Still, better than the alternative. Who's next?'

'They postponed, Doctor, just this morning. They took poorly over the weekend and their GP says bedrest is required.'

'No last-minute replacements?'

The receptionist shook her head.

'Oh, well. I have a mountain of files to tidy up. May as well do a few now.'

'Shout if you need help.'

'I will.'

She returned to her office and set to dividing the dozen folders into three piles: one for archiving, one for filing in her room, and one for further thought. The first pile she took to the receptionist and asked for her to place the folders into the central registry run by the practice. The second pile she slotted neatly into the relevant sections of her filing cabinet.

She hummed tunelessly, enjoying the buzz more than the sound. Filing was a simple job, and so rewarding. She really didn't know why she didn't keep on top of it, not that a dozen folders made a mountain. She always made it seem much worse than it ever was.

One folder remained on her desk, the one she needed to mull over some more.

'Alistair Lethbridge-Stewart. Brigadier. (Retired.) What to do with you?'

She flopped into her chair and read the file from the start, and all the way through. The incident in 1977 that hospitalised him concerned her. Slightly erratic behaviour on one day, found knocked out cold the next. No signs of an attack. No bumps on his head, and no memory of why he lay where he fell, who he'd been with, and great chunks of his past torn from his mind. It wasn't like any form of amnesia described in textbooks.

She knew from what the Ministry of Defence didn't share with the clinic that the Brigadier's record could be described as colourful, active, and highly secretive. She judged him to be a good leader, solid and caring. The type of person ordinary people would follow.

'Who are we but the sum of our memories? And when those abandon us, who are we then?'

She put his file back on her desk. She would keep it in her office. Despite his assurances that her advice had put his bad dreams to bed, she knew she would see him again. The demons that haunted him were too big for him to fight on his own.

Two days after seeing the picture of the car he desired, the Brigadier telephoned John Benton. Benton gave him the name of a dealer in Ramsgate when he'd been unable to help. 'Sorry, sir. My focus is on the newer old car.' The Ramsgate dealer, a Mr Sneddon, told the Brigadier about Mr Abbott who restored 1920s and 1930s cars to roadworthiness. He operated from his home near Broadstairs.

A ghost whispered to him not to trust the used car salesman. The Brigadier ignored the warning voice. He made an appointment for eleven o'clock, Friday morning, to see what Mr Abbott had available for sale. Abbott asked for cash-in-hand, should he like what he saw. The Brigadier blinked at the price Abbott quoted, and he debated the pros and cons while Abbott prattled on about the value of the car and his work to restore it.

The Brigadier tightened his grip on the telephone receiver and ground his jaw. The Edwardian car that bounced along in his memory made up his mind for him.

'Mr Abbott.' He interrupted. 'Consider this a firm acceptance of your offer, pending me seeing it and taking it for a test drive.'

'Delighted.' Abbott gave him the directions to his home. 'I look forward to meeting you on Friday.'

Having finished the call, the Brigadier held a hand to his forehead. He didn't keep that sort of cash on hand. He would have to sell his sensible car, and see about a loan.

Friday dawned like Christmas morning for a five-year-old. The Brigadier barely slept, and when he did his dreams taunted him with that short clip on a loop of his partial memory of the vintage car.

He set off earlier than planned and took the fine, sunny weather as a good omen. He caught a train to Ramsgate. There, he waited for the bus and pondered if he should take a taxi. The wads of cash weighed heavily in his jacket pocket. He borrowed the money from a lender his conscience warned him about. Wary, he watched other people mill about.

The bus arrived. He asked the driver to announce his stop, and the man grumbled that he would. Forty-five minutes later, he did.

A childish glee lifted his steps as he followed Abbott's instructions to his house, a ten-minute walk from the bus stop. He found the place half an hour before his appointment. He strolled on past the open gate, but glanced inside the forecourt. The car gleamed and he stopped. He gawped at it and felt the flutter of excitement.

Dogs barked and a man shushed them. The Brigadier turned his attention to the laneway along which he'd walked. A man his age walked six hunting dogs that all strained, quiet now, at their leads. The dog walker doffed his flat cap. 'Are you the gentleman after my old car?'

'Sorry. Yes. I'm early.'

'No matter. Come in and have a look while I put the hounds in their kennels.'

The Brigadier smiled and nodded. 'Thank you.'

He crunched behind Abbott and his pack until they peeled off to the right around his house. The Brigadier examined the car, admiring the polished leather seats, the shining paint and metal trim. The tyres looked good and he itched to look under the hood.

Abbott returned. 'Open her up.'

He did so and beamed at the machine that gleamed. Abbott talked him through the engine, what he restored and what was original. He told him the miles to the gallon, and its quirks. They both got in to take it for a test drive, the Brigadier at the wheel with Abbott navigating through the lanes and out to open country.

On their return, Abbott disappeared into his house to retrieve the paperwork. The Brigadier handed over the cash, signed the documents, and accepted the receipt. They shook hands.

'You've done a fine job with her. Why sell?'

'Thank you. I've my eye on a real challenge and I need the readies. She's brought me a lot of pleasure. Treat her well and she'll do the same for you.'

She drove like a dream all the way back to the school. He parked her in the car park next to his old reliable car.

Mr Grey emerged from the main building, cigarette in hand. He trotted down the stairs. 'My, my.'

The Brigadier grinned. 'She's a Humber 1650 Imperial. Made in 1929, but fully restored and operational.'

'I didn't know you liked cars, Brigadier.'

He frowned. 'We all have our secrets.'

'Quite, quite.'

His telephone rang. He excused himself from Mr Grey and strode into his quarters. He picked up the receiver. Dr Pelham-Rose greeted him and after the usual platitudes, he said, 'I've bought a car.'

'I thought you already had one.'

'A proper motor car, not a modern thing. Bit of a splash out, I'll admit. But why not? What can I do for you?'

'I was thinking we might schedule an appointment, just to check progress.'

Thunder rumbled in the distance. His temple pounded. He rubbed at it. 'No, I don't think I need one. I'm fine. It's all fine.'

'Okay, but you know where I am if you do need to talk.'

'I do. Yes. Thank you.' He dropped the receiver onto its cradle. Another clap of thunder rumbled louder and he went outside to put the roof up on his lovely new car.

Most of the boarders returned to her brother's school on Sunday. That same day, Jacquie crept up to the obelisk. Jack lay in the grass and chewed on a blade. 'Hey, hey.' She flopped down beside him.

'Whatcha.'

'We've got a problem.'

'What?'

'One of Mother's friends told her about a summer camp on some small island off the coast of Scotland. It's for girls like me, apparently. Whatever that means.'

'Super smart and bored, you mean.' Jack tossed the blade of grass away. 'For all of summer?' He propped himself up on an elbow. 'What about me?'

'What about you? It's always about you.' She ripped up a clump of grass and threw it at him. 'It's me who's being sent away.'

'When?'

'Don't know. Not until the holidays start, I expect.'

'We've got a few weeks to plan something, then.'

'We do.'

'Hey! You there.'

Both twins swore.

Jack sat up. 'Yes, sir?'

'Get down to the school. Mr Newton wants to have a word with all students. Who's that with you?'

'No one, sir.' Jack stood up and brushed his clothes. He winked at Jacquie. The grass was long enough to shield her and the teacher stood far enough down the hill to not be able to see. Jack set off towards the buildings.

Jacquie waited a few minutes before making her move. She raced down the other side of the hill, through the trees and out to the road. She collected her bike where she'd left it, mounted it and set off home. Around a corner she swerved into the hedgerow to avoid a car travelling way too fast towards her.

'Watch out!' called the driver.

Jack's blasted maths teacher. He and his car disappeared around the corner before she had time to react. Jacquie let loose a string of swearwords, flipped the finger, and then checked her bike for any damage.

CHAPTER FIVE
Lovely Lightning

FINALLY, THE end of the school year dawned. Jack woke in his dorm and took a few moments to ponder the fact that this would be the last time in this creaky old bed for a while. Home, home, home. His own bed. His own room.

No Jacquie, though. That hurt.

Their olds plotted so hard to keep them apart, but there'd be a week when they couldn't. Unless they took her out of school and sent her to Scotland sooner. His forehead scrunched up. There were rules and laws about that, surely.

A pillow whacked the back of his head. Someone leapt on him and a set of teeth clacked at him in his ear. Jack lashed out. 'Gerroff.'

The weight left. So did the pillow.

'Alfie.'

'Jaws!' Alfie held up a set of plastic teeth and wound them up to chatter in his hand. 'He's alive and after Bond.'

Jack scrabbled up and for his own pillow. He flung it at Alfie to knock the stupid toy to the floor. It landed upright and chased an imaginary enemy with the same single-mindedness as the Bond villain.

'You're no fun.' Alfie hugged his pillow to his chest.

Jack raised his eyebrow. 'You want to fight?'

'Boys!' Ms Peters stood in the doorway, her arms crossed. 'Time to get ready for the day.' She tapped her wristwatch. 'After breakfast, you only have a couple of hours to pack everything before your families collect you. Mr Granger, I understand you'll be visiting Venice.'

'Yes, Ms Peters.'

'For real?' Jack glared at him.

45

Alfie shrugged.

A smile played on Ms Peters' face. 'It's not all spy chases in the canals, you know.' Her smile vanished. She clapped her hands. 'Get a move on, you two.'

The Brigadier opened the shutters of his holiday flat. He stepped out on to the balcony and gazed out over the azure sea. The sunlight dappled off it, and he narrowed his eyes to watch the ant-sized men below swarm over a launch before a limousine arrived. A couple emerged and stalked through the workers up the gang plank.

He turned back into the flat he'd been lucky to get last minute. Dr Pelham-Rose suggested it during her last telephone call to him. Another of her patients couldn't make it this summer and would prefer their modest flat was used by someone trusted rather than rent to a stranger. 'They own it outright and only expect you to pay for what you use. Fair?'

'More than fair.'

He clenched his jaw. The repayments for the loan he took out for that blasted car wiped out most of his pay. What had possessed him? His temple twinged and an eyelid twitched. He rubbed them, disconcerted by it no matter how often it happened.

Mr Grey had talked him out of driving the car to the Riviera. He trusted the old man to look after her. At least he had enough money from selling his perfectly serviceable motor to cover a fair proportion of the loan repayments. At the school during term time his salary and Army pension covered his normal outlay. He would just have to be extra frugal.

He sighed.

Dr Pelham-Rose insisted he relax for a few weeks. 'Lie on the beach, maybe see some of the sights. Live the Mediterranean lifestyle for a couple of months. You deserve it, Brigadier. Let go of the cares and worries of your past career. I will give your money back if your dreams don't stop on your return to teaching.'

Doctor's orders to rest and recuperate. He hadn't told her he took up the offer. Time enough for that later.

Tension ached in his shoulders. He rolled them as he considered his wardrobe. He picked out a light suit suitable for the summer sun and a long stroll along the sea front. A recce, of sorts, to see what's what and to stretch out his muscles from the long journey across France by train and coach. At least he was able to doze, only he couldn't shake the weird waking dream of a different long journey. Small plane, then larger. Champagne service, with attractive young women attending to his every whim.

A dream. Pleasant, but weird. Virtually real, yet patently not so.

He shook himself of the memory. Last night he dutifully described it in his dream journal. Dr Pelham-Rose assured him the act of writing it down would rob it of its power to unsettle him. That made sense when she said it, but in practise he couldn't shake the idea that the dream strengthened into memories. He huffed. There were enough gaps in his actual memories for these interlopers to set up home.

Outside, he crossed to a café and ordered a breakfast croissant and coffee. He paid over the francs, and dropped the centimes returned as change into the tip saucer. He found a table and consulted his guidebook. He decided to go to the marina he could observe from his flat, and then stroll to the east.

Jacquie looked out at the grey sea smashing against the rocks below. Giant seagulls screamed above and below as they wheeled and darted. The sun's rays beat down from a bright blue sky and burned her skin. The stiff breeze did little but keep the clouds of midges at bay.

She picked up a small rock and threw it at a hovering gull. She missed. The blasted bird ducked, and screeched its anger at her.

Tears leaked from her eyes. She scrunched up the letter in her other hand. The letter from her brother, Jack, who in open language told her about his trips to London, and to the coast. Happy days of too much sugar and drizzle. The coded message hidden in those words told her a different story. It seemed their olds dropped their guard around him. Twice he earwigged them planning how to keep the twins apart. Their father hoped for a transfer with his job to Manchester – Manchester! – with a salary large enough to keep Jack at Brendon, but move her to some nasty sounding place up north. They planned to sell their current home and buy cheaper in the north.

'Jacqueline Lee Bouvier Armstrong! Return here this

minute.'

Jacquie shoved the letter back into her pocket, wiped her eyes, and turned. She glared at Miss Mackintosh who stood, hands on hips. Jacquie barely contained the invectives she wanted to pour at the woman who ran this hell-hole.

She arrived a fortnight ago with the dozen other girls, tired and sick from the coach and ferry ride north from London. Instead of being allowed to rest and recover, this bloody woman got them cleaning their dormitory, and hiking around their bit of the island to learn the limits of their new world. While they yomped, Miss Mackintosh listed out all the rules and punishments, and her expectations of the girls in her charge over the summer.

Two of the girls were pregnant, and their sentence to the island was longer than for the others. Three of the others got so sick the first few days with the shakes, sweats, and screaming. Jacquie swore off even considering trying any of that. All the other girls told variations on her story: behavioural issues.

Jacquie dragged herself towards the woman who ran the place. She failed to dodge the clip around the ear.

'Back to the house, you utter disgrace. You'll tidy up and fix the damage you caused. There'll be no luncheon for you.'

Jacquie glowered, but said nothing. Two weeks under Miss Mackintosh's iron rule had taught her the futility of protest. Felicity broke the ugly vase when she barrelled down the stairs to get the post. Jacquie arrived on the scene just after, and right when Miss Mackintosh appeared from the other direction. Felicity, excited and oblivious, tossed the envelope addressed to Jacquie, who caught it and ran out to the cliff.

She got ten minutes to herself. Now she shook and clenched her fists.

'After you've finished that, you can darn the sacks sent up from the village.'

Jacquie dragged her feet. The weekly delivery brought letters – their first since arriving – groceries to supplement what the Mackintoshes grew and raised on their land, and huge loads of needlework repairs for the girls to do.

'Mr Mackintosh said I could help with the shearing.'

The woman's meaty, calloused hand grabbed Jacquie's ear. She twisted. Jacquie yelped. 'You are here to learn skills suitable for a girl, not to muck about like a boy. That's what your parents have paid good money for, and I will deliver on that.'

Jacquie stumbled when Miss Mackintosh released her ear. She rubbed it, and conjured up an image of her olds with her and Jack hurling rocks at them, each one finding its target and doing damage. They would get what's coming, she vowed.

Three weeks in and the Brigadier's day saw him rise, and breakfast at the café where the waiters praised him on his improving French. He read the local paper on a bench that overlooked the marina, where he enjoyed watching the super-wealthy and their boats. He chatted to the crews, who shared scandalous tales about film stars and European royalty. He imagined the thrill on Miss Nugent's face when he passed along the stories on his return to the school.

He took his lunch at any one of a dozen seafood restaurants along the beach, then devoured a paperback thriller as he lazed on the sand. He cooled off with a swim in the surf.

One day, a young woman caught his eye and returned his attention with a little smile and fluttery finger-wave. She strolled off and he resumed reading. He thought about her light brown hair, her summery dress and wide-brimmed hat. Her smile that didn't dismiss him, or laugh.

Two days later, their eyes caught again. Like the other day, she seemed to be on her own.

'You only live once.' He shushed the ghostly, chiding voice that whispered in his mind.

He ambled towards her, a smile on his lips. He expected a young man to join her, or her to shake her head and move on. Neither happened.

'Bonjour, Mademoiselle.'

'Bonjour, Monsieur.' Her voice sparkled like the sea.

He introduced himself, and apologised for the French he spoke so poorly.

She gave him her name, Sandrine, and told him his French was better than her English. At his quirked eyebrow, she pointed to his novel. He laughed, and asked her if she would like to accompany him to lunch. His heart leapt when she said yes.

They spoke mostly in French, but occasionally he resorted

to English when a local idiom defeated him.

Sandrine told him she grew up in a small village in the Dordogne region, and this summer tried her luck on the sea front. 'Perhaps a Hollywood star would find me, no?'

'Well, I trust a British soldier will do until then?'

They both talked about hopes and dreams, and past regrets. They drank wine, and ate shellfish, bread and olives. They strolled, arm-in-arm, along the beach and joked about the people they saw. As dusk fell, Sandrine invited him to her hotel room. He threw caution to the wind and joined her.

She ordered room service, and he stayed the night. In the morning, he overhead part of a rapid conversation she had with the man on the reception desk. She chided the desk clerk for his concerns.

They breakfasted at a different café. Sandrine told him she needed to go away for the day on a modelling shoot, but tomorrow her schedule was free.

He let her go and wondered if he would see her again.

He resumed his day. A super yacht crewman invited him on board while its owners tried their luck in Monaco. The crewman teased him about the lightness of his step, and invited him to a cruise the next day.

Back on shore he sent flowers and a note to Sandrine's hotel. He reserved a table at a decent restaurant within his budget for the next evening and included those details on the card with three hopeful question marks.

Next day after his day on the sea, he dressed for dinner. He prepared himself for an embarrassing solo meal, but to his surprise Sandrine arrived just as he did. She radiated health and bubbled over with excitement about the photo shoot. He listened as she described it all.

He caught the glances of a group of French men and women, about his age. If they were English, they would be tutting.

'So, my dear, what did you do?' She touched his hand with her fingertips. Her smile captivated him. He told her about the boats, and the novel he finished reading. She listened, and asked questions, and he forgot about the table of disapproving French people.

They lingered over their meal, and their wine. They spoke of films seen, books read, and art exhibitions attended. She spoke more about her dreams and aspirations, and he told her to not let anyone or anything hold her back.

The table of tutters stood and began the ritual to depart. The Brigadier watched them from the corner of his eye. As they passed by their table, one of the men leaned over Sandrine and told her off. The Brigadier followed the gist of what the stranger said. The others nodded, their mouths pressed together in thin lines.

He stood up. He gripped the linen serviette in his hands and twisted it. He spoke in his most formal French.

'Sir, you are out of line. We are both adults, capable of making our own decisions. We enjoy each other's company. It is none of your business.'

Some of the group hurried away. A woman and a man remained with their friend. He straightened up, puffed his chest out and glared at the Brigadier. A medal glinted from his jacket lapel, which the Brigadier recognised as a *Légion d'honneur*. Before the stranger could speak, the Brigadier nodded at the honour.

'I choose not to wear my medals in public, sir. If that truly meant anything to you, I suggest you leave us in peace.'

The Brigadier refused to break eye contact. His opponent spluttered, and swore quietly. The second man glared at the Brigadier, but turned away and whispered something to his friend. The woman clutched her purse to her belly. When the first man finally turned and left, she paused. She said in perfect English, 'To think we fought once on the same side. How dare you insult one of our heroes.'

The Brigadier drew himself up to his full height. 'Madam, how dare you insult one of your own.' He threw the cloth down onto the table. Waiters hovered. The restaurant chilled into silence. His hands clenched and unclenched. A ghost in his head egged him on to stand his ground. They should respect him, after all he'd done.

Sandrine broke the awful silence. 'Alistair, please. They are not worth it.'

The voice in his head turned on Sandrine, but he stifled it. Shook his head, then nodded and smiled at her.

A waiter herded the offending group out and away. The normal restaurant noises returned, although the chatter focused on what might have happened as well as what did.

He sat back down. Sandrine reached for his hands and with her thumbs she stroked them gently. She insisted he focus on her and not the whispers and talk. She smiled, but he saw a sadness behind it.

'I know them. Not well, but my uncles have dealt with them. They would have sided with the Vichy if it wasn't for a false arrest and shooting early on in the occupation. Now they give money to neo-Fascists. The woman is an Australian, but pretends to be more French than any of us. She complains about the English and Americans who come here. She is the worse type of bigot. She is a hypocrite.'

The ghost in his head stirred, its anger palpable. He swallowed against it.

'I don't like the assumptions they made.'

'Neither do I.' Sandrine laughed. 'But they are a dying minority.'

The maître d' approached them. He apologised for the rudeness of the departed diners and offered them liqueurs, on the house. They accepted.

Once they finished up, the Brigadier paid and tipped generously for the restaurant staff rescuing their evening.

Afterwards, he and Sandrine meandered along the seafront and gazed at the twinkling lights of distant boats and buoys, above them the stars. A gentle breeze brought the smell of brine to the shore.

They paused. The Brigadier rested his hands on her shoulders. 'I'm only here for a few weeks more, but I am falling in love with you. I can't offer you any way in which you could fulfil your dreams and my heart aches.'

Sandrine laid a finger on his lips. 'Alistair, part of me wants to say, no, no. Too soon for such talk. You bring me much happiness, but I want my memories of this summer to be wistful of what might have been. I do not want to be the wife of a retired soldier, much as I have also fallen a little bit in love with you.'

He kissed her, and she responded. They resumed their amble until he invited her to his flat. She agreed.

For the next fortnight, they spent most of their time together. They visited other towns along the coast, ventured a little way inland. Not as far as to visit Sandrine's home, which he respected. He took her out on a boat one day, a trip organised by one of the crew he befriended.

She had two more photo shoots that kept them apart. At the end of the third she didn't want to see him until the day after when they met for breakfast. She wore sunglasses, even though the sky clouded over. Frost iced her conversation, and he delayed asking her what happened. He asked instead what she wanted to do for the day. She sighed heavily.

'Can we just sit on your balcony and watch the world go by?'

They bought groceries and wine. After half an hour of companionable quiet, Sandrine removed her sunglasses to reveal her puffed up and reddened eyes.

'What happened?'

'A bad reaction to the make-up. The shoot was for a commercial for one of the big brands, but my stupid skin. I will be going home tomorrow. I will work on applying for university and become an intellectual.' She pouted and frowned, and looked so earnest until she burst out laughing. She laid a hand on his arm. 'Oh, Alistair. I will miss you, but I will treasure our summer together. You help cushion the blow to my dreams.'

For a moment, words failed him. His emotions jostled about. He wanted to tell her to stay with him as long as he had left. The strange, ghostly whisper demanded he control her, but he stared that one down. 'Sandrine, I am so sorry about your dreams. You have been a balm for my soul, and I will treasure knowing you even as briefly as this.'

They made love for the last time together that afternoon. Afterwards, they ate and drank, and as the dusk descended he walked her to her hotel. He bid her adieu before they kissed.

They never spoke about it, but they both agreed to not write to each other. To not pursue anything more than what they shared; a summer fling, too good to ever last.

It wasn't the Brigadier's first holiday fling, but it was certainly one of his best.

Over the August bank holiday weekend, Jack meandered into the town centre and local record shop. Jack didn't find anything he wanted that he could afford, and the shop owner started to pay attention to him. He sauntered out, hands in his pockets.

He whistled the tune of *Are 'Friends' Electric?* as he passed the group of men as if to say he shared their musical tastes.

Outside, he considered his options for the day. His last day of freedom before being carted off back to Brendon, a week before the other boarders. All because his sister's school started a week before his did, and their olds ambitious plans to relocate had been scuppered. Thankfully. Even if it did mean a return to the less than optimal status quo. At least their olds and Jacquie weren't moving away.

Their olds had screamed at each other when their father came home with the news his company had shrunk, not grew. He'd clung on to his position, and salary, when dozens hadn't. At best Jack could stay at his school, and maybe they could convince Jacquie to work for a scholarship to the place up north they had their eye on for her.

Jack laughed at that, but managed to bottle up the guffaws until he escaped their earshot. He wrote about it all in his last letter to Jacquie. In her last return letter, she failed to hide her glee, despite the continued awfulness of her summer. She couldn't wait to return on the Bank Holiday Monday, even if they would have to plan their reunion carefully.

A man bumped into Jack as the boy stepped onto the footpath. 'Watch out, lad.'

Jack scuttled back. That voice. He looked up to see the man stop beside a vintage car. 'Sir?'

The man, the Brigadier, glanced up at him. His sun-browned face screwed up in a deep frown.

'Sorry, sir. I didn't expect to see you here. Have you been away?'

The Brigadier beamed. 'I have. Yes. Caught a bit of sun, but looking forward to seeing you all back in class. Not long to go, but I must dash.' He saluted and got into the car. Its engine roared to life and in moments the Brigadier sped off.

Jack stared after him. He scratched his head. Something didn't seem quite right. He shook his head, jammed his hands back into his pockets, and wandered without aim along the high street, pondering what it could have been.

CHAPTER SIX

Empty Spaces

HOME, SWEET home.

The Brigadier sank into his armchair and surveyed his digs. The converted shed might not suit everyone, but he'd lived in worse. In the years since he arrived at Brendon, he turned it into a cosy home in which he felt safe.

He gazed at the pictures of friends, old colleagues, and his African family on the wall, and smiled. Only a few of them had visited him at Brendon, and a few more he kept in contact with. Christmas might be four months away, but he ought to make a note of those he'd fallen out of the habit of keeping in touch and write to them. In particular his son, Mariama.

The Brigadier sighed. He didn't have Sandrine's address, and despite their unspoken pact he now wanted to thank her for everything. Those few weeks were different to his other relationships, but it restored a bit of confidence in himself missing since the incident that stole parts of his memory.

A smash from outside dragged him back from his reverie of the Riviera. Two boys chattered to each other in hushed tones, loud in their desire to be quiet. The Brigadier struggled up and he left his quarters to see the damage done.

Granger and Armstrong stood outside, Granger clutching a cricket bat. They whispered urgently at each other, the last phrases about his arrival on the scene.

Granger stepped forward and set his shoulders. 'Sir, sorry, but I accidentally hit the ball into one of your flower pots.'

'I see.' He regarded the boy who gripped the bat. In his experience, Granger rarely volunteered guilt about anything.

The Brigadier glanced at Armstrong, who stared back at him with a peculiar expression on his face. The Brigadier put that to one side and turned to look at the damage. He suppressed a wry grin. Mortars minus their explosive content might do similar damage. One of the large terracotta pots now contained a hole at its side that dribbled dirt. His eyebrows danced upwards. He couldn't see the cricket ball, which had no doubt lodged itself deep within.

'Judging from the trajectory and force, would I be correct in suggesting you two were not sufficiently far enough away to avoid causing such damage?'

'We didn't mean it, sir.'

The Brigadier winced at Granger's whine. He turned to face the student. 'I will need to assess the damage done, Mr Granger. I'm not so worried about the pot, but that plant took me a great deal of patience to nurture and grow. It's entirely probable that your cricket ball has damaged its roots. Mr Armstrong, you're being unusually quiet. Cat got your tongue?'

'No, sir.'

The ghostly voice whispered that he should drag both of them to the headmaster's office and insist they both receive half a dozen stripes from the cane. That would teach the insolent layabouts some responsibility.

He shook his head.

'Can we have our ball back, sir? Please.' Granger's hands gripped the bat so tightly his knuckles whitened.

'New kit, is it, Mr Granger?'

'Yes, sir.'

The Brigadier nodded curtly. He glanced once more at the oddly silent Armstrong. The boy gawped like he'd grown horns or a tail. He returned his attention to Granger. 'You'll get the ball back once I've dealt with the damage. Now, on your way. Both of you.'

'Yes, sir.'

The Brigadier walked back towards his home.

Armstrong whispered to Granger in a voice that carried. 'How long does it take for a 'stache to grow?'

'How would I know?'

As he reached his door and opened it, the Brigadier touched his moustache, not that he needed to. Still there. Boys. He snorted to himself.

*

Jack gaped after the older man who hadn't berated them for destroying his property. But that wasn't the full reason for why he stared.

Beside him, Alfie hefted his fancy new bat signed by Ian Botham. A gift from a family member who went to see the Ashes played out in Australia earlier that year. 'We should go before he changes his mind.'

'Seriously. When I saw him on Saturday he had no moustache.'

'What are you on about?'

'I saw him and his new motor in town on Saturday. It was weird, like old Stewpot didn't clock who I was, but then he sort of did. He was clean-shaven. No stupid 'stache.'

'You must have imagined it. Army bores like him never do anything radical like changing hairstyles. That's what Pa says, anyway. Oh, hey, did you see what the IRA did?'

'Lord Mountbatten?'

'Yeah, and twenty of our soldiers. I hate them and hope they get what's coming to them.'

Jack shoved his hands into his pockets. He tore himself away from his maths teacher's quarters and sauntered back towards their sports field. Granger followed.

Jack picked up his pace. No matter what Alfie prattled on about, he knew what he saw. The Brigadier had shaved his moustache off. He'd got a tan, too, so he must have shaved it off before he caught the sun. Yet, today, the blasted thing was back.

Unless it was a fake.

He clenched his fists in his pockets and wished his sister could be there. She'd know a way to find out. Or tell him to ignore it. Did it really matter? Only, something was off, and that had to matter.

Alfie followed him all the way. Drizzle dampened everything, and the grey skies hung low.

'Have you seen your sister?'

'Not yet.' Jack flung himself down in the grass. A caterpillar attracted his attention. Alfie's bat just missed squashing the thing as it landed, followed by Alfie. 'I know she had an awful time of it.'

'Wales?'

'Worse. Some island off Scotland.'

'Why do your parents hate her so much?'

Jack rolled over to his side. He picked at the grass. 'She's smarter than them and she scares them. She's the smartest person I know.' He pulled out a handful of grass and tossed it towards the obelisk. 'If the world was fair, she'd be here. Not me.'

'Are you a feminist?'

'No.' Jack spat the word out instinctively. He didn't know what it meant. Not exactly. Jacquie would. He scowled.

Alfie shrugged. 'Hey, did you see we've got a new boy starting in our form. Oliver Floyd-Jones.'

'Sounds like a right laugh.'

Friday. Finally. First week of the new school year and Jacquie sat outside the headmaster's office. She bounced her heels against the chair legs. The thump and squeak of her shoes against the metal annoyed the busy-bodies in the administration office.

Mr Beavers, her old history teacher, passed by and sneered. His delivery of those lessons was as dull as the brown corduroy everything that he wore, so she dismissed him.

Thankfully, the livelier Miss Starr replaced him as her history teacher this term.

The Head's door opened. Maureen Gill mooched out and smirked at Jacquie before she left.

Mr Locke loomed over her. 'In my office. Now.'

She stood up and slinked by him and to her usual spot in front of his desk.

'Well?' His eyebrows furrowed behind his old-fashioned glasses as he took up his usual position beside his desk. So, he was going to play it as a version of the prisoners' dilemma, only from Maureen Gill's smirk, she'd already been betrayed.

'I'm waiting.'

She huffed a sigh. 'Sir, Maureen wanted some help on the set problem, but Mr Merrill was clear he wanted us to work on our own.'

His eyes narrowed. 'Miss Gill says you disparaged Mr Merrill and she told you to show respect.'

Her eyes widened. Wow. Total lie.

He picked up a wooden ruler from his desk. 'The thing is, Miss Armstrong, if you weren't so intent on disrupting your classes, you could be at a much better school for your talents.'

She glanced up. What?

'It's evident your home life isn't ideal. It wasn't easy to fit you back in after your parents withdrew you.' He placed the ruler back on his desk. 'I'm letting you off with a warning this time. Next time you're back here, you'll get ten, plus whatever else necessary to get you to pay attention.'

'Thank you, sir.'

'Get back to class.'

The first Saturday with the full complement of boarders back saw the Brigadier leading his new contingent of cadets to a ceremony. During the week, he drilled the boys on marching, saluting, and standing to attention. He inspected their uniforms and got them polishing their boots so they shined. They were far from perfect, but he didn't grumble. None of the other teachers cared too much about the cadets and what they stood for, and the boys all tried their best. He couldn't really ask much more.

Alfie Granger surprised him by turning up in good kit, on time. His assistance with the younger boys impressed the Brigadier even more. He recalled the cricket ball incident on the day the boy returned to the school after his summer holidays and nodded. Chances were the lad sought forgiveness. Maybe, just maybe, the lad was growing up.

Shame the same couldn't be said of Granger's friend, Mr Armstrong. The boy wore his martyrdom of having to board even during most holidays as a gloomy old cloak. The Brigadier wanted to tell him that if he joined the cadets, he would gain a group of steadfast friends for life. Then he wouldn't pine after his sister all the time.

Mr Newton warned him off about pressuring young Mr Armstrong. 'I can't divulge the details, but the family's plans didn't work out over the summer. I have passed on your argument to his parents, but right now they are opting to let sleeping dogs lie. Go easy on him.'

Working with the students who joined the contingent quickly took up all of his spare time, anyway. Teaching, drilling, examining, fixing.

The Saturday dawned misty, but the sun burned it off. The unit assembled after morning tea. Later than he liked, but the opening ceremony was scheduled for noon. Mr Weller wanted the band and marching displays just before the ceremony itself. While the Brigadier moved the boys into line, Mr Newton and a few other teachers herded another twenty boys in their school uniforms into two mini-buses. Some of those boys called out to the cadets, which caused three of them to break their stance and gesture rudely. He shouted at them to restore order.

The mini-buses puttered off.

The Brigadier led the cadets in a march from the school grounds towards the estate. In contrast to the times last term when they went to help clean up and rebuild after the fire, he wore his parade uniform. The boys wore their sixty-eight pattern smocks and trousers, and they carried their brand-new unloaded rifles on their shoulders. They settled into a good pace.

When they reached the outskirts of the estate, he heard a brass band belting out tunes. A wistful smile tugged at the Brigadier's lips. Cheers erupted, and the bunting and little flags waved by the crowd conjured the image of a triumphant army's return. He brought the boys to a halt in front of the dais full of local dignitaries. The boys performed the most basic of rifle drills tolerably well before crashing to attention. The band played sombre music. Speakers talked about the community, and a councillor's wife cut the ribbon to the new community centre that looked like a clean version of the one burned down.

Done, the cadets stowed the rifles in the luggage compartment of one of the mini-buses. Freed from their commitment, the cadets joined their school chums and wandered about the fête for the afternoon.

Miracle of miracles, Mr Locke refrained from telling Jacquie's olds about her visit to his office as a result of Maureen Gill's fit up. She didn't volunteer any of that information, but she desperately needed to see Jack to interrogate him about everything he witnessed during the holidays. On Friday afternoon, she planted her note. On Saturday morning during her paper round, she checked his reply.

That blasted maths teacher playing soldier and that stupid community centre. She had no time to leave a note for Jack before his trip to the estate. She considered going there, but not with the Brigadier and the plod. Not after their escapade before the summer holidays.

She told her mother she was out to meet a friend.

'Who?'

'Molly.'

'Be back by dinnertime.'

'All right.'

Jacquie looked to see if she had the change to call Molly in case her mother checked on her. She used the telephone box on the corner two blocks away. Screwing up her nose from the smell of old booze and pee, Jacquie dialled. Molly answered like she usually did, her mother out working. Jacquie outlined her proposed deal, and Molly acquiesced. She asked for a copy of *I Don't Like Mondays*. 'If you can find me *Friggin' in the Riggin'* I'll cover you next weekend, too, yeah.'

'For serious?'

'For serious.'

'Deal.'

Jacquie made a beeline to the record shop and flicked through the vinyl and found both records for Molly. She asked the guys who ran the shop for any tips on acts to watch. One of them mentioned a solo effort from Gary Newman. Or The Clash, if punk still appealed.

She left and meandered up the high street to the cinema. She paused when she saw that hideous vintage car that had nearly ran her down before she left for Scotland. She stared, open-mouthed, as the maths teacher who owned it emerged from the cinema with a girl half his age on his arm.

'No way.'

Both got in the car.

'No frigging way.'

CHAPTER SEVEN
Cruel World

AT LUNCHTIME, Miss Nugent found Jack in the dining hall. She handed him a note, her lips pursed. 'I don't know why your mother called the headmaster's office to ask you to call her, but kindly remind her to use the telephone in your dormitory within the scheduled time. The general administration office can be used for emergencies. Understand?'

He half stood. His chair scraped back loudly. 'Yes, miss. Sorry, miss. I will, miss.' He clutched the note in his hand as he blushed. She nodded, curt and prim, before she turned on her heels and clicked out of the dining hall.

'That's you told.'

Jack sank back down on his seat. 'Shut up, Alfie. It's not my fault my mother broke the stupid rules.'

He unfolded the paper. He read it twice, his frown deepening. His mother normally wouldn't be the type to break the rules like that, and the message itself didn't sound like her. 'Do you need a set of mathematical instruments? There's a sale on. Let me know and I'll drop you a set. Love, M.' He owned the required set, which she knew. Oh. Ohh!

'Jacquie.' He laughed, scrunched the paper up again and shoved it into his trouser pocket. He picked up his fork and speared a slice of roast beef.

'What's so funny?' Alfie gawped at him.

'Jacquie called. Not our mother. She wanted to get my attention.'

'Who's Jacquie? Your girlfriend?'

Jack scowled at Oliver Floyd-Jones who sat next to Alfie opposite him. 'It's not polite to earwig.'

'Wasn't.' Floyd-Jones paused. 'So, is she your girlfriend?'

Alfie swallowed. 'She's his sister. They're twins.'

'Traitor,' Jack said.

'Ollie's all right.'

'Thanks.' The new boy in the form sounded sullen. He shovelled more of his food in his gob. 'Who likes their sisters, anyway?'

Jack placed his knife and fork down on his plate. He clenched and unclenched his fists a few times. He looked up at Floyd-Jones. 'Butt out.'

Floyd-Jones clasped at his chest like Jack had shot him there. He flung himself back. Alfie sniggered, then glanced at Jack as though for approval.

Mr Grey back-handed Floyd-Jones on the side of his head. The old history teacher jabbed a nicotine-stained finger at the new boy. 'Practice a bit of decorum in the dining hall, young man.' He waggled his finger at all of them.

'That's us told.' Alfie glanced back at the teacher who intervened.

Jack finished his lunch and, with permission, he scarpered ostensibly to go to his dorm to return the call. He disappeared inside, swapped his blazer for his denim jacket. No time to change fully. He escaped through a window, clambered down, then ran out to and down the lanes to the bus stop just as the bus lurched into view. He got on, sat near the front, and jumped off at the stop nearest to Jacquie's school. The church clock struck one. Kids screamed and shouted in the front yard. He saw Jacquie near the gate and jogged up to her. A few teachers patrolled and one looked like she noticed him.

'Whatcha?'

'Hey, hey.'

'When and where?'

'After school, but before the olds get in. Say, four?'

He nodded.

'New community centre?'

'Perfect.' He glanced up. The teacher moved towards them. 'Better scarper.'

Luck stayed with him as he retraced his steps back to Brendon. The only close call was the Brigadier's new old car, which nearly clipped the bus as it pulled out after Jack left it.

'Blimey.'

But the driver didn't stop and didn't seem to have noticed Jack as he ran back to his favourite place to break in and out of his dorm. Inside, he swapped jackets and then moseyed to his class. Maths. At least his teacher would be as late as he.

Only, old Stewpot stood at the front and droned on about trigonometry like he'd been there all day.

'Mr Armstrong. Good of you to join us.'

'Sorry, sir. I had to call my mother. It took longer than I expected.' He slid into his seat and pulled out his books.

'It's true, sir.'

Jack quietly groaned. He didn't need Oliver-flipping-Floyd-Jones to defend him.

Their teacher carried on. The afternoon dragged, but they made it to the end. Jack raced to his dorm and changed out of his uniform into jeans, a Tubeway Army t-shirt and his jacket.

Alfie arrived. 'Where are you off to?'

'Out. Cover for me? I'll be back before tea.'

'You owe me.'

'I know.' Jack flashed a grin. 'But look out for Floyd-Jones. I don't trust him.'

'Why?'

'Got to dash.' Jack escaped the same way as he had earlier.

This time Jack went his usual way to the estate. He arrived before Jacquie and kicked his heels against a new brick wall. The local kids moved away when he snarled at them. None of the adults who hung around said or did anything.

Jacquie arrived. They greeted each other. 'Let's stay out in the sunshine while it lasts.'

'All right.'

'Missed you.'

'Same,' Jack said.

'The olds are being suspiciously nice, but quiet. I've learned nothing new since I got back.'

'That place they sent you sounded horrible.'

'It was.' She shuddered and glanced away from him. 'Back now, but.'

'Back now, and not going away.' He flung himself backwards so he stared up at the sky. He laughed.

'I saw your maths teacher on Saturday.'

'Can't have.' He sat back up again. 'He was here with his little soldiers.'

'I know what I saw. He was with some dolly-bird half his age. They came out of the cinema. They were all over each other and got into that stupid car of his. You know. The one that nearly ran me over before the holidays. He's a menace behind the wheel of that thing.'

'Did he have a moustache?'

'What? Yes.' She shook her head. 'Like most men do these days.'

'I swear I saw him during the holidays and he didn't. He looked like he shaved it off before he went somewhere sunny. It's not like him. It's just weird.'

Tuesday morning dawned with a mist that caressed the sports grounds and hid the treetops. The Brigadier stepped out for his morning walk to clear the cobwebs and to stay trim. He adjusted his flat cap and set off.

He paused as he passed by his car. He frowned. Mud clung to her tyres, but he didn't recall driving anywhere where such mud would be collected. Not only that, it was parked at more of an angle than he liked. The mini-buses got too close for his comfort too often, and he really did not want to add any expensive repair bills to what he owed the man who loaned him the money to buy her. He shook his head. He must be imagining it. No one else drove her. He would just have to be more careful.

Setting a pace to raise his heart rate, the Brigadier marched out of the school grounds and towards the estate. He startled a flock of small birds from one of the hedges. They flitted and darted about, chittering and calling to each other. He passed them by with a smile. The things he barely noticed as a young man with more important things to do than watch birds.

He reached the estate and nodded at a few of the residents as they headed towards the bus stop. They returned his greeting with nods and smiles.

A woman wearing a dark grey head scarf emerged from the off-licence shop. She wrestled with a trolley. He picked up his pace. 'Madam. Let me.' He held open the door. She darted a quick, uncertain glance at him. She appeared younger than he first thought. He tipped his cap, smiled, and wished her a good day. She stammered a thank you, and scurried away with her liberated trolley rattling behind her. She headed towards one of the remaining towers that the clouds swallowed.

The shopkeeper greeted the Brigadier on entry. 'Bad news about British Leyland.'

'What's that?'

'As of autumn next year they'll stop making MGs.'

'Oh, yes. Terrible.' He picked up his newspaper and made his usual show of looking for something else to buy.

'Mark my words, but that will be just the start.'

The Brigadier made a non-committal grunt.

'Although I suppose you're a Tory and all, teaching at that posh school.'

'I keep my political views to myself, but no one can say that any of us have had it good for a while now. I believe it the fault of many poor decisions made by every government since the war and not only in this country.'

'Fair enough.'

The Brigadier snatched up a chocolate bar and bought it along with his newspaper. He smiled briefly at the shopkeeper, and left just as quickly to return to the school.

As he strode, he pondered over the shopkeeper's comments. While he appreciated a good motor car, it wasn't his passion. So much had happened during the decade now nearing its end to fixate on a type of car unlikely to be owned by the complainer. He frowned. He couldn't help but worry the outrage was manufactured. Provoked. Not genuine. Dangerous territory.

He turned into the school's driveway. A gaggle of boys ran around one of the ovals accompanied by the sports master. Mr Ellis waved at him as they passed and the Brigadier saluted with his rolled-up newspaper. He turned towards his quarters, having decided to breakfast there. As he turned, the sunlight glinted off the front left fender of his car.

He stopped. Gaped. Every muscle in his body tensed up and his blood pounded. He strode forward. Ran his hand along the curve of the fender.

Someone had dented the metal. No scratch or scrape, and he'd been careful when driving. The mini-buses hadn't been used since Saturday, so the damage must have been done after they'd been parked. He traced the shape of it with his finger. He straightened up and caught sight of the pot he had yet to replace from the destruction caused by Granger and Armstrong, and their blasted cricket ball.

He'd extracted the offending item and returned it to Granger. He warned them about playing cricket so close to the buildings and vehicles. They promised not to, and he believed them. He'd let the matter drop quietly.

Idiot.

Give those boys an inch and they always took a mile. Spare them the rod and they never, ever learned.

Worst was they didn't volunteer the information about the damage to his car. Even after he gave them the benefit of the doubt. If it wasn't those specific boys, surely they would have told their fellow pupils he was fair. More than fair.

Well. No more. The headmaster wanted to tighten up the discipline code, and he would contribute to the review.

Wednesday afternoon saw Jacquie drag her feet to Miss Starr's classroom. Jacquie knocked on the doorjamb and Miss Starr waved her in. She pointed at the desk and chair directly in front of the teacher's desk. 'Sit.'

Jacquie scowled, but obeyed.

'Mr Locke issued a staff memo about you. He's instructed us to report any and all infractions. I haven't yet informed his office about this morning's incident.' She glanced at her watch. 'You have ten minutes to write me an essay about why you need to pay attention in class.'

Miss Starr pulled a book out from her desk drawer, opened it, and began to read. After a few moments, she glanced up. 'Get writing.'

Jacquie snorted and wrote about teachers exacting inter-generational revenge on those who couldn't fight back. Just because they'd been bullied and belittled didn't give them the right to do the same to the next generation. As for not paying attention? Fine. Her mind wandered while other kids played up, but she'd done her homework. She hadn't heard Miss

Starr's question, but she could have repeated it. She apologised for her reaction during class.

'Time's up.'

Jacquie stopped writing. Sullenly, she handed the paper to her teacher, and sat back with her arms crossed.

When she finished reading, Miss Starr looked at Jacquie with a grim smile. 'You are clearly intelligent.'

Jacquie shifted in her seat.

'You're not incorrect in your observations about too many of my colleagues, and I know I am not perfect. I apologise for the mistake I made earlier, and I accept your apology. Dismissed.'

Jacquie stood up. 'You won't report this?'

'I don't think it serves anybody's interests, do you?'

Jacquie shook her head.

'Off you go.'

Jacquie left the classroom with a frown. She headed towards her home, deep in thought about Miss Starr's words and actions. A car horn tooted, breaking into her reverie.

Her brother's maths teacher sat once more in his ridiculous car. She was about to flip him a finger when a woman tottered on high heels from a dress shop. She flung two large bags onto the car's back seat.

'Come on,' the old soldier said. 'I need to be getting back.'

'All right, duck. Keep your hair on.' The young blonde got in the front passenger seat. She leaned over and pecked him on his cheek, leaving a red impression of her lips. 'I can't help it if Mavis Marple or whoever wants to tell the world about all the problems of this bloody borough.'

He gunned the engine of the car and pulled out without looking. He gesticulated at two other car drivers, who slammed on their brakes. He sped off.

'Blimey.' Another incident to share with her brother about his teacher.

Thursday afternoon carried on with a cool drizzle which started that morning. After a warm summer, the plummeting temperature proved a shock. Yet, the school demanded the boys dress in shorts and t-shirts to run around the cross-country track.

Jack played up a sniffle and cough to bunk off the run. He balanced it just right to avoid the sport, but not enough to send him to the nurse or the doctor. He went to his dorm room and dressed in jeans, a shirt and jacket. He headed out his usual way, and went to the new community centre. He met Jacquie there, who already drank from a can of fizzy pop and crunched on some new crisp flavour. After their customary greeting, he sat and popped his own can.

'Your maths teacher is out and about a lot,' Jacquie said.

'You've seen him again?'

She nodded. 'With the same dolly-bird. Definition of vacuous, if you ask me.'

He mouthed the word 'vacuous'.

She sighed and flopped back in her chair. 'Air head. Vacuum where her brain should be.'

'Oh, right.' He opened the crisp packet she bought for him. He looked inside. 'Was he in his vintage motor?'

'He was.'

'The new boy, Ollie, heard him go off about me or Alfie denting it with a cricket ball. We didn't, as it happens, and he's not said anything to us.'

'Maybe he really knows it came from his own reckless driving.'

Jack shrugged. 'Alfie swears the Brigadier didn't go AWOL from here last Saturday.'

'He must've.'

'Well, when I applied a bit more pressure, old Alfie did admit to not having his eyeballs on him for the whole time.'

'The truth will out.'

As Jack skulked back into his school, he heard raised voices. One belonged to his history teacher. The other he couldn't quite make out. Young. Probably one of the new intake into one of the Middle School forms. Jack crept closer.

'But, sir.' The boy squeaked. 'We've seen teachers outside, too, and Papa says that's not allowed.'

'Who?'

Jack stopped. Through the bushes and trees he saw two young boys, both snivelling, but one stood up tall while the other studied the ground. Mr Grey resembled his name with his expression dark and stormy.

'The Brigadier for one.'

'That is a serious allegation. Both of you, go to your form master and explain.'

Jack stared as Grey motioned for the two boys to move. The old teacher hurried them along with a clip around their ears.

Jack waited for a few moments to ruminate over what he heard. It seemed the boys verified his sister's stories about his maths teacher.

The Brigadier sat in his usual seat for the weekly staff meeting. Mr Newton rattled through a summary of the first week back, and highlighted the existence of a waiting list of students to the school. He noted the generous donations to the library from a London university, and turned to a paper he gave out to the gathered teachers.

'The waiting list I mentioned is useful. It means that if a boy be expelled, we can more freely consider the options and not be constrained by the risk of financial loss.'

The Brigadier's eyebrows darted upwards. He grunted, and shifted in his seat. Expulsion was a serious matter with the potential to ruin a boy's life. He took his copy of the distributed paper and passed the remaining pile on to Ms Peters.

'The paper is a proposal to tighten up the Discipline Code, now that we have an idea about the government's intentions on school reform. If you can, please read it over the weekend and submit any final comments by five o'clock on Monday afternoon. I would like to thank you all for contributing your comments and ideas to date. Any other business?'

The headmaster looked at each teacher in turn and, to the Brigadier's relief, no one prolonged the meeting. He folded the draft Discipline Code and jammed it into his jacket pocket.

His lessons that afternoon sailed past with little to make them remarkable. He strode back to his quarters. Inside, he put the kettle on for a cup of tea. Once made, he settled in his armchair with it, and pulled out the Discipline Code to read. Much of it remained the same as the old Code, as it ought, in his opinion. When he turned to the pages of transgressions and the rising scale of punishment for each, his blood ran cold. He skimmed to the end, stood, and stormed from his digs to the office block. He powered up the stairs and down the corridors. Miss Nugent stood outside the headmaster's office and she stepped back.

'Brigadier?'

'Is he in?'

She nodded, and turned back to the open door. She repeated his title.

Mr Newton emerged from his office. 'Whatever is the matter?'

The Brigadier waved a rolled-up copy of the draft new Discipline Code. 'This is too much.'

Newton glanced at his watch. 'I can spare you five minutes, but I did say I would take comments up to the end of Monday.'

'I know, but where has this viciousness come from? You know I'm not one to spare the rod, but this contains nasty and brutal stuff that I cannot in all good conscience accept or support.'

He followed Newton into the office. He shook his head at the headmaster's indication he should sit. He made to open up the document to show the other man what he meant.

'Brigadier, I am puzzled. Most of this draft is what you yourself gave Miss Nugent on your return from the summer holidays.'

Anything the Brigadier was about to say deserted him, like a sail without wind. He spluttered. 'There must be a mistake.' He shook his head. He cast about in his memory. He had intended to work on it, but between Sandrine and needing an actual break, he hadn't.

Newton drew a copy from one of his filing cabinets and showed it to him. He recognised his own handwriting. His ideas. He clutched his head. Shook it slowly.

'I'm sorry, I must have…'

Mr Newton waited. 'Must have what?'

'My mistake.' The Brigadier quickly retreated from the headmaster's office.

CHAPTER EIGHT
Message in a Bottle

TUESDAY MORNING saw the boys in Jack's form inspected for shiny shoes and ties knotted the right way. Boaters and blazers had to pass muster, too, before they were allowed to board the mini-buses. Mr Grey, Ms Peters and the Brigadier all had chaperone duty.

Jack wanted to sit beside Alfie, but the Brigadier had other ideas. Ollie joined Jack up the front and stared around him. Alfie sat at the back in the same mini-bus. Jack folded his arms and slumped in his seat.

'If you're going to sit like that, do you mind if I sit by the window. Please.'

Jack grunted. Shrugged. He looked up at the teachers who conferred about their lists through the open doors of their mini-bus. He stood up and indicated Ollie could do as he asked.

The Brigadier looked back. 'Mr Armstrong. Sit down.'

Jack fell back into his new seat and flipped his middle finger up in the teacher's direction. Only Ollie saw and his eyes widened. 'You shouldn't be so disrespectful.'

Jack glared at the boy, who shrank from him. Jack resumed his slump.

Finally, the three teachers finished their fussing and they set off in convoy.

As they drove through the countryside, and then into London, Ollie stuck his nose on the window like a little kid. Despite himself, Jack appreciated the boy keeping quiet and not invading his space. The rest of the boys in the mini-bus erupted in boisterous singing to stave off boredom. After a few minutes, the Brigadier bellowed at them to quieten down.

'Have you ever been to central London?' Jack asked Ollie.

'No. Is it all this boring?'

Jack grinned. 'Naw. The bit where we're going is all right. It's just the way in that's rubbish. Where have you been before?'

'I was born in Kenya, but we moved to India and then Singapore. I only arrived in England a few days before school started.'

'Wow. I've never been anywhere. My olds promise a lot, but they never come through.'

'They live near the school, don't they?'

Jack hunched over and nodded.

'How come you board?'

'I've got a twin sister and our olds don't like it when we get together. They say we're trouble.'

Ollie scratched his head. 'Are you much alike?'

'Identical.'

'How does that work if you're a boy and she's a girl?'

Jack gave an exaggerated shrug. 'It's super rare, but it does happen. Jacquie knows the details. We look alike, but she's got the brains.' He nodded towards the Brigadier. 'Last term she pretended to be me in one of his classes. Got away with it, too.'

'Golly.'

Jack told Ollie all the details and about some other mischief they'd got away with. The new boy listened attentively, his shock and surprise egging Jack on. He tried and failed to raise a laugh, but he did conclude that Ollie was all right.

The mini-buses arrived at a place they could park and everyone trooped out. First port of call would be the Houses of Parliament. To reach Westminster, they needed to walk down Whitehall. Mr Grey pointed out the parts built by the Tudors, which no one could see. Ms Peters and the Brigadier herded the boys.

As they passed the Ministry of Defence building, a man in a three-piece suit and bowler hat called out. 'I say. Lethbridge-Stewart. That you?'

Everyone paused and stared.

The Brigadier shook hands with the man.

'You're looking well. The grapevine said you'd been to

warmer climes over the summer.'

'Uh, yes. You're looking well, too.'

Jack noted the Brigadier used no names, and seemed to be at a loss.

The man nodded at the boys, who Mr Grey and Ms Peters tried valiantly to move away to give the Brigadier and his friend privacy. 'I heard you'd taken up teaching. Enjoying it?'

'Ah, yes. It's a fulfilling second career. We must get on, though, if you'll excuse me.'

'Of course, old boy, of course.' The man tipped the brim of his bowler hat.

The Brigadier nodded, touched the peak of his flat cap, and returned to his colleagues and students with an apology. They continued on to the Houses of Parliament.

At some point on the tour, Jack earwigged the Brigadier and Ms Peters in quiet conversation. He only heard a little that interested him. The Brigadier had no memory of the man who greeted him on Whitehall. He mentioned something that occurred in 1977, before Jack arrived at Brendon. Frustratingly, neither teacher elaborated. Jack stored the information to pass it on to Jacquie. She would know what to do with it. Alfie wouldn't, and while Jack now regarded Ollie with less suspicion he guessed the new boy wouldn't approve of gossip.

The tour proved dull. They only saw the prime minister from a distance. They weren't allowed into a few places, and had to be quiet everywhere else. Still, a day out was a day out.

They trooped back to the mini-buses. No mysterious men approached anyone this time. Their drive through to Hyde Park for a picnic lunch stalled in traffic. The Brigadier snarled at a herd of tourists, and then at cabbies cutting in. The old soldier's caution drew Jack's attention. It didn't add up to the damage done to the old car newly bought, or Jacquie's tales of narrowly avoiding being knocked down by him. He shook his head and carried on with the jokes and japes with Ollie and the boys around him.

After lunch, they trotted to the Science Museum. The teachers divided the students into three groups and took turns to show them around the exhibits based on what they taught. Despite himself, Jack almost enjoyed some of it. Jacquie would be better at explaining it, though, and he hung back and scowled at the injustice of it all.

They were allowed half an hour to go to exhibits they wanted. Jack followed Alfie to the rooms that showed animal and human remains. Ollie tagged along behind them. At a display case filled with old surgical tools, Ollie crowded up to it. He pointed out the different tools and told Jack and Alfie all about how surgeons used them. He gloried in describing the blood and crunch of the bones, and both Jack and Alfie leaned in.

'How do you know all this stuff?' Jack asked.

'One of Daddy's friends is an old surgeon. He had a set like that and told me all about it.'

Mr Grey arrived, huffing and puffing. 'Mr Armstrong, Mr Granger and Mr Floyd-Jones. There you all are. You're five minutes late. Get a move on.'

Jack joined Alfie and Ollie in their chorus. 'Yes, sir. Sorry, sir.'

The Brigadier led the little convoy of three mini-buses through congested central London, then to an arterial road where he could relax a bit. So long as he kept the vehicle in lane and at a steady speed, and no other driver did anything untoward, they ought to return to the school in under an hour. His shoulders ached with tension rather than exertion. He'd driven less responsive and heavier vehicles in his army career.

Exhaustion subdued the boys. They chattered and laughed at a decent volume, but some snored. No fights. No singing. No whining.

The traffic around his mini-bus kept pace. A few cars swapped lanes, but none ventured near his.

He changed gears to climb an incline. He checked for and saw the other two mini-buses as they kept with the pace he set. All good. All in place.

They reached a plateau and he adjusted the gears accordingly. Smooth operator. He allowed himself a smile.

His mind drifted.

The man who approached him on Whitehall vexed him.

From his clothes, he had to be a Civil Servant. He assumed from the Ministry of Defence, but he couldn't rule out C19, the Foreign Office, or possibly even the Army. If the last option, he was probably high ranking given the way he addressed the Brigadier. The man knew him, but his own mind refused to fill in the blank.

He shifted his position and tightened his grip on the steering wheel. His shoulders twinged.

The man knew so much about him. His change of occupation. His travel to the Mediterranean during the summer. The stranger's knowledge disturbed him.

Maybe if he could remember who the man was it would all make sense.

They neared a pedestrian overpass that marked the point to shift lanes to the next exit. He saw silhouettes of a small group of people on the overpass. He registered the way in which the group moved, and how they weren't walking across the pedestrian bridge but gathered above the lane along which he and the two others drove.

Something hit the roof of the mini–bus. More missiles rained down from above. Glass from bottles shattered around them.

The Brigadier kept his nerve and prayed the other two teachers would, too.

Rebecca farewelled her final patient of the day. She returned to her office to tidy her files ahead of a weekend away and she looked forward to the long chats with former research colleagues. She hummed a tune in the charts that she would be hard-pressed to name.

The intercom buzzed. She answered. The receptionist told her that Brigadier Lethbridge-Stewart was on the line. 'Can you take the call?'

Rebecca glanced at her clock. 'Put him through.' She collected his file and sat at her desk. She opened the folder and picked up her pen as the call clicked to announce the connection. 'Brigadier?'

'Apologies for the late hour. I'm not keeping you, am I?'

'No, not at all. How can I help?' She noted he always dissembled when he needed to confront a deep problem. She could give him a comfortable half hour of her time, which she could stretch for an extra fifteen minutes. More than that she would have to convince him to visit in person.

'I'm sorry. I'm wasting your time.'

'Brigadier, that is the last thing you are doing.'

He sighed. She pictured him looking troubled, but trying to hide it behind his stiff upper lip. She let him work up the courage he needed. 'Have you heard the news today?'

'Uh, no. Not yet.' She winced at a hardness she hadn't meant to convey. 'What's happened?'

'Oh, um.' He paused. 'I don't know them, but there was an accident this morning in Cambridgeshire. Two Harrier jets crashed into a few houses in Wisbech.'

'Oh, gosh.' She hadn't heard, and she decided to avoid the television news that evening because it sounded horrible. 'Did it bring back memories?'

'I, uh. This is silly. I'm not sure.'

'Are you frightened it will?'

'No, of course not!' he snapped.

'Sorry, Brigadier. I made a poor choice of words.'

'No, I'm sorry.' His voice softened. 'I am. Daft as it is to be scared of my own dreams.'

'It's what the dreams represent that scare us. Dreams bring to the surface our memories, and some of those memories are of unpleasant things. You've nothing to be ashamed about.'

'We were attacked. Two other teachers and I. We were returning from a school trip and some local teenagers threw bottles at the mini-buses.'

'How awful.'

'Oh, the police are trying to find them, but I don't think they will. They don't think we were targeted, but it's obvious we were. Otherwise they would have thrown the bottles at other vehicles, which they didn't. I keep seeing the carnage.'

Her heart thudded. She felt sure she hadn't missed news of a fatal crash involving his school. 'Was anyone hurt?'

'No. We all kept our heads, and the glass shattered on impact. The tyres withstood the barrage. No, the carnage I can't let go of is what might have happened.'

'I see, and I understand.' She saw how the two separate

incidents would link up in a former soldier's mind. She entertained no doubt he associated both with traumatic events from his soldiering days. He was right to call.

'I suppose you're thinking that I'm recalling events from my past?'

She started. Frowned. 'You are an intelligent man and I certainly do not take you for a fool.'

'I know.' He sighed again. Down the telephone line he sounded so vulnerable and alone. Her heart ached. 'The thing is, I could consider a few incidents from my career. I can recall a few, but if there's one thing I've learned from you is that would be too easy. My problem is my memory. Specifically, the holes in my memory. Like Swiss cheese, isn't that what they say?'

'You have been paying attention.' She kept her tone light.

'Yes, well.' He took a deep breath. 'Earlier that day of the school outing, I met a man who knew me, but I have absolutely no recollection of who he is.'

'Ah, I see.' She wrote it down and drew a line to connect the ideas.

'I've racked my brains for days. I've spoken to a few old friends, but all to no avail.'

She nodded as she contemplated her notes of his concerns.

'Thing is, he knows so much about my life now. I've been teaching for a few years, so that was less of a surprise. But he knew where I spent my summer.'

'Are you certain about that?'

'I know what he said!' he snapped again.

'I'm sorry. Of course. Look, did you want to reconsider coming in for an appointment?'

'I'll think about it. I'm sorry for wasting your time.'

'You haven't.' She spoke into the buzz of the disconnected line. She swore.

Jacquie hung her Sunday best dress up in her wardrobe. She put on her jeans, and pulled on a jumper over her shirt. An autumnal chill fought and won against summer's last hurrah of sunshine. She told her olds she was heading to a friend's place to do some homework and would return in time for tea.

She pretended not to hear her mother call after her. She

grabbed her bike and set off in the direction of her friend's house. This time, Jacquie had planned the subterfuge on Friday at school. She just needed to remember to give over the second half of the payment.

At the corner, she checked for signs of pursuit. Nothing. She continued on to her friend's house. A man mowed the lawn out the front. She pulled up and smiled.

'Is Shirley in?'

He turned the mower off. 'Who's asking?'

'A friend from school.'

He wiped his sweaty brow. 'You've missed her. She's off seeing a picture with other friends.'

'Oh, yes. That's right. She did say we should meet at the cinema. Thank you.' She peddled off.

The deceit gave her a little thrill as it all came together. If her parents followed her, which she couldn't disregard, then her cover story was in play. Next stop was the cinema where she chained her bike up. She saw Shirley and her friends gathered near the snack bar. Jacquie and Shirley swapped cash for a ticket and Jacquie left them to it.

She checked outside and saw no one she recognised. She sauntered towards the record shop and approached her brother who flicked through the singles with a concentration she reckoned his teachers would love to see. The boy did love his music.

'Hey, hey.'

'Whatcha.' He looked up at her. 'They sold out of Gary Newman's *Cars*.'

'Why's he split with his band for?'

Jack shrugged. 'Did you bring it?'

'Couldn't. Both the olds are watching like hawks.'

He swore under his breath.

She tapped the side of her head and grinned. 'Memorised it.'

He half smiled and removed himself from the records. 'Obelisk?'

She shook her head. 'Too far. I'm seeing a dull, but long film with a new school friend.'

'Huh?'

She tilted her head and watched him as he worked it out.

'Isn't that paranoia?'

'Not if they really are out to get us.'

He play-punched her on her upper arm. 'Library, then?'

'Thought you'd never ask.'

The twins left the record shop and walked towards the library. Jacquie scanned for any threat, and only breathed easy once they reached their usual table.

'How long's the film?'

'Three hours.'

Jack whistled. 'Would I like it?'

'I didn't.'

'Why'd you see it?'

'Get your paper out.'

Jack opened his satchel and pulled out an exercise book and a collection of differently coloured pens. He scattered them on the table. She grabbed the book and opened it at the first blank page. She picked up a black biro and scratched out what she remembered of the paperwork from the school he boarded at. It was mostly guff to do with his choices for the next school year and preparation for it. Her own school didn't operate that far ahead, although this year she had overheard some of her teachers moan about new government policies. Like they cared about the effect of those changes on their pupils.

Done, she passed the book back to him. His face creased up while he read it.

'It boils down to what you want to concentrate on next year,' Jacquie explained.

'But we've only just started this year.'

'What subjects do you want to ditch out of that lot?' She pointed to one column of two.

'Why have the olds got it and not me?'

'A conspiracy of adults.'

'What?'

She huffed. 'They don't think you know you, and what you want to do when you're all grown up. They want you to be able to get a good job so you can get married, have kids, and replicate their lives. Only without screwing up like they think they did with us.'

His upper body sagged. 'Why don't they leave us alone?'

She shrugged.

He picked up a green pen and doodled around her words. 'So, why did you go see that film?'

'I told the olds it was for school. It got me out of the house for an evening. Plus, it got me a good alibi for today.'

'Why'd your friends see it?'

She snorted a sharp laugh. 'They're not my friends. We struck a deal. One of the many reasons why we're not friends is because they love that pile of steaming rubbish as if it's art of the highest order. It really isn't. Pretentious twaddle is the technical term.'

'Oh.'

'God, I am so bored.'

'Sorry.'

'Not with you.' She raised her shoulders and arms, leaned back, then curled forward and slumped over the table, her hands outstretched. She knocked a few of his pens flying. Jack collected them and dropped them back into his satchel. She looked up at him. 'Can we play another trick on your maths teacher? That was fun, but we could do better.'

'Yeah, I guess.' He grinned. 'On our school trip something weird happened.'

'Oh?'

'Yeah. Some geezer talked to him. He knew who the Brigadier was, but I swear old Stewpot had no idea who he was. He lost his marbles a few years ago, so I think it might have something to do with that.'

'You feel sorry for him?'

'Not really.'

'Good,' Jacquie said. 'I don't think he should be smooching about with a girl young enough to be his daughter.'

CHAPTER NINE
Gimme! Gimme! Gimme!

FIRST CLASS of the day saw the Brigadier in front of the board attempting to get the fifth formers to concentrate on solving a problem of the type that would feature in their exams.

The revised Discipline Code didn't really help, not that he wanted to revisit that fiasco. Not when he'd only just managed to coax a correct answer from Mr Armstrong about how to approach the set problem on the board. The boy looked tired. Pale, drawn skin. Bags under his eyes. The Brigadier debated whether he should suggest to the boy to go see the nurse.

Mr Granger interrupted the class with a braying laugh.

'Mr Granger! What is it?'

'Nothing, sir.'

A headache thumped in the Brigadier's temple. *Give me strength.* He strode to Granger's desk and slammed his hand down on the piece of paper that lay flat on the boy's text book. All of the boys jumped. Silence descended on the classroom. The Brigadier glanced at Granger and picked the paper up. He read it quietly to himself and suppressed a smile.

There once was a soldier turned teacher
Who spied a girl and wanted to teach her
But for his vintage car
That couldn't travel far
He genuinely thought he could reach her

'Very droll. Whoever the poet is should report to Mrs Young.'

He returned to the front of the room and hit the board. Chalk dust bellowed out from it, followed by outbreaks of sniggers from the students.

'Back to the problem and its solution.'

Miss Nugent smiled at him when he arrived outside the headmaster's office. 'Go on in, Brigadier. He's expecting you.'

He nodded, knocked, and pushed the ajar door fully open. He closed it behind him.

Mr Newton waved at him to sit on the comfortable chairs that surrounded a coffee table. On the table sat a manila folder embossed with a modern-looking logo he didn't recognise. He frowned as he struggled to decipher the words.

Newton sat opposite him. 'That arrived in the last post yesterday.' He indicated the folder. 'It's from one of the most influential think-tanks with the government on education policy. I am led to believe that its chairman is a friend of the prime minister.'

The Brigadier nodded as he leaned back.

'Go on. Pick it up and have a read.'

The Brigadier did as Newton asked. He skimmed over the letter on the top, addressed to Newton and the school trustees. As he read, Newton summarised.

'They are keen to put us forward for a research study that will provide a funding stream for at least two years. Longer if we are selected as an exemplar school.'

'So I see.'

'Yes. They are particularly pleased with what you've done with the CCF and want to expand that.'

The Brigadier allowed himself a brief smile as he shifted in his seat.

'I spoke with the think-tank's chairman this morning. Mr Woolton is his name. I don't know him personally, but he impressed me with his vision for this country. I wanted to share two points with you before I take their proposal to the full teaching staff. The first is to do with the Irish violence. He believes that the training possibilities afforded by the CCF should be better used to protect ourselves from the terrorists. He believes we have a moral duty to train as many of our boys as we can to prevent such violence as occurred against Lord Mountbatten.'

The Brigadier's eyebrows danced upwards. He chose to hold his tongue and listen to what Newton had to say. He didn't wholly disagree with the proposal. Training boys how to fight tended to bring discipline to otherwise chaotic responses. The more boys knew how to fight, paradoxically, the less inclined they were to express their views through violence. Despite that, butterflies fluttered in his belly at the idea of using the cadets to counter the IRA's terrorist cells.

Newton kept on, oblivious to the Brigadier's reaction. 'I took the liberty of sharing the main points of our new Discipline Code with Woolton and he was very impressed. He would like a copy of the complete document.'

'*Draft* Discipline Code.' The Brigadier grunted and shifted in his seat once more.

'I know you've had second thoughts about your proposals, but so far they are proving effective.'

There it was. The yawning gap in his memory. The Brigadier touched his forehead for a moment. Just as the identity of that man in Whitehall refused to surface, any memory of the work Miss Nugent and Mr Newton proved he'd done failed to come to light. The butterflies in his belly whipped up a storm.

'Are you all right, Brigadier?'

He swallowed, and sat forward. 'Yes, yes.' He waved Mr Newton away. He paused for a moment for the world to settle down around him. 'I'm fine, and it does all sound encouraging.' He gestured at the folder he put back on the table.

'Good, good. Couldn't do it without you. You really have proved to be an asset to the school. We'll discuss it formally at the next meeting of the teaching staff.'

Miss Starr set her Fifth Form history class a project to research a local person, institution or event connected in some way to the Great War. The project intrigued Jacquie, more by its open nature than the topic itself. Her teacher gave the whole class the rest of September and most of October to complete it ahead of Remembrance Sunday. She wanted everyone to do their own, but they could pool together to help each other if they liked. Miss Starr gave them a list of ideas and a schedule of things to do and dates she would check on their progress.

Jacquie loitered after the bell rang. Miss Starr raised an eyebrow at her. 'Is there a problem with what I've set you?'

'No, miss.' Jacquie twisted the strap of her satchel in her hands. 'Do you mean it when you say we can choose anything?'

'Within the guidelines, yes.'

'There's a retired old soldier I know who I'd like to look at.'

'If he served during the Great War, then that's the sort of project that would be ideal. I don't need to know just yet.' Miss Starr smiled warmly. 'I am glad to see you taking an interest, after our conversation last week.'

'Thank you for not reporting me, miss.'

'You're welcome. If you want any advice or help on this, or anything else, just ask me. Okay?'

Jacquie didn't answer right away. She finally nodded, and left for the school library. There, she scribbled out her ideas and questions in the code she and her brother used. She wanted to make his maths teacher the focus of her project, but figured his age precluded him. But, if she could find out more about him, then she could find something interesting for Miss Starr and for her and Jack to exploit.

The school library contained nothing of use. The reference books were too old, or too general. The librarian, on the other hand, could help. Mr Devereaux dabbled as a local historian, so Jacquie learned years ago from observation. Like usual, no one else bothered the man. Jacquie collected her thoughts and approached him.

'What can I do for you, young lady?' He peered over his thick, square glasses.

'Miss Starr set us a history project to do with World War One and the local area.'

'I see.' He straightened up.

'How might I go about finding old soldiers who live around here?'

'Let me see.' He glanced up at the ceiling. 'Any soldiers surviving that war would be in their seventies or eighties now.' He looked down again. 'You could try the old person's home. I've spent many an hour there listening to the tales told by them about this part of England, and they enjoy the company. I can't think of any old soldiers there, but they don't always volunteer that information.'

'Why's that, do you think?' She cocked her head, genuinely

interested.

'Have you heard of shell shock?'

She nodded and frowned.

'They simply don't want to be reminded of the horrible things they experienced. In some cases, they may just have forgotten.' He tapped out a little rhythm on the desk with his fingers. 'They closed the local army barracks around here, but you could write to the Ministry of Defence to find out which regiment was stationed here. There's a fellow who teaches at Brendon School who's a retired officer. He could help.' He paused and his brow furrowed. He pushed his glasses up his nose. 'Your brother's at that school, isn't he? Perhaps you could ask him.'

Jacquie rewarded the librarian with a bright smile. 'I will. Thank you.'

As she turned away to go to her next class, she pondered his words. Clearly, Mr Devereaux had filtered out the details of the headmaster's instructions about her and her brother. Interesting.

Jack had received and decoded Jacquie's letter, and waited until two o'clock in the morning when the boys in his dorm room slept deeply. He crept out and along the corridors, up and down flights of stairs to traverse the maze to the administration offices. The trusting fools didn't even lock the main door.

They did lock the filing cabinets where they kept examination papers, assignments, and private documents. Not that the locking system proved too much of a challenge to Jack and his picking tools. The full moon, clear night, and curtain-less windows meant he didn't need a torch, and he knew better than to turn a main light on.

He found the cabinet where they kept the personnel files on the teaching staff and opened it. The clunks and clicks made his heart leap into his mouth in case the noise would summon an insomniac teacher.

None came.

He found the Brigadier's file and took it with him so he could peruse it at his own leisure. He planned to return it on the weekend. Before heading back to his bed with the contraband, he shut the cabinet drawer and manipulated the locking mechanism so it would seem whoever opened it last hadn't shut it properly. He had the impression from the dust and stiffness of the drawer that the administrators didn't open that cabinet all that often, not like the cabinets of immediate interest to the students.

As he stole up the final flight of stairs, the sound of shuffling feet and wheezing breath warned him Mr Grey patrolled. Like a clockwork soldier, the old man kept to his usual route and Jack ducked out of sight. Once he passed by, Jack waited for a few moments to get his heart rate back under control. With a soft huff, he headed back to his dorm room and hid the file in his locker.

The Brigadier spent what spare time he had since his meeting with Mr Newton earlier that week trying to think of the reasons why he felt uneasy about the think-tank's proposals. He failed to identify anything concrete. It just felt off.

He trudged into the common room with Mr Grey and Ms Peters. He slumped in his usual place and shuffled through the papers that Miss Nugent handed them all. The think-tank's proposal took up an entire agenda item and it generated a buzz of conversation among the teachers. He skimmed over the typewritten summary of the documents Newton showed him earlier in the week. It included the additional information that the trustees all gave their verbal agreement, pending provision of details, and recommended a teacher take the lead in liaising with the think-tank. To his relief, his name was not included anywhere on the summary paper.

Mr Newton called the meeting to order, and they ploughed through the agenda items with little fuss. Until they reached the item before that about the think-tank. Ms Peters spoke about a chance for the boys to get involved in a fun run to raise money for a charity close to her heart. A London-based charity to help young women struggling to make ends meet, having been thrown out of their homes, or having left because of violence. The gathered teachers erupted with arguments for and against. Ms Peters sat back, her mouth in a determined line, and her arms crossed. Mr Newton called for order and selected two teachers to present the main case for either side.

The Brigadier let it all wash over him. He had every sympathy for the women Ms Peters spoke about, but he couldn't see why a public school for boys should raise money for that cause.

Mr Newton turned to the next agenda item and ran through the summary, spinning it as positively as he could. 'I had wanted to discuss this more fully, but the previous item took up more time than I expected. I am proposing that the Brigadier take on the position of liaising with Mr Woolton of the think-tank. Much of it is about the CCF, which the Brigadier leads with the utmost professionalism. Any objections?'

The Brigadier inched forward, then stopped. He glanced around at his colleagues, who all looked bored as they shook their heads.

Mr Newton smiled. 'Excellent. Brigadier, I'm sure you'll represent the school well with this opportunity to secure a funding stream as well as put Brendon on the map as far as the government is concerned.'

'Thank you, Headmaster. I'll do my best.'

'Hey, hey.'

'Whatcha.'

'Did you get what I asked for?' Jacquie shivered into her rain coat. Jack, unusually, arrived late to their meeting. The cold seeped into her bones, and the rain stopped her from walking about to warm up.

He dug in his satchel and gave her a packet wrapped up in a plastic bag. She made a gimme, gimme gesture with her hands.

'I copied it out for you.'

'You're a gem.'

'It doesn't say much.'

'If it's got his date of birth and full name, then that'll help,' Jacquie said.

'I've got to go.'

'Already?'

'They're cracking down on us leaving the school grounds without permission, and they are reducing the number of times we can get permission. We're going to have to think of other

88

ways of meeting up.'

She regarded him. He looked terrible, all hunched over and pallid. 'Are you sleeping okay?'

'Yeah.' He sniffed. 'No. They're making a huge fuss over the exams and putting the pressure on.'

She screwed up her face. 'Unfair. We've got ages, and they're barely mentioning it at my school.' She chewed at her lip. 'Tell you what, I'll think of something to address both problems.'

He brightened at that. 'You always do. That fake letter from that Persian guy was genius.'

'Don't forget you need to write to "him" so they don't get suspicious.'

He nodded. 'I really had better scarper.'

'All right. Thanks again for this.' She held up the package. 'You are brill.'

She watched him slouch away back to the school. It really was so unfair that she couldn't go to his school where they could help each other. She huffed, and turned to find sanctuary from the rain in the library.

She went to a different desk than normal and carefully opened up the packet Jack gave her. He'd done a good job of copying the personnel file neatly. She put asterisks next to the information she needed to write to the Ministry of Defence to find out more about Jack's maths teacher. She read the file in case there was anything else that might help, but there wasn't much.

After half an hour, she left the library and returned home. In her room, she carefully typed the letter to the Ministry asking for information about regiments stationed near her home and school active from 1914 to 1918. She added that she was also interested in information concerning a retired brigadier, and provided the details from Lethbridge-Stewart's personnel file.

She checked over the letter, signed it, and folded it into an envelope she'd pinched from Mr Patel's shop that morning. Downstairs, she rooted through her mother's desk and found a second-class stamp. It would have to do. She applied it to its corner, and then left the house to post it in the nearest pillar box. She wished it good luck and returned home.

*

A week later, Jacquie's mother told her a packet had arrived for her from the Ministry of Defence. She demanded an explanation as to what it might be, and Jacquie told her about the history project Miss Starr set the class. Her mother hovered while she opened up the official-looking envelope. The covering letter thanked her for her questions, and trusted the documents enclosed would assist her enterprise. The first few pages listed the military units stationed nearby during World War One and suggested a few places where she could find more information. They knew of no veterans still alive, but perhaps the regimental societies could help.

They enclosed five pages about Brigadier Lethbridge-Stewart and his career. They listed dates and notes about his enlistment, training, his first few postings. Then it got weird, with lines blacked out. Geneva featured a few times, but loads of other place names were obscure parts of England and Scotland. She scratched her head.

If she could work out a way of removing the blacked-out bits to find out what they wanted hidden, then she had struck gold.

CHAPTER TEN

Nobody Home

JACQUIE SPENT as much time as she could working to remove the black ink that covered the words she wanted to see. She ended up going in to the Reading Room in the British Museum to try to find a book that could tell her how it might be done. She'd already exhausted the local libraries, which yielded a few clues.

To do it thoroughly would require chemicals and equipment way beyond what she could afford or had the wherewithal to obtain. However, with extensive cross-referencing of chemistry books and a couple of perfectly phrased questions of her chemistry teacher, she managed to discover a way in which to coax out the lettering beneath the black ink. It required much patience and a steady hand. She had to do it letter by letter, gentle dab by gentle dab. Too much, and the paper would disintegrate. It already had in a few places. Her sheer concentration made her tremble and shake, and the chemicals produced itchy eyes and a headache.

By the end of the first week, she uncovered the words 'UNIT' (in capital letters, no less), 'fifth' and 'great intelligence'. Strictly speaking, she guessed 'intelligence' based on the first five letters and the context of the secrets. She wrote up what she could based on the Ministry of Defence document and listed a series of questions. She put it to one side to complete her normal homework, and the household chores her olds set her to do. 'Either them or we charge you rent, young lady.'

She argued against her father's new edict, but her logic and facts fell on two sets of deaf ears. She knew it was because they couldn't really afford to keep Jack at Brendon, but they didn't want to remove him and send him to her school. Not while she went there, too. She also knew they tried to work the numbers to get her into a boarding school far away, and figured that if she gave them any excuse then they would, and the impact on their lives could go hang. So, she did the set chores.

Her Saturday morning paper round became her only source of income. She liked it more because it got her out of the house every Saturday morning, and she could race up to the obelisk on the hill to leave and collect messages with Jack. She racked her brain over ways in which they could meet up in person, but between their olds and Jack's school, a solution proved elusive.

She took a copy of what she'd learned about Brigadier (ret'd) Lethbridge-Stewart and her list of questions with her. It was all in plaintext. She hadn't had the time to rewrite it into their code.

Jack hadn't mentioned anything about anyone from the school due to be up there, but nothing stopped any of the teachers from turning up. She parked her bike against a tree in the forest and crept towards the top of the hill. She looked out, saw no one, and stole across to the obelisk where she and Jack had found a hidden little door. It looked like there might be something behind a second door, but neither of them had managed to prise that open. The hatch proved enough for them to stash papers and small things to exchange.

Jacquie closed the door on her papers and stood up.

'Well, well.'

She started and turned around. The bloody Brigadier had sneaked up the hill and found her. She backed away a few steps. Hopefully he hadn't seen exactly what she'd been doing. He closed the gap between them, and held a hand up to shield his eyes from the glare of the rare October sunshine.

'What have we here?' He squinted into the sunlight behind her. 'Are you from the estate?'

'I was only having a gander, guv'nor.' She matched his stance. Surely he must recognise her, but she played up a working-class London accent. Maybe he couldn't really see her because of the way the light angled.

'This is private land and you have no business in being

here.'

'You're that soldier, ain't you? The one in charge of the soldier boys?' She took a punt he hadn't recognised her, or maybe forgotten. Jack said he'd forgotten loads and seemed distant at times. Like he'd lost bits of himself.

He narrowed his eyes. 'What of it?'

She took a breath. 'What does UNIT mean to you?'

'What?' He spoke low and mean, somehow making the single word sound menacing.

She backed up a step, but kept all her attention trained on him. 'Or the fifth?'

He laughed, but it had an edge to it. 'Seriously, girl, are you all there?'

His sudden shift in tone startled her. She saw his dart forward begin before he lunged, and she dodged backwards.

'Oi, watch it, mate.'

He lurched for her again, and she turned on her heels and ran into the forest. 'Don't come back!' he yelled after her.

He didn't pursue her, so she stopped, checked, and doubled back for her bike. She looked back and saw him head down the hill to the school buildings. His hands in his trouser pockets, looking for all the world like he was just out for a casual stroll.

Following his last meeting with his sister, Jack established a pattern of going for a jog around the school grounds every evening after classes finished and before tea was served. That way he could check on the hiding place in the obelisk for messages, and leave them there for Jacquie in return. The school used every opportunity to remind him and all the boys that truanting would not be tolerated. To underline the message, two second formers caught larking about in the lanes got six whacks each in front of the whole school assembly.

Both Alfie and Ollie wanted to join him, but he growled at them that he needed space. Alfie knew better than to press him when he was in that mood. Ollie needed some extra lessons in that department, but the new boy was a quick study. Jack hammered home the point that no one liked a grass, either, and Ollie promised not to tattle on him. It had been months since he last needed to physically follow through on a threat, he worried he missed the sweet spot of maximum pain for no markings on the boy when he squirmed. He needn't have worried. Alfie told him Ollie didn't squeal.

Saturday was the day he expected a drop, and the expectation of contact with his sister lifted his spirits and his running legs. He slowed when he saw the Brigadier wandering around at the top of the hill. Jack wondered how he got up there so fast, because Jack was sure he'd seen him washing his car when he set off on his daily run. Jack scratched his head, humphed, and kept on up the hill like normal.

The Brigadier turned away from the obelisk and headed down the hill towards him. He tipped his flat cap and nodded at Jack. 'Afternoon, lad.' He strode on past.

Jack slowed to a jog and pretended to nurse a stitch as he reached the obelisk. He used it to lean against to catch his breath as he watched his maths teacher leave. Thankfully, he didn't look back and, once he'd reached the halfway point, Jack fell to his knees and opened up the hatch. He pulled out the paper and shoved it into his shorts pocket. He put a brief note of his own, neatly written and encoded, before closing the door up once more. He stood, checked around, and performed a few stretches. His note didn't say much because he didn't have much to say, except about how awful things were going at the school. He felt trapped, but didn't want to complain too much.

He waited until he reached the school buildings before he looked at the paper. His mouth hung open at the words in Jacquie's handwriting, all in plain English, and all about the Brigadier's military career.

There wasn't much, and what was there was weird. She'd written a load of questions which Jack had to, somehow, get from the man himself.

'And pigs will ruddy fly.'

Unit, fifth, and *great intelligence.*

All nonsense words. He remembered something Alfie mentioned once when he babbled on about stuff. Operation names and codes, like D-Day and Overlord. Nonsense words the military liked to use to hide what they were really doing. Maybe those words Jacquie wanted to find out about were operation names and codes, and maybe it all explained why the old soldier had gone a bit peculiar over the last few months. Jack couldn't think of anything that sparked him going doolally now rather than years ago.

Unless, maybe he had. Maybe he did break down, and enough to leave the army, and get a job as a teacher. Jack recalled the notes in the Brigadier's personnel file about a breakdown during '77. He'd been hospitalised then, his memory shot to pieces. The Brigadier had recovered fairly quickly, but not completely. Maybe he was starting to flip out again.

Jack kept Jacquie's notes hidden on him while he ate his tea with his friends. He said nothing about any of it to Alfie and grunted he wanted to study for an hour or two in the library. 'No, I don't want to talk about bonfire night and sodding Guy Fawkes.'

He collected his maths books and hunched over them and Jacquie's notes. He cradled his head in his hands as he thought about ways he could find out the answers to her questions. Just asking his maths teacher wouldn't cut it. Not with the school's current policy on thwacking students first and asking questions later, if at all.

He sighed, and packed up, and hid Jacquie's notes in the most secure place he could find.

Half-term approached rapidly and the Brigadier wrote in his journal questions about the fleeting nature of time. Where had the endless summer days of his youth gone? He included a few lines that sounded a bit poetic, read them back and grimaced. He shut the journal with a grunt and put the book in its place. He frowned at the books on the shelf, and returned them to the order they ought to be in. No one visited, and surely he hadn't misplaced them. He shook his head. Perhaps he should call Dr Pelham-Rose again, but she would only insist he come in for an appointment and he didn't need that.

The weekend arrived with heavy grey clouds, and most of the boarders left for their holidays. The usual half dozen boys who stayed on waved their classmates off and trooped inside. The school had organised for a guest later that day, and Miss Nugent press-ganged the boys to help tidy up.

During the last staff meeting, Ms Peters had insisted to Mr Newton that if the boys' freedom was to be curtailed, then they needed incentives to make their lives tolerable. 'Teenagehood shouldn't only be about preparing for work. They should have some fun, too.'

'That's what games are for.' Mr Newton meant organised sport.

Ms Peters gave him her best scowl and most of the other teachers murmured and muttered their support of her point. No doubt all with their own particular reasons that none of them aired. The Brigadier quietly agreed the boys needed to be able to let off steam, or they would explode. He'd seen it with his life in the army. Lived it, a long time ago.

'All right, all right. We'll alter the policy for next term.' Mr Newton looked around the gathered teachers. 'And organise some entertainment for the boarders staying in over half-term. However, they are not to receive additional passes to leave school grounds without supervision. It's dangerous with all those bombs.'

The Brigadier was pleased he avoided the first shift of looking after the boys. In fact, he was pleased to have that whole day free of school responsibilities. He wanted to wash and polish his car before the heavens opened.

The physical work of scrubbing off the dirt that accumulated far too fast and readily for his liking made him feel good. He rinsed the soapsuds off and dried it with a chamois. He collected the polish and applied it with plenty of elbow grease. At least he found no extra dents or scratches this time.

Next, he turned to the inside. He frowned at the tube of lipstick he found in the footwell of the front passenger seat. He picked it up. It looked used, but the shade of lurid pink didn't match that used by any of the women who worked at the school. At least, as far as he had noticed. Even if it did belong to one of them, it didn't explain how or why it turned up in his car. He'd not given any of them a lift.

Granger and his limerick. Not that Granger wrote it. The boy didn't have that sort of talent. He suspected Armstrong's sister of the penmanship, but couldn't prove it. He'd actually not pursued it, harmless jape as the limerick was. But leaving lipstick in his car... That strayed into going too far for a joke.

He sighed. He didn't want either boy to get into trouble over it, but he would have a word when Granger returned.

On Monday afternoon, during his allotted time to patrol the grounds, the Brigadier strolled up the hill to the obelisk. A man crouched by it, but the sunlight's angle made him appear in silhouette. He didn't recognise the profile and suspected he might be a stranger ignorant of the boundary. He waved. 'I say. You there.'

The man stood up. He said nothing, but brushed down his trousers.

The Brigadier shivered like someone stumbled over his grave. He walked forward a few more paces and glanced at the obelisk. A small door hung ajar. He looked back up at the man, a frown creasing his forehead. He held up a hand. He still couldn't see who the fellow was.

The man turned and dashed towards the forest. The Brigadier harrumphed, and turned his attention to the little door in the base of the obelisk. He hunkered down and pulled it fully open. Inside sat a manila folder. He pulled it out, stood up, and opened it.

His mouth hung open and his heartbeat skittered about. He reached out to hold the obelisk to stop from fainting.

The papers contained in the folder weren't marked Top Secret, but they ought to be. Not so much for the personal information about him – his date of birth, the bare bones of his military career, the names of his family members – but for the annotations. Brief descriptions of the Fifth Operational Corps and UNIT, and mention of the Great Intelligence, rocked him. Worse, he recognised the handwriting as his own.

He fell to his knees as a darkness rushed at him, knocking his life from him.

Jack set out for his afternoon run. He quite enjoyed the games the school put on for him and the other students, and he looked forward to seeing the film they organised for later that evening. It made a change for the better, but not as good as being allowed out. He missed seeing the world beyond the school grounds.

He missed his sister.

As he jogged up the hill, the sunlight dipped when clouds covered that part of the sky. He paused to gaze up at the bright orange and pinks that reminded him of his own house after his olds' last redecoration binge. Only nature did the colour scheme better.

He powered onwards. As he neared the obelisk, he saw the Brigadier crouched beside the hatch. He swore. Stopped. Turned around with his head in his hands. If the Brigadier had found their dead letter drop location, they were done for.

The Brigadier didn't call out to him.

Jack turned back to face his teacher. The former soldier leaned against the obelisk, his forehead pressed to it. He moaned softly, and muttered. Jack stepped closer, careful to not spook the old man.

The Brigadier clutched an open manila folder in his left hand, the papers attached to the thin cardboard with treasury tags. Both his hand and the folder drooped beside him, like the teacher had lost all power to the left side of his body.

Jack couldn't work out what the Brigadier moaned.

'Sir?'

The Brigadier made no response.

Worried now, Jack closed the gap and reached out to shake his maths teacher's shoulder. 'Sir? Are you all right?'

The Brigadier sobbed. 'I've breached the Official Secrets Act, only I don't remember doing it.' He turned to face Jack, who stepped back. His teacher's face paled and shone with sweat, his red-rimmed eyes brimmed with tears.

Jack's stomach flipped. He recognised the paper in the folder as the notes Jacquie delivered to him so he could ask the Brigadier some questions. He'd not thought of a way yet, and hid the paper away in the safest place he could. Someone had scribbled on it. That same someone must have brought it here, but now the Brigadier found it and Jack had to get it back off the Brigadier.

'Sir. That's unlikely. Give me that, let me help you go back to the school.'

The Brigadier shook his head, but he struggled to stand. He stared at the folder in his hand and moaned once more. 'All my working life I've been careful. I don't understand.'

The Brigadier rolled the folder up and shoved it into his jacket pocket. Jack's heart sank. Plan B would have to swing into operation. He grabbed his maths teacher's arm as he flailed about, unsteady on his feet.

'It was here, you know. I don't remember, but it was here.'

'Whatever you say, sir. I'll take you back to your quarters and you can have a rest. Maybe you might remember then.'

Jack took hold of his teacher's arm and led him down the hill and straight to his quarters. He watched the Brigadier hide the folder, then lurch towards his telephone.

'I'll be all right, Armstrong. Don't mention this to anyone. All right?'

'Yes, sir.'

Jack backed away and left. Seeing an adult so vulnerable took his bravado from him, but at least he knew where the document was. He could retrieve it later.

The Brigadier barely registered the student backing away and out. Everything beyond his immediate focus on the telephone appeared fuzzy to him. Peripheral. Not real anymore.

He dialled Dr Pelham-Rose's number. The receptionist answered and he asked to speak to the doctor. The woman seemed to detect something in his voice, something he hadn't said. 'Do you need someone to collect you? We can send a car.'

'I can get a taxi.'

'We'll be waiting for you.'

He dialled the taxi company's number and they said they would be there in fifteen minutes. Enough time for him to pack an overnight bag, which he did quickly. Next, he called the administration office and Miss Nugent answered.

'I need to go away for a day or two. It's unexpected, I'm sorry.'

'Oh, I'm sorry. Is there anything we can do to help?'

'No, no. It's fine.' He hung up, and surveyed his digs. He scribbled a note as to where he was going and taped it to his fridge door. Then he locked up, collected his bag, and set off to the end of the school drive. He only waited for a minute before the taxi arrived.

The Brigadier sat back and let the journey to the clinic wash over him. It eased the strange panicky feelings he felt since seeing that man near the obelisk. He hadn't seen who the man was, but he couldn't shake the idea he knew him somehow.

The obelisk. The hatch at the base didn't surprise him, even though he'd never seen it before.

The papers, though. He shuddered. This amnesia. He pressed a hand to his temple that pounded.

They arrived and he paid. The taxi left.

The Brigadier turned towards the clinic and saw Dr Pelham-Rose sweep from the entrance way. He thought of giant purple butterflies launched from the sun and sweeping down to the earth, focused on him. He sensed them rushing towards him. He looked up, raised his arms and dropped his bag. They stole the air that he breathed and he deflated. The ground rushed to meet him and he barely got his arms out to protect himself.

Dr Pelham-Rose knelt beside him. She called his name and sounded a million miles away. Her touch, though, felt heavy and hot. The fragrance she wore cloyed in the air around them.

People manhandled him up and into a wheel chair. His consciousness returned and he protested.

'I'm all right. I'm fine. Leave me be.'

'It's okay, Brigadier. We have you. I'm just going to give you a sedative to calm you down. You'll only feel a little sting.'

It felt like the entire contents of a wasp's nest stabbed at him. The warmth of the poisons spread fast throughout his body and his eyes closed.

'I'm fine. I'm fine.'

'No, you're not, old boy. Time to roll over and let the professionals take over.'

His eyes flickered open. The bright white lights hurt as they seared into his brain. He smelled the tropics and heard reggae beats and calypso singing. The heat rushed him. Burned him. He tried to cough and splutter and move, but he couldn't. Cotton wool stuffed his mouth and up into his brain.

Two voices spoke. One he recognised as Dr Pelham-Rose. The other he didn't know.

'I've given him a shot. We'll settle him in and work out a plan from that.'

'I saw him two years ago. Something must have happened for him to regress this far.'

'I've conducted a few sessions with him, but he's stubborn and refused to come in after the first two. I should have insisted.'

'You weren't to know. We'll do our best for him.'

'Of course we will.'

CHAPTER ELEVEN
A Brick

THAT EVENING, after eating his meal, Jack did his share of the tidying up. That was a new thing, having to clean up after students and staff on a roster. The headmaster said he was trying it out over the half-term break with every intention of introducing it to the whole school on their return. Jack didn't mind so much, but he knew of at least a dozen boys who would kick up a stink over it. In his mind, he played out a likely scenario while he wiped down the tables. Alfie would moan to his olds, and his olds would protest to the trustees that they handed over enough in fees for the school to pay for cleaners. Maybe he ought to set up a book as to how long the initiative would last.

He watched the first episode of the new *Quatermass* on ITV, the station was back after a strike that began in the summer. Afterwards, he mooched up to his dorm room and read a couple of comics that Alfie left behind. He dozed off, but woke up from a nightmare in which the Brigadier stomped into his bedroom at home. He might have called out or did something equally as embarrassing. For once, he felt relieved no one else was there during the half-term break.

The Brigadier didn't show for breakfast the next morning. Not so uncommon as to cause a stir. Jack ate his breakfast and joshed around with one of the boys who had clean-up duty. He worked through how and when he could get into the Brigadier's quarters to recover Jacquie's papers.

Outside, the day promised to be one of those autumnal days ideal for roaming free. Cool, crisp, and bright. The constraints on his freedom bit deep. Next best thing from leaving the school grounds was to grab the work set for revision and find a place outside, but within the school boundary. He wanted to avoid trouble – maybe he might get a pass for good behaviour – and keep an eye on the Brigadier's digs should an opportunity present itself. He settled on a bench that overlooked one of the sports grounds.

Jack lost himself in his work. The subject he revised was physics, specifically a unit on astronomy. The information about the planets and stars clicked and made sense. He powered through the questions with a sense of achievement, and when finished he wondered if this was what it was like being Jacquie. This stuff always seemed so easy for her to grasp.

A noise attracted his attention. He looked over towards the Brigadier's hut and saw the man out near his car. Jack squinted. He didn't look as though he was going out. Ah, drat. Off came his jacket, up rolled his shirt sleeves, and out came a cloth and tin of polish. Polishing his beastly car might take a while, but it wasn't the same as him leaving the grounds. No time right now for stealing in and recovering the papers.

Jack turned to his next subject for revision. Maths. He frowned at the equations and hoped the same revelation that he just experienced with physics would repeat, but no. The numbers, letters and symbols danced around in a confusing conspiracy against his understanding. With a grunt, Jack closed the book and shoved them all back in his satchel. Half an hour of study on a half-term break day was enough. He shivered. The sun's rays were too weak to keep him warm. Maybe he could convince one of the other boarders to join him in a practice session in the nets. He wanted to improve his bowling to shut Alfie up.

As Jack strolled across the field towards the school buildings he studiously ignored the Brigadier and his car.

'You, boy.'

Jack stopped in his tracks. He turned around. The Brigadier waved his polishing cloth at him. 'Yes, sir.' His shoulders dropped.

'Care to earn a bit of credit?'

'Sir?' Jack stepped closer to the Brigadier.

'I want to make my car shine, but I don't have the time right now to put in the work myself.'

'You sure, sir?' He furrowed his brow. To his knowledge, the Brigadier never asked for help like this.

'Sure? Of course, I'm sure. I wouldn't ask otherwise, would I?' The Brigadier scrunched up the cloth in his fist and his face turned a horrid puce colour.

Jack backed away. 'Sorry, sir. I didn't mean it.'

'That's the problem with boys like you. You talk too much. No time to think about what you're about to say, and what the consequences might be.' The Brigadier tapped the side of his head. 'You just have to rush it out. And as for your hair. When was the last time you got it cut?'

'What...?' Jack stepped back again, but the Brigadier exhibited a speed Jack didn't think possible for the old soldier's age. The Brigadier grabbed Jack's hair and yanked it hard enough to make tears spring from his eyes. 'Sir, please.'

'Or are you a girl?' The Brigadier tugged Jack's hair once more, then flung his hand down. Jack fell back and hit the ground. He blinked up at the Brigadier towering above him, fists at his side, an awful sneer twisting his face. He flung the cloth at Jack. 'Get to work, you lazy so-and-so.'

Jack picked up the cloth and scrambled to stand up. He stumbled over to the car and followed his teacher's directions on polishing it. The teacher harangued him, got him to repeat the work again and again until his muscles ached. Any chill he felt from the autumnal day burned away from the repetitive work. All the while, the Brigadier grumbled about slovenly boys showing disrespect and what he planned to do to fix it.

Dr Rebecca Pelham-Rose stood with her colleague, Dr Kevin Kent, over the bed in which Brigadier Alistair Lethbridge-Stewart slumbered. Dr Kent reviewed the patient's chart. It indicated a man in good physical health for his age and present occupation. His vitals were all within normal range, and he showed no evidence of self-harm. On his arrival at the clinic he showed signs of chronic sleep deprivation, which is why they sedated him.

Kent glanced up at Rebecca. 'I think we should ease off the sedation and see how he is when he wakes up. Two years ago, he exhibited signs of suppressed rage, but he wasn't violent to himself or others. Has he exhibited any signs of violence this time?'

Rebecca shook her head. 'I think he's very good at bottling up his emotions.'

'He returned here because of bad dreams?'

She suppressed a smile. Bad dreams as a term belied the seriousness of what brought the Brigadier back to the clinic earlier that year. 'I believe they were his suppressed memories leaking into his subconscious mind. His distress wasn't caused by the content of them so much as how visceral they felt. We got as far as him understanding that he has no reason to feel shame about his amnesia, or his reactions to past trauma. I had hoped we could have worked through what that trauma was, which might address his amnesia.' She glanced down at the sleeping man. 'But, as I said to you yesterday, he stopped coming in. We spoke on the telephone a few times, which helped him. He told me the dreams had gone.'

Kent nodded. 'When he wakes, keep going with your talk therapy. You've worked miracles with the others here.' He flashed her a warm smile. 'What concerns me is his sudden relapses. What happened two years ago came out of the blue. Now this. We'll keep an eye on his behaviour and consider a medical intervention should it look like another breakdown is underway. Are you good with that?'

'I am, yes.'

Kent slotted the chart back in its holder. He nodded at Rebecca and left the room.

She looked down at the Brigadier and folded her arms. 'I hope it doesn't come to that. Please don't let it come to that.'

Jacquie owed Shirley and Molly. Before the holidays started, Molly mentioned a bonfire night on a common not too far away from their part of the world, but not in the usual place. Shirley pooh-poohed the idea of Guy Fawkes and demanded they do something for Hallowe'en instead. Jacquie kept out of their spat because neither festival interested her, not without her brother.

Poor Jack. Trapped in his school and finding it impossible to sneak out.

The last message she received from him at the obelisk told her about the compromise to their dead letter drop. At first she thought he left no message, he'd made the scrap of paper so incongruous. The message itself was in code, written in invisible ink. It took her a while to work out the message from his messy handwriting. The gist of it was the Brigadier had found the hatch in the obelisk, and the documents about him. Jack worked on a way to recover the papers, but the Brigadier was acting really strangely. She sensed her brother held back on his description.

It all meant they had to find a new place where they could exchange messages. The adults in their lives imposed stricter controls, which shrank the locations where they could both reach at reasonable times. She cursed them.

Then, she remembered Molly's bonfire night. She could convince her olds that she was going with school friends, but organise for Jack to be there. She wrote a coded letter under the guise of a letter from Behzad, a refugee from Iran. In it she advised Jack to reply and send it to Mr Patel at the shop where she did the paper round. She would tell Mr Patel that she was forwarding the letter to a refugee boy in London as a favour.

The subterfuge worked, although Mr Patel did warn her not to use the shop address for too long.

Jack convinced Alfie Granger to invite him along to the bonfire night, and Alfie convinced his olds to let him go with Jack. Bonus, Alfie's olds convinced the school to let Jack out. Jacquie's and Jack's only true heart-in-mouth moment was over whether the school would check with their olds, but they didn't.

Jacquie found Alfie first, then Jack. She blinked at him. 'Your hair? What happened?' He looked like a skinhead.

Jack grimaced and rubbed his hand over the bristles. 'The Brigadier.'

Alfie glanced away. 'My pa will have words if they try it on with everyone next week.'

'The Brigadier says they will.' Jack's shoulders rounded and he gazed down at the ground. 'It's been awful this term, and worse during the break.'

'Why'd he shave your hair off?' Jacquie crossed her arms.

'Because he said I looked like a girl, and then ranted about how everyone lacks discipline, and it's no wonder this country is going down the tubes with long-haired layabouts everywhere. He's seriously lost it. I think I was only let out tonight because one of the office ladies took pity.'

Jacquie swore under her breath. She shook her head. 'He can't get away with that.'

'He has, though.' Jack looked up at Jacquie.

Alfie kicked at a clump of grass with his boot. 'Pa doesn't like the new Discipline Code, either. He's told me that a bit of discipline doesn't hurt anyone, but it's a thin line to sadism.'

Jacquie stared at Jack's friend. 'Do you even have a clue what those words mean?'

Alfie hunched his shoulders. 'Yeah. Course I do.'

'You don't.' Jack sniggered. 'Not fully.'

'Sod off.' Alfie mooched away to join Molly and her friends who he said he knew from Sunday School.

'I got the papers back.' Jack reached into his jacket pocket and took out a folder. 'I didn't write in it, but. It's all really weird what's happened.' He told Jacquie about seeing the Brigadier finding their hiding place in the obelisk, but how the teacher took a funny turn. 'To think I took pity on the man and helped him back to his quarters. It's the only reason I knew where he put these papers. He shooed me away, but I thought he left the school. He told me he was fine, but getting some help. Only he was back the next day and turned really nasty.' He told her about his behaviour with the car, and then every day since getting him and the other boys to do odd jobs beyond the new roster of duties. 'He patrols the school at night at random times, and he's getting the other teachers to do the same. He cut my hair off on Thursday and did the same to two other boys that day.'

Jacquie gazed open-mouthed at him. She shook her head slowly. 'It's assault, or something. Criminal, anyway. Or should be.' She opened up the folder and looked at the papers. 'Thanks for getting this back, given all the risks.'

'I don't think he looked at it. I've only been in his quarters a few times, and it was messy. Books and papers all over the place. It surprised me, him being an old soldier. Now it's more like what you'd expect – all tidy and really clean. But, the place where he put these papers looked like he hadn't gone anywhere near it since he put them there. I got them back on Wednesday evening when he was out and he's not given any clue he's noticed.'

'That's something.'

'Yeah, but I didn't add anything to what you got.'

'What are these notes then?'

Jack shrugged. 'They look like the Brigadier wrote them, but it was like he was furious about it at the obelisk. He kept going on about the Official Secrets Act, and stuff about something that happened at the obelisk before. He seemed really frightened, which scared me, to be honest.'

'Not like you to be rattled by something like that.' She studied him through narrowed eyes.

'You didn't see him. It was like a bunch of ghosts got him, and now it's like he's turned into a caricature of himself.'

She shoved the papers into her jacket pocket. 'Oh, hey. I got you this. It's a new comic called *In Other Words*. It's pretty cool, but hide it from the teachers. Not sure they'd approve of its anti-establishment themes.'

Jack beamed as he flicked through it. 'Very cool.'

The Brigadier felt like he woke from a nightmare, but he couldn't recall it all. Parts played in his mind, and crashed into his vision and his hearing. Shouts. Bangs. Flashes. Leering monsters. Slimy beasts. Robot armies goose-stepping. Laughter – unkind and cruel. Spinning tops and bright red clown shoes. Daffodils and stony-devils.

He thought he lay in a hospital bed, a hospital gown draped over him. Everything shone white and clean. The antiseptic smells drowned what else might be there. All those human smells. Animal smells.

Mud and blood. He'd crawled through plenty of both in his life. Dragged fallen comrades to safety through it.

A giant wasp buzzed at him and a centipede snapped its jaws. A Buddhist chant kept time.

Peace became the soft hum of air-conditioning and buzz of overhead lights. The rhythmic clank of a trolley wheel that needed to be unstuck. The smell of institutional food. Quiet chatter. Distant.

The smell of roses, gently nudged away the scents of horror.

'You're awake?'

Barely. He struggled to free his mind from the mire and chaos. He opened his eyes and saw the butterfly smile down upon him. 'Doctor,' he mumbled. His throat raw. He struggled to ask for water and failed.

'Shh, now. You're safe. Do you know where you are?'

'Clinic.'

'Yes. That's right. The clinic. Do you remember who I am?'

'Doctor.'

His memory slipped in the mud that reared up and rushed him, turned into a wall of flames. Things with great claws reached out to grab at him. Snapped and caught his clothes, his skin. Bit and burned. His father and mother waved to him. His brother grinned. Platoon after platoon of dead soldiers saluted him, flesh dripping from their outstretched arms.

'Brigadier?'

The smell of roses wafted through his visions and made them disappear. He blinked and tried to focus on the butterfly that spoke his title.

'Alistair, tell me what you're seeing when you close your eyes.'

'Bricks.'

'Bricks?'

Rubble of an old house in the country smashed to pieces by something he no longer remembered. That's the problem with amnesia. Leaves holes. Mind like a sieve, or Swiss cheese, or, or...

'Get a grip, man. Call yourself a soldier? An officer, no less? You are a disgrace to the crown.'

He blinked to focus on the man who screamed at him, but his face shifted and changed and he couldn't see or remember.

Rebecca watched over the Brigadier as he drifted into what looked like calm slumber. His breaths deepened and slowed, and his face relaxed. His fists loosened their grip on the bedsheets and he shifted position to lie on his side in not quite a foetal position. She waited a few moments before gently unsnagging the IV line.

He didn't stir. Didn't murmur anything. His forehead

smoothed.

She stole to the foot of the bed and quietly took out the clipboard. She made her notes about the partial conversation she had with him. The only word he spoke with clarity was 'bricks', which made no sense to her. Everything else he tried to say remained indistinct and unintelligible. However, it did seem as though he tried to respond to her questions, which was something, and he knew he was at the clinic.

Everything else about his case concerned her. She concluded that he had buried his trauma deep, and perfected masking it even to himself. The strange amnesia he suffered cloaked part of it, but she thought he used it as an excuse. She didn't believe he did so consciously, and berated herself for not pressing harder at his appointments.

'No use crying over spilt milk.' She shook her head slowly as she watched over him for a few more moments before turning and leaving the room.

She stopped by the nurses' station and told Gloria, the matron, that their patient slept and shouldn't be disturbed. 'All his vitals are fine, but he needs real rest. If we can, I'd like to avoid using restraints.' She gave a small sigh. 'But, if he needs them then he'll need them.'

'I understand, Doctor.'

Gloria handed her a slip of paper. Rebecca skimmed it quickly. Dr Kent wanted to discuss treatment options for the Brigadier.

'Dr Kent is in his office now, and free.'

'Thanks, Gloria.'

Rebecca strode towards Kent's office and knocked on the doorjamb. He waved her in with a smile. 'How is he?'

She settled herself in one of his chairs meant for patients and visitors. 'Sleeping.' She told him about the Brigadier's obvious distress when he woke earlier. 'I'm not sure that talk therapy will work right now. Whatever trauma is causing the amnesia is buried deep, but surfacing through his dreams, and those dreams are exhausting him.'

'I agree. I wanted to discuss the possibility of using ECT on him.'

Electro-convulsive therapy. She shivered. It had changed considerably from when it was first introduced in psychiatric treatment, but she remained wary of it. She frowned. 'I'm uncomfortable about using it without his informed consent, and at the moment he's incapable of giving such consent. My instinct is to enable him to sleep, then work through the options.'

'You're not against it in principle?'

She sighed. 'I'm not a fan, but I have kept up with the research about positive results in cases like this. I am willing to try it, but not until he can give his informed consent.'

Kent smiled. 'He is your patient.'

'Thank you.' Her shoulders eased. The fights she'd fought over matters like this in other clinics and hospitals where she worked drained her just thinking about them. She straightened up. 'He needs deep rest. What are your views on induced comas for situations like this?'

Kent's eyebrows darted upwards. 'We've used it successfully in the past, when it's been warranted.'

'Do you think it might be warranted in this case?'

He pursed his lips and glanced up at the ceiling. He returned his gaze to her. 'I think you are correct in that he needs rest, and his nightmares are making that impossible. Yes. I concur with your treatment suggestion.'

Rebecca nodded, smiled, and thanked him.

That Monday's resumption of lessons brought some relief to Jack. After the freedom of seeing Jacquie and Alfie at the bonfire night on Saturday, his Sunday started with the Brigadier rousing him up early to replace the boy rostered on dining hall duty. He'd taken ill, apparently.

Then came the usual chapel service, only this time the Brigadier inspected them before they went. He harangued them to wear their ties properly, to tuck in their shirts, and to polish their shoes to military parade standard. The boys who stayed over the half-term break bore it all, but the students who returned a day early all looked stunned. After the service, those boys lost their hair to the Brigadier's clippers wielded by Jack and other students already shorn.

The remainder of the boarders arrived back on Sunday afternoon. Those in the CCF were called out by the Brigadier. He inspected their hair and trimmed those he deemed wore it too long. Alfie told Jack later that those who protested had their rebellion thwacked out of them. He rubbed his own knuckles.

'You weren't wrong. He has lost it. Pa will have a word with the headmaster.'

Every class that Monday ran the way they usually did, except for maths. Like with everything else, the Brigadier ran the lesson as though his students were his squaddies on parade. He brooked no disturbance, and demanded they all sit up straight. He used his wooden ruler to prod their compliance. Weirdly, though, he seemed to have lost his place in the syllabus.

After their tea, the headmaster allowed the students to change into their weekend clothes and told them to gather on the main sports field closest to the buildings. The teachers organised a display of fireworks for Guy Fawkes night, which everyone agreed was pretty good.

Mr Grey's First Form class wheeled out their effigy. 'Penny for the Guy, penny for the Guy.' Everyone dropped coins into buckets. Mr Newton said the money was for charity, but he didn't say which one. Ms Peters glowered.

Mr Grey told the assembled school about Guy Fawkes while a couple of the Upper Sixth boys wrestled the effigy into its place up on an impressive wood pile. Mr Grey finished his story and indicated that Mr Newton should light the bonfire. Everyone oohed and ahhed, but without excitement.

Jack surveyed the crowd and pondered the changes. To one side stood the Brigadier, his arms folded. Jack couldn't see his expression, but he didn't look impressed.

The Brigadier visibly shuddered, almost as if frightened by the flames.

CHAPTER TWELVE
A Wall

REBECCA WATCHED Dr Kent as he prepared the cocktail of drugs that would ease the Brigadier into a coma. He injected it into the drip bag so it would be slowly administered. Too fast and the Brigadier's body could react with shock. Rebecca chewed at her thumb knuckle as she stared at the Brigadier's face, the man oblivious to all the attention paid to him.

Gloria looked on as well. She checked the Brigadier's vital signs, and noted them down as their patient sunk into a deeper sleep. While Kent and his team had successfully used this treatment on a handful of their patients, it was a radical thing to do. So much could go wrong, but Rebecca really couldn't see what else to do to help the Brigadier. His brain needed to recover from the mysterious trauma that caused his problems before her preferred therapy could have any chance of working.

Rebecca stood back while Gloria and her team worked to insert various tubes that would keep the Brigadier's body in as good health as they could maintain while his body and mind shut down. She glanced up at Kent who remained in the room with them. He had put together a fine team at this clinic, and she felt strengthened to be a part of it.

'You like him, don't you?'

Rebecca looked away from the senior physician. 'I do, yes.' She chuckled softly. 'I like all my patients here, but there is something about the Brigadier beyond his sense of duty. He seems so unassuming and modest. We haven't spoken about his career – oh, I know all the usual caveats apply – but I get the feeling he's done more than most.'

'I know no more than you, I assure you. I tried to get his service records two years ago when he first arrived here, but the Ministry clammed up tight. The school wasn't much help, either.'

'He's a stickler for the rules.' She sighed. 'He was concerned about breaching the Official Secrets Act when he arrived. I can't imagine him ever doing that.'

Kent raised an eyebrow.

'I think the Brigadier was worried he would, but his head is so muddled up. I do hope this treatment works.'

Kent smiled. 'He's a good candidate for it. Comparatively young for our patients, and fit and healthy. It's not our first time doing it, and Matron and her team are excellent.'

'They are that.' Rebecca flashed Kent a warm smile. Even though she felt reassured, she still chewed at her knuckles.

'We'll leave him under for forty-eight hours and review the situation. Okay?'

Rebecca nodded, but she didn't look at the senior physician.

Jacquie managed to avoid trouble at her school after her less than illustrious start to the Fifth Form. Miss Starr took her under her wing and kept her focused on all her studies, not only history. It involved a few stretches of detention-in-all-but-name after school, and quite a bit of talking and sharing home truths.

'A year might seem like an eternity to you, but it isn't. I suspect you could do better than your O-levels, but at least once you have them you can consider leaving school and making a life on your own.'

Miss Starr told her all that during the third time she was held back. In that moment, Jacquie resented it, but the point her teacher made churned around in her head and she understood what Miss Starr meant. Her sixteenth birthday was at the end of November. Legally, she could leave school at the end of this month. She hadn't considered that as an option to escape. She hadn't really thought that much about her future since she'd been so caught up with her olds, her brother, and preventing being sent to horrid places like she endured over the summer. All that, and having a bit of fun during what were supposed to be the best years of her life.

Yeah. Right.

During the half-term break she thought through what

might happen if she did leave when she turned sixteen. She'd have to get a job – a *real* job – and the market for that wasn't great. No qualifications worsened her prospects. She would either have to leave home and risk a life on the streets of London, or be stuck at home with her olds. She shuddered at that. Their olds acted as though they were trapped because they didn't have the types of jobs to get a better life. They both had qualifications and experience and all those things she didn't. She had the brains. They didn't. They dumped her in the rubbish school while they wasted their money on Jack's school. Not his fault, and he really did not deserve the horrors he told her about in their letters.

She took her frustrations out on arcade games, destroying wave after wave of alien invaders. It ate her coins, until she found a place that didn't mind her hustling and she played for free.

She made up her mind. She would stick it out and get as many O-levels as she could. Maybe she and Jack could then quit and leave, and set up home together. He could get a job, and she could earn a degree. She buckled down and finished her project on the Great War for Miss Starr and handed it in on time.

Tuesday morning saw all of the students at Brendon roused from their beds earlier than usual. Told to wear their gym clothes, they assembled outside in the half-light of dawn. Jack shivered in the cold drizzle.

Their form masters lined them up. 'Come on, come on. Faster you do this, the faster we can all get inside and have our breakfasts.' Mr Grey used a stick to encourage the boys to do as he instructed.

The Brigadier strode up the stairs and stood halfway up the flight. 'Attention.' He wore his army uniform.

Jack fidgeted like everyone around him. He hugged himself. The thin tracksuit he wore did nothing to keep him warm.

The Brigadier pulled a pistol out, held it aloft, and fired it.

Jack jumped. Swore. He wasn't alone in that. Consternation rippled through the assembled crowd, but everyone turned to face the Brigadier.

'Stand to attention. That means legs together, shoulders back, chests out, and arms by your sides. Face front. Chins up, but tucked in. *Move!'*

Everyone moved, and tried. Honest. The Brigadier moved through them and guided those who hadn't got it right, which was almost everyone. Those in the CCF got it right. Jack wondered why the Brigadier didn't get them to help him, but it was like the man blanked people he knew. Jack shook his head, glanced at Alfie, and copied him. He exhaled quietly when the Brigadier passed him by without castigation. Three boys down the line, the Toad wasn't so lucky.

The Brigadier returned to his place halfway up the staircase. 'The headmaster has instructed me to get all of you ready to take part in the Remembrance Sunday ceremony.'

A few students murmured. More moved.

'Quiet!'

Shocked silence blanketed the ranks.

'I am proud to say that this school has attracted the welcome attention of the government. In no small part, that is down to the school's contingent in the Combined Cadet Force. However, it should not be down to twenty-four boys to carry the weight of the entire student body. Those of you who failed to volunteer ought to be ashamed of yourselves. This changes today. Every student is now expected to enrol in the school's contingent forthwith.'

Discontent broke out in a few small pockets. Muted, but the Brigadier reacted fast and loud. He bellowed, 'All you boys moaning about this expectation, get out to the side now!'

No one moved. No one said a word. The Brigadier surveyed the school with a calmness akin to a coiled cobra. He nodded. 'Mark my words. You dissenters who are too cowardly to stand up for your convictions, I will find you and you will be sorry.'

Jack swallowed and risked a quick glance around.

'Let's get to work.'

The Brigadier blinked a few times to clear the fuzziness of his sight. He coughed to ease his raw and dry throat. He struggled to sit up. A hand rested on his shoulder, light, but it kept him down.

A shape formed. Human. A woman. He smelled a soft rose scent and he smiled. Dr Pelham-Rose.

'There, there, Brigadier. You're waking up from a deep sleep. How are you feeling?'

He coughed, then cleared his throat.

'Here. Sip this. It's water.'

A drinking straw batted against his lips. He grabbed it and drank. The liquid soothed the rawness of his throat. He focused on Dr Pelham-Rose, who withdrew the cup and placed it on a bedside table. She sat beside his bed and leaned forward.

He cleared his throat once more. 'I feel like I fought several rounds against a Chieftain tank and lost.' He tried a smile. 'What happened?'

'Do you know where you are?'

He frowned. 'The clinic.'

'Good. Do you remember how you arrived here?'

His frown deepened. He lay back against the soft pillows and gazed up at the ceiling. He recalled one of the boys at the school helping him to his quarters, but he couldn't remember which boy, or why he needed help. He recalled calling the clinic, then a taxi arriving. He couldn't remember if he paid the taxi, or whether the clinic organised it. He remembered next to nothing of the journey, or his arrival. Except for something about butterflies. Preposterous.

'Very little.' He coughed again. 'I had another breakdown, didn't I?'

Dr Pelham-Rose rested her hand on his lower arm. 'We are not mechanical things that break down, Brigadier. We do suffer when we experience traumatic circumstances and sometimes that lays hidden in our minds. We want to heal, to get better, but we don't always listen to our bodies or brains when they need rest. We soldier on.'

He turned his head to look at her. She looked serious. Worried.

'You haven't answered my question. What happened?'

She sighed. 'Dr Kent and I decided to put you in an induced coma for a couple of days.'

'A coma?' Immediately thoughts of his nephew, Owain, rushed into his mind. Over a decade, and still in a coma...

'Yes. It is a radical treatment option that we didn't take lightly. You were in a great deal of distress when you arrived here, and unable to rest.'

'Did it do the trick, this coma?' His throat caught and he cleared it. He needed more water to quench it.

'You seem to be rested and calm. Who is the prime minister?'

He nodded to himself, and told her.

'Good, good. Your name and date of birth?'

He grumbled both to her.

'Current job?'

He blinked a few times. 'I teach mathematics and rugger at Brendon Public School, as well as lead the CCF contingent. Does the school know I'm here?'

She leaned forward with a frown.

'Oh, they must do. I remember telling them.' The student knew, but he couldn't recall which student. A fifth former in running clothes. Half-term. One of the boarders who had to stay. 'Armstrong. John Fitzgerald Kennedy Armstrong.' He beamed and looked at Dr Pelham-Rose. 'He is known as Jack. He has a twin sister who causes trouble.' He shook his head. 'Jack told the school what happened. Yes. He must have.'

'That's quite a name.'

'They were born the day his namesake died. His sister's name is Jacquie.'

'Jacqueline Lee Kennedy née Bouvier?'

'No idea. Probably a variation on the theme. She attends a local comprehensive school.' He huffed a sigh. 'Does this mean I'm better?'

'If only it was that easy, Brigadier.' She patted his arm a few times and then removed her hand. 'Now the hard work must begin. I was too easy on you before.'

'I was afraid you'd say that.'

Jack dragged himself from his warm bed when the bell rang. Blearily, he dressed in his full school uniform. His fingers ached with the cold. The other boys in his dormitory stumbled about as they did the same. A few muttered about their ties, or boaters, or whatever. Alfie checked Jack's tie and Jack returned the favour by checking Alfie's cadet uniform and telling him to slightly move his beret.

'Why can't we have the heat on?'

Ollie sighed heavily. 'It's character building.'

'It's freezing is what it is.'

Jack snorted, but he didn't join in with the moaning. Ollie sounded worryingly like the Brigadier did these days.

'Quiet down, boys.' Their form master, Mr Ellis, stood at the door. Jack reckoned he looked as tired as they all felt, and he looked uncomfortable in a suit rather than his usual sports gear. But, get through today and this pseudo-military nonsense would be over. Alfie had complained to his olds about it, and his olds held sway over the school.

Ollie pushed them all into their lines so Mr Ellis could inspect them. He found little to correct and marched them outside to where the Brigadier waited. The cadets moved away from their dorm-mates and flanked the Brigadier. He inspected them, and berated those he found wanting. Two he ordered onto the ground to do a set of press-ups. At least Alfie wasn't one of those getting punished for imaginary crimes this time.

The Brigadier ordered the cadets to inspect and guide the ranks of students in their final drill practice before their performance. They stomped through it all without much haranguing and verbal abuse. The Brigadier dismissed them with a warning to keep their school uniforms in tip-top condition while they ate their breakfast. Everyone had to be back at ten o'clock sharp. Everyone scurried up to their dormitories to ditch their jackets and boaters and put on other jackets to protect their shirts and ties.

In the dining hall, everyone ate what was served by Alice and the boys on kitchen duty. Conversation rumbled through the large room at a dull, subdued level. Jack lingered over his breakfast to warm up.

Mr Newton stood and tapped a spoon against a glass. The conversation stopped. 'Not long to go now until you can show the town what this school represents. I commend the Brigadier for his work in transforming you all this past week. I didn't think it possible, but he held the faith that you would be able to achieve this. Keep that in mind this morning. Brigadier?'

The Brigadier stood up as Mr Newton sat back down.

'Thank you, Headmaster. Do not forget that you are doing this to show your appreciation of those who sacrificed their lives for this country. You owe them your respect. Do not disappoint them.'

Jack heard none of the whispers or sniggers that once would have greeted such tosh. It didn't take long for everyone to toe the line, him included.

At ten o'clock, everyone stood to attention and passed muster. They marched out and towards the cenotaph in the nearby town where they performed what the Brigadier drilled into them relentlessly that last week.

Jacquie lay on her bed and listened to the record she played while she dipped into reading a novel borrowed from the library. A fanciful thing she knew she'd forget once read and returned, but having read it would give her social currency.

Her olds were going out. They told her they were off to attend a Remembrance Sunday service and gave her permission to stay at home.

'Well done on completing your school projects.'

'Thanks.' She always had, and not only her own.

'And for avoiding the headmaster's office.' Her mother didn't look at her when she said that. She fiddled and fussed with her coat and scarf. 'For most of the term, at any rate.'

'We'll be back in the afternoon.' Her father put his hat on.

'Okay. Bye.'

Later, after she ate a sandwich for lunch, Jacquie pondered whether the service they referred to was at Brendon. She put it out of her mind and flopped back on her bed and dozed while she listened to her music.

Her thoughts drifted to Jack. If their olds did go to the school, maybe they might see the awfulness she couldn't tell them about.

She'd written a note to him using their new system, but nothing arrived from him at the shop. She hoped and worried that the Brigadier hadn't tumbled that the papers she'd got from the Ministry of Defence were back with her.

She studied the notations, which Jack said looked like his maths teacher's hand. They didn't say much, but added a bit more to the words she'd uncovered from the Ministry's censors. She figured she would have more luck with the Fifth Operational Corps than the other words, but also worked out that the Ministry would not help further. They might even panic that they'd sent her too much the first time.

The record on the turntable finished playing. The needle automatically lifted up and returned to its rest position. She couldn't be bothered to get up and play it again, or select something else.

The front door opened. Her father called up to her. 'We're back.'

'I'm reading.'

Well, she had been. She checked the time. Half three. She would stay ensconced in her room.

After a few moments, she heard them both tread up the stairs to their bedroom. They didn't close their door.

Her father said, 'It was good to see the Grangers.'

She couldn't hear her mother's reply, but it went on a bit judging from the length of her father's silence.

'Maybe, but Jack would say if there was trouble.'

Jacquie sat up on her bed.

'I thought they looked good. I wasn't convinced about…'

Jacquie frowned. Her father must have wandered away from the part of their bedroom where she could hear him clearly.

'Well, maybe a little bit of discipline like that will do him some good. Something's happened to make Jacquie behave, too.'

'Shhh.'

'What? She's probably got music on, or her head in a book. She said she was reading.'

Another pause broke the conversation. Her mother probably kept her voice low. Jacquie grinned. Her mother knew her daughter well.

'All I'm saying is we should feel good about a bit of peace at last,' her father said. 'That Brigadier chap seems to have found his feet and is making his military experience count. Like I said, I thought they looked good and it was nice to see them all pay their respects like that. I've felt for a few years that people weren't taking Remembrance Sunday seriously with the crowds dwindling at the services. I'm only saying it was a good thing of Brendon to turn the whole school out and not only rely on their cadets for a good show.'

A short pause this time.

'Look, I had to do National Service. That marching up and down and saluting instils discipline. It might look easy, but drilling to get everyone in time like that takes work. Hard work. I've a good mind to write to the headmaster to thank him for what they did.'

Jacquie stared at her bedroom door as her olds walked past and back down the stairs. She would have to feign interest in their activities to find out what on earth Jack was going through. She shuddered.

CHAPTER THIRTEEN
Silly Games

THE HEAVY mist rose by mid-morning, burned off by the weak November sun. The Brigadier wrapped his dressing gown around himself and wandered to the sun lounge. He was the only patient there and he settled into one of the chairs. He clutched a magazine in one hand, but he didn't open it. He rested it on the chair's arm, his arm on top of it, and he gazed out at the gardens.

He started when a man entered the room, the bucket he carried rattling. The Brigadier squinted at the man as though that might help his memory to return. He recognised the man, and knew he worked here.

'Good morning, Brigadier. Nice spot.'

'Yes, thank you. Reggie.' He beamed as his memory produced the man's name in the nick of time.

'I just need to look after the plants in here, too. Give them a good feed.'

'Of course. Carry on. Don't mind me.' The Brigadier picked up the magazine and opened it, but the words and pictures swam. He blinked a few times, but shook his head and put the magazine back down.

Reggie had put his bucket near the three large pots wedged up against the wall near the window. He scooped out dirt from the bucket and spread it at the base of each plant. He whistled a tune that the Brigadier couldn't name, but he smiled at it. He leaned his head back and closed his eyes.

The sunlight warmed the room and as he drifted into a doze, a feeling of calm caressed him.

Jack and the boys thought they would be left alone after they returned to the school on Sunday. Instead, Mr Newton spoke to them about his pride in their behaviour. He passed them on to the Brigadier and disappeared inside the main building with the small gaggle of dignitaries and teachers. Their form teachers remained, and watched while the Brigadier pointed out every mistake they made.

What did he expect? He'd had years to knock the cadets into shape and they were rubbish. Why on earth did he think he could get the whole school marching and standing perfectly in a week? They weren't soldiers. They were students. It might be a posh school, but it wasn't pseudo military. Jack railed at the Brigadier's quibbles.

'The headmaster has instructed me to extend the discipline brought to you all for today's ceremony to all parts of your life here. You have one week in which to get rid of anything that might bring disrepute to the school's name. That includes clothes, reading material, music... everything. Next Sunday, we will search your belongings to ensure that you have complied.'

Jack's eyes widened, both at the Brigadier's words and the silence with which they were greeted. No one, not even Alfie, shouted out any opposition. No one grumbled. No one did as much as move.

'Dismissed.'

Everyone breathed with relief and slunk to their dormitories to change into their normal Sunday clothes.

Ollie pointed at Jack's t-shirt collection. 'You're going to have to get rid of them.'

'You what?'

'They don't exactly match the school's ethos, do they?'

'Says you who only turned up here a few weeks ago.'

Ollie folded his arms. 'Not my views, but the Brigadier's, and he has a point. Most of those bands you like are anti-authority figures and this school is preparing us to become the leaders of this country. It's contradictory.'

Alfie approached. 'Huh.' He scratched his head. 'I guess he has a point, put like that.'

'No he blinking doesn't. And I don't like them because of their politics, but their music. They're musical artists, and that's what I like about them.'

Ollie set his shoulders. 'If it's just the "music" you like, why have their t-shirts?'

'What do you mean "music"?' Jack drew himself up to his full height and set his jaw. He heard the dismissive tone in Ollie's voice when he said the word.

'That noise you like to play with singers who mumble so that no one can understand the lyrics, and if you can they're dire and full of sex.'

'You don't know what you're talking about.' Jack kept his voice low and made fists of his hands.

Alfie stepped forward. 'Hey, chill, lads. Ollie, the t-shirts just show who we like.'

'The Brigadier says that sort of thing leads to violence.' Ollie kept his arms folded, and his gaze locked on to Jack.

'What about football strips, then?'

Jack darted a glance at Alfie, as did Ollie. Alfie held a jersey in the colours of his favourite team, and Jack stifled a laugh at how innocent Alfie tried to look.

'Maybe they should go, too,' Ollie said. 'Maybe we should only wear the colours of the school's team.'

'You can't be serious.' Jack swivelled back to Ollie, who shrugged.

'What's wrong with showing our pride in the school?'

Jack shook his head. 'Sod off.' He turned away to end the conversation, and Ollie backed away.

Next day, the teachers in their first classes for the day expanded on the Brigadier's announcement. People grumbled and moaned, and questioned the edict. Jack wanted them to shut up because every time they questioned a definition, that item unequivocally turned up on the banned pile. It got to the stage that the teachers may as well say what they were allowed to wear or have with them at the school because that list would be shorter.

Then came the kicker. Certain items were defined as material that would warrant expelling the student from the school. Jack didn't need to be told that the copy of *In Other Words* Jacquie gave him would fit that bill.

Rebecca completed her list of out-patient sessions by lunchtime. She ate her sandwich in her office, using the excuse of filing to escape socialising with the other staff members. She liked them, and enjoyed a bit of chit-chat, but she needed activity without the presence of people to quieten her mind. Her three patients that morning all made breakthroughs about their respective issues, which she loved, but for the toll it took on her to reset herself for the next patient.

She had a tendency to ruminate too much over every individual case, so her teachers and mentors informed her. She argued it made her a better therapist, which she still contended. But she did concede how much it drained her afterwards now she wasn't as young as she once was.

Filing proved to be a good compromise. She channelled her natural inclination to go over her sessions into preserving a thorough record of the breakthroughs and observations. It further allowed her to consider potential next steps.

The old railway clock in the reception area chimed to announce it was two o'clock. She packed up the folders and put them away in their places. She left her office to walk through to the in-patient clinic where she met her sole patient for the afternoon. He stood at the doorway to his room. He might be wearing pyjamas, slippers and a dressing gown, but he somehow managed to retain a military bearing. He straightened up when he saw her.

'Brigadier, sorry I'm a little late.'

'Not at all, not at all.' He flashed a smile. 'I'm not one for lying about.'

'I know.' She stopped herself from saying any more. In the week since they woke him from his induced coma they both repeated the same arguments several times. She told him he needed to be careful, that even the forty-eight-hour coma damaged some of his internal organs and they required rest for healing. His rejoinder was that he felt as fit as a fiddle and always surprised his doctors at how quickly he recovered. 'Shall we take a stroll out in the garden? It's a lovely sunny day.'

He held out an arm. 'Delighted.'

She tilted her head and shook it, smiling to remove the sting of rejection. He smiled in return as if to say 'no harm done' and dropped his arm to his side.

*

The sun shone in a cloudless sky. At this time in the afternoon it was warm enough for a turn around the garden, but the chill in the air warned them to not dawdle. The Brigadier delighted in sharing with her the names of plants and a few pointers on how to take care of them through an English winter. Rebecca recognised the words of Reggie, and smiled at the evidence of the Brigadier forging a friendship. She steered him towards the pavilion that overlooked the pond. On days like today she enjoyed using it for extended therapy sessions. The sunshine warmed the space, and the glass walls lent it an open feeling. The views of the pond and surrounding gardens in late autumn made her feel as though the world wasn't a crowded place full of concrete buildings and machinery.

They both sat on the wicker chairs.

'Down to work, now, I'm afraid,' she said.

'It doesn't feel like work, all this talking.'

'Perhaps not the work you're used to, but did you know our brains use up most of our body's energy during an average day. More when we do what's called "deep thinking". Our talks involve quite a bit of deep thinking. During one of our last sessions, you used an analogy of walls protecting the memories affected by your amnesia, and how some of the bricks were loosening. It's an analogy I really like. Would you care to describe the state of those walls?'

The Brigadier made a grumbling noise and stared out towards the pond. She let him be for a few moments. He cleared his throat, but didn't redirect his gaze to her.

'Those bricks are crumbling, but slowly. The walls are thick, like those of castles. I don't know what caused them to spring up the way they did, and the way they seem to me they are perhaps better left alone.'

'I see.'

He turned to her. 'I'm not sure you do.' He sighed and looked outwards once more. 'I don't.'

On Thursday night at the dining table, Jacquie's mother mentioned that the school rang. For a moment, Jacquie froze. Her school? Or Jack's? It took a second before she recalled her mother used 'the' for Brendon. Her school was dismissed in a derisory tone as 'your school'.

Her father asked what about.

'They are doing a belts and braces clean-up. They don't want the boys wearing anything that might bring disrepute to the school's image when they're not wearing the uniform. So, no music or sports t-shirts or football strips. They would prefer the boys to wear shirts and trousers rather than jeans and t-shirts. Trainers should only be for playing games.'

'Blimey,' said her father. 'Well, I can't say I can complain. We pay for our son to be transformed into a gentleman.' He nodded. 'I approve. He should look the part at all times, and not only during lessons.'

Jacquie blinked and put her knife and fork down. She sipped her drink to stop from blurting out how stupid it was what Brendon was doing.

'There's more. They'd like us to pick up Jack's record collection and his comics. They don't believe that either are good influences on the other students.'

The blood ran from Jacquie's face as she thought of the magazine she'd given him. She would have to work out a way to get to the school and rescue it. Their olds wouldn't understand.

'They suggested Saturday, if we could.'

Her father dabbed at his mouth with his serviette. 'That suits, yes. In the morning?'

'That's what they would prefer. Good. Otherwise, they would have to destroy it all and I don't think that's quite right. He can enjoy it when he's home.' Her mother glanced quickly at Jacquie, but said nothing more.

Jacquie said nothing, too, but her appetite vanished. Her parents applauding all this like it was a good thing. Jack loved his music and comics. He already withstood having to stay at the school during holidays. She asked to be excused, and they let her go. She didn't try to earwig what they might say about her, and about the two of them together. She could guess.

She put her mind to how to rescue what she could of Jack's things, and how to let him know. Their current method of letters containing hidden codes wouldn't work because of the time involved. She couldn't telephone because of all the restrictions placed on them specifically, and the practice more generally. She would have to skive off and get into the grounds.

She touched her hair. She couldn't cut it off to copy the extreme look the bloody Brigadier forced on all the students at Brendon, not without attracting a lot of attention.

How dare he do that. He really did deserve to get what was coming to him. Maybe when she next saw his car in town she might do something to it.

Desperate times called for desperate measures. She'd work out something. She always did.

Sunday arrived, and the teachers woke all the students pre-dawn. Everyone stood in the dining hall, shivering in their dressing gowns and waiting for the heating to kick in. They also waited for the teachers to finish their search of the school for anything now declared contraband.

Jack hugged himself and stared down at the table. His olds collected his things yesterday morning. His mother fussed over him, and his father admired his new haircut. Jack overheard his father approving the changes in the school to a couple of other parents visiting to take away the little things that made boarding bearable.

Seeing his parents made him miss Jacquie even more than he usually did. Two weeks had passed since they last saw each other. They'd written, using their code and the cover of a pen pal relationship with a fictional refugee. But one letter a week each way wasn't brilliant when all this was happening, and so fast. His hatred of the Brigadier grew, a lot of it from the compromise of the hiding place in the obelisk.

Desperate measures saw him hiding his favourite t-shirt and the first edition of *In Other Words* in separate places. While the search went on, he worried they'd be found. Maybe it would be good if they were. Maybe if he was expelled from Brendon he could go to the comprehensive his sister went to.

Yeah, that was not going to happen. Their olds would find a way to keep them apart, and that would screw up their lives. Jacquie, as ever, concluded that a long time before it even dawned on him.

Jacquie's letters counselled him to keep his head down and focus on getting through the school year. With a collection of O-levels, they could escape school, and their olds, get jobs and start living their own lives on their own terms. What was a year, after all?

He nestled deeper into his dressing gown. She wasn't living in a militarised nightmare like him. He blinked back a tear and scowled.

The teachers returned and congregated at the front. Jack glanced up, but the way the teachers huddled meant he couldn't see what they found. Despite the silence of the student body, he couldn't hear what the teachers muttered about until Mr Newton's voice exploded with the word, 'Filth.'

Jack's stomach twisted in on itself.

Mr Grey, Mr Wade and Ms Peters launched themselves into the student body. Mr Wade thundered past Jack, and Jack breathed out. He angled his head to watch Mr Wade's progress. He grabbed a first former by his ear and pulled him back from the table. Jack frowned. He half-turned, and tensed as Mr Wade dragged the kid back past him. The kid's face twisted, all red and blotchy with tears, and he batted uselessly against the man's arm. Jack pulled his own arm back, his hand balled into a tight fist, but Alfie grabbed his shoulder and he whispered urgently into his ear.

'Don't.'

Jack eased back and shrugged Alfie off.

Three boys stood at the front with the teachers. They were the first former hauled up by Mr Wade, a fourth former named Johnson, and a student named Fawcett with a shock of blond hair in the Upper Sixth. The first former and Fawcett rubbed their ears, while Johnson rubbed his shoulder.

Mr Newton told the assembled students to turn to the front and listen. He rambled about being simultaneously pleased and disappointed about the amount of questionable material found and removed during the week.

'The staff have searched high and low and despite the clean-up found three disgraceful items. Mr Fawcett, as a student in the Upper Sixth, we expect you to set an example for the younger boys. A good example.' Mr Grey handed Mr Newton a t-shirt, which the headmaster held up so the boys could see. Jack frowned. It was only an ABBA t-shirt. 'Mr Fawcett, this will be destroyed and I will give you twelve. However, you may remain at the school to complete your A-levels. We will be watching you.' He stabbed at the student with his finger.

He next turned on Johnson. His crime was hanging on to the Boomtown Rats' single, *I Don't Like Mondays*. He, too, was sentenced to twelve lashes of the cane. He could remain at the school, but this was his last chance.

Lastly, Mr Newton turned his fury on the first former, named Duffy. The headmaster brandished a copy of a magazine. 'But this, this is depraved filth.'

Even from where he was standing, Jack recognised the cover.

'It wasn't mine, sir, I found it and was going to throw it out, sir.'

'You disgust me, Mr Duffy. Trying now to blame it on someone else. You do not deserve to remain in this school. You will get twelve, and then you will leave. This… this rag will be destroyed.'

Jack paled. Stupid kid should have left it.

They all had to watch and count aloud as one while Mr Newton delivered the twelve blows to each of the three students. Jack flinched at each thwack and mumbled each number.

Later, back in their dorm room as they changed into their sports clothes for their Sunday morning run, Ollie sidled up to Jack. 'What do you know about that magazine?'

Jack shrugged. 'Nothing.'

'No, you do know something. I'd wager it's yours, but that first former stumbled across it.'

Jack swallowed, but drew himself up to his full height. 'Are you threatening me?' He kept his voice low.

Ollie shook his head. 'No, but you've just confirmed it.' He grinned. 'And now I *own* you.' He sauntered off and out of the room.

'You don't "own me", you little oik.'

CHAPTER FOURTEEN
Heart of Glass

ON MONDAY morning, the Brigadier asked the matron if anyone from his school had been in contact. She flicked through a folder and smiled at him. 'Why, yes. The headmaster's office has telephoned a few times. They didn't leave any messages and said not to disturb. Just asked after you.'

He nodded. 'Did they seem concerned about my return?'

She shook her head. 'Quite the contrary. They said that you need to take as much time as you need to get better. They miss you, and look forward to your return, but your health is paramount.'

His eyebrows danced. 'Can you please thank them? When they next call?'

'Of course, Brigadier. Consider it done. They seem like they're a nice group of people to work with.'

'They've been good to me, yes. Thank you.'

He ambled to the sun lounge and picked up a discarded copy of *The Echo*. He skimmed the news pages with a light frown and didn't take long to put the paper down on his lap. He gazed out of the window. The heavy rain stripped the deciduous trees of what remained of their leaves and he felt for Reggie and the main gardeners who toiled in the cold weather to keep the lawns clear of rubbish.

His thoughts drifted to the therapy sessions with Dr Pelham-Rose, and the group therapy sessions he attended with the other in-patients. The latter Dr Kent led, most often. Dr Kent kept a tight rein on the group, curtailing the tendency of a few to meander on in their reminiscing. Most of the other in-patients were older than the Brigadier and suffered from the various ailments of old age. Forgetfulness and irascibility, and a strange nostalgia for a past that didn't exist in the way they remembered.

His peculiar amnesia marked him as different to the others. His short-term memory worked decently well, and he clung on to the proof of that with the results of test after test after test.

Each night as he wrote in his journal, he couldn't help but feel a ghost poke at one of the bricks in the wall around his forgotten memories. Dr Pelham-Rose warned him to not force even the loose bricks free. She agreed with his worry that his mind protected him from something, and he would remember when it was safe for him to do so and not before. She told him that all the therapy sessions were making him ready for that moment.

He smiled as he thought of her, his butterfly.

Jack plodded through his morning routine as though on automatic. The Brigadier disabused the students of thinking they were free of the military drilling. They enjoyed their week off after Remembrance Sunday, so far as old Stewpot was concerned, and now they needed to get back to it.

So, well before dawn all the boys dressed in their sports clothes and met outside in their forms. The Brigadier, aided by the members of the Cadet Corps dressed in their uniforms, drove the students to perform an hour's worth of physical fitness exercises, marching, and practicing loads of useless drills. The Brigadier harangued them, and berated them about every imaginable mistake. Quite a few wholly imagined, Jack reckoned.

They showered before dressing for breakfast. Jack dawdled for no real reason except to take a moment for himself to think.

Ollie didn't let him. The toe rag came from nowhere and clapped his arm around Jack's shoulders. 'Orright?'

'Sod off.' Jack shrugged himself free and picked up his pace.

'Not nice.'

Ollie grabbed Jack's arm with a tight grip. Jack swung around with his fist up, but Ollie batted it away with his free hand, twisted, and held on to his wrist. Jack stumbled, but Ollie did not let go.

'Now, now, Jack my lad. I want to make sure you understand the nature of our friendship now.'

'I thought you were all right. Seems I was wrong.'

Ollie twisted the arm he held and Jack bent over to ease the pain that lanced through his arm.

'Oi, oi, ow. Leave it out.'

'Are you going to pay attention?'

Jack grunted. Ollie twisted his arm like he'd dislocate his shoulder, and Jack relented. 'Yeah, okay, all right. I'll listen.'

Jack straightened up when Ollie released his arm. Jack scowled and resisted rubbing at where Ollie had gripped him and twisted. He didn't want to give any clue about the damage done.

'Good, Jack my lad.' He waved a finger at Jack. 'Now don't test me again.'

The little oik manoeuvred Jack into a corner and, while he could easily win a fair fight, he figured that Ollie wouldn't let that happen.

Ollie grinned. 'Good to see you learning, my man. Word is you're a bit slow at times, and that your sister got all the brains.'

Jack squared his shoulders and gritted his teeth. 'Watch it.'

Ollie put his hands up, palms forward, and his grin widened. 'I told them I didn't believe it. I told you knew how to look out for yourself. I told them that you are feared by many out there in the real world. Not just feared by kids, either.' He nodded. 'It's impressive, and by barely lifting a fist.'

Jack lowered his shoulders and allowed himself a cautious half-grin.

'And I thought to myself, I could do with a bit of that. Not outside the school. Not since we can't go out as much as you used to. But in the school. I thought to myself, I'll have a word with Mr Armstrong who strikes such fear in people outside and see if we can spread a little of that magic inside the school. Only every time I got ready to say something, something would happen and I couldn't because I didn't know if you'd listen to my proposition. Until now.'

'You what?' Jack shook his head slowly. The lad was missing something.

Ollie's smirk returned. 'You and me can bring a bit of discipline to this school the way the teachers can't. Oh, the Brig is making a good start, but he is only one man.'

'Did Newton put you up to this?'

'What?' Ollie scoffed. 'No, not the old Newt. None of the teachers "put me up to this". It's my very own style of school pride. Not pride at what is, but what could be. My school in Singapore showed me the way it ought to be. Singapore's Prime Minister, Mr Lee Kuan Yew, is an inspiration, if people here could just push aside their racism.'

Jack blinked at him. The kid really wasn't the full quid. Singapore was hot, and maybe the heat had got to him. He'd been in India before that, and that was hot, too. A life-time of heat on the brain.

Ollie rubbed his hands together. 'You and me, a team, a dream team, yeah? Or I might let slip that you owned the *Other Words* mag that got that little kid expelled.'

'You can't prove it was mine.'

'Oh, Jack my lad, I can. Your sister gave it to you. I've worked out your silly little code.' Ollie laughed, turned, and stepped away. 'Oh, that's something else I could tell the old Newt about, how you and she disregard the rules.' He waved with his fingers. 'See you at breakfast, my lad.'

Jack stood there, jaw dropped. He swore. He had to tell Jacquie to stop writing, that their way of communicating had been compromised. He swore again.

'Why can't I just have this one little bit of something nice for me? Huh? Why'd he have to ruin it?'

The empty corridor mocked his words in the way it echoed them back.

He picked up his feet and went to the dining hall for breakfast. Ollie, acting like their little chat hadn't happened, stood up and waved him over. Jack trudged towards him and sat in the empty space next to his blackmailer. He saw Alfie blink at him as if to say, 'What are you doing next to him?' He shrugged, but turned his attention to his breakfast.

Ollie clamped his arm around Jack's shoulders. Jack flinched, and Ollie squeezed. 'Now, my lad Jack has opinions about us all joining the CCF. Care to share them, Jack, old son?'

Jack looked up at the students sat around Ollie. 'Uh.' He glanced at Ollie.

'Come on, come on. We were only just talking about it. It's why we were late for breakfast.' Ollie shook Jack.

'Uh, yeah.' Jack swallowed, and then he lied.

Jack broke the pattern of letters. He wrote a follow-up to his last one the day after he sent it. Jacquie only knew about it because Mrs Patel saw her on her way to school and yoo-hooed her, waving the envelope. 'Another letter, dear. But, please, can you organise for a new address for them to send their letters to? We are not a post office.'

'Yes, Mrs Patel. Sorry. I am working on it.' Jacquie accepted the letter with a smile and shoved it into her satchel.

'If you need more pocket money, we can offer you a job in the shop.'

That made her pause. 'Really, Mrs Patel? That's very kind. Can I think about it?'

'Yes, of course. Study hard today.' Mrs Patel disappeared back into the shop.

Jacquie continued on her way to school. She figured the Patels wouldn't pay her that much, but it would be better than what they paid her for the paper round. She could save a bit, which would help her and Jack for after they got their O-levels and could leave school. The offer opened up quite a few opportunities, which occupied her thoughts until she arrived at her school and headed to the library.

Inside the warm space, she took out Jack's letter and read it. He described what happened on Sunday, with the search and the punishments. She checked the stamp. Somehow her brother had managed to send it first class, and somehow the Royal Mail delivered it to their promise of next day delivery. That hadn't always been the case before the General Election.

Then came the kicker in Jack's letter. One of the other kids knew the *In Other Words* was Jack's, and the toe rag threatened to use that over him as blackmail. 'It's horrid here, J. It happened so fast, and I'm scared.'

Jacquie scrunched up the letter. She stared into the middle distance while she organised her thoughts. She couldn't rely on the Royal Mail repeating their fast delivery trick twice in the one week. She would have to risk making a telephone call and leaving a message, and then going to the school.

The first bell rang. It jolted her and she shoved Jack's letter back into her satchel. On her way out of the library she waved at Mr Devereaux, who smiled and returned her greeting. She trudged, deep in thought about what message to leave for Jack. One that would protect her and their communications, but also one that he would understand. One that would bring him a bit of comfort. Whatever was going on at Brendon needed stopping.

Ollie insisted on sitting next to Jack in every class they shared. Jack complied. If any of the teachers noticed, they said nothing. Mr Grey looked like he was about to say something, but he didn't. Jack caught the looks exchanged between Ollie and Grey, and he shuddered. He knew what the little oik had on him, but what must he hold over old Mr Grey?

During the day, Ollie kept nudging Jack to openly promote the new regime of unquestioning obedience, and to encourage membership of the CCF. After they ate their tea in the dining hall, Ollie whispered to Jack about how pleased he was. 'Don't do anything silly to undo all that good work today.' He nudged him hard in the ribs. 'Jack, my lad.' Ollie left the room.

The Toad sidled up to Jack. 'There's a call for you. Third Form dormitory.'

'Who?'

The Toad shrugged.

Jack nodded and thanked him before he bolted from the dining hall up to the dorm room. He scooped up the receiver. 'Whatcha?'

'Hey, hey.'

Jack sank down onto the chair and cupped the mouthpiece to his face. 'Can't talk long. The toe rag knows our code, and he's got me on a tight leash.'

Jacquie swore. 'Look, I'll still write and send stuff, but it'll be diversions. A trick. Yeah?'

'Okay.'

'I'm working on something to help you.'

'I know.' Whistling announced the arrival of a student outside. 'Got to go.' He hung up, and darted down. He released his pent-up breath.

It wasn't Ollie.

Jack crept out and went to where he should be on a Monday evening. The library, to do the set homework.

Ollie sauntered in a few minutes later. He grinned at Jack, and waved, and headed to the stacks. Alfie and the Toad arrived a minute later. The Toad raised an eyebrow at Jack, who nodded quickly and put his finger to his lips. He darted his head in the direction of where Ollie stalked. Alfie and the Toad crossed to a different table.

Ollie emerged. 'Mr Granger and Mr Merrem. Delightful evening. Care to join me and Mr Armstrong?'

Alfie shrugged.

Ollie clamped a hand on Jack's shoulder. 'Go on, invite them over.'

Jack scowled. 'Come and sit with us.'

Alfie and the Toad moved to join them.

'Mr Granger, have you been doing your bit to encourage everyone to join the CCF?'

Alfie shifted in his seat. 'Uh, yeah. Of course.'

'Great.' Ollie slapped Jack's shoulder. 'Care to explain why my lad here still hasn't.'

Jack grimaced. 'I'll join tomorrow, all right.'

Rebecca's Monday list occupied her all day with her out-patients. As she finished up for the day, she turned to think about her in-patients. She would see them for appointments tomorrow, but her worry about two drove her up and out to see Dr Kent. She knocked on his door, but no one answered. No light leaked out from below the door. She assumed he'd already gone.

She should go, too. Tiredness seeped into every cell of her being, and Tuesday shaped up to be equally as exhausting. But she felt the need to check up on the two patients she worried about.

With a little humph, she carried on down the corridor to where the clinic became a lying-in facility. At the nurses' station, Gloria packed up her things. She looked up as Rebecca approached. 'Is there a problem?'

'I won't rest tonight if I don't check on the Colonel and

the Brigadier.'

Gloria smiled. 'The Colonel is having a bath, but he's fine. The Brigadier is in the television room with some of the other patients. They are watching the news, I think. He's fine, too.'

Rebecca smiled in return. 'Thanks. I'll just put my head around the door. I won't be long.'

'Of course, Doctor.'

Rebecca's smile faltered at the sound of hardness in the matron's voice. 'I don't doubt you. It's purely for my own peace of mind.'

'Of course, Doctor.' This time Gloria sounded softer.

Rebecca put the interaction out of her mind as she strolled to the room from where she could hear the serious tones of the newsreader and reporters. She entered and saw four of the patients. Three watched the television intently, the fourth nursed a newspaper on his lap, but his head leaned against the backrest and he snuffled quietly asleep. The Brigadier. She paused, and turned to leave. One of the other men glanced up and waved.

'Hello, Doctor. To what do we owe the pleasure?'

The Brigadier started awake and looked about him. 'Butterfly,' he mumbled. He shook his head and smiled sadly.

The two other men shushed everyone else in the room. One of them turned the volume up on the television.

Rebecca put her finger to her lips and winked at the Brigadier. His eyebrows jumped and his eyes twinkled as she crept towards him. 'I only wanted to check in on you.'

He kept his voice as low as hers. 'I'm feeling fine, Doctor. Dr Kent had us all share something we enjoy in our group session today. I thought of butterflies, for some reason.'

She lay a hand on his upper arm, and he laid his hand on top. He patted it.

'I always think of butterflies when I think of you. Butterflies and roses.'

Rebecca extricated her hand from under his. Her heart sank. She leaned in to whisper to him. 'That's very kind, Brigadier, but I'm sure you'll understand that I must maintain a professional relationship with all my patients.'

His brow creased. 'I didn't mean anything by it.'

'My mistake. I've had a long day.' She covered up a yawn.

'See you tomorrow.'

'See you tomorrow.'

Rebecca walked to the door. 'Goodnight, all.'

Somehow, Jack made it through the morning drill without collapsing from exhaustion. He hadn't slept the night before. During the night, his mind churned through everything that had gone on, and what might happen next. His dreams lurched into nightmare territory. Flames from the estate up the road licked at Ollie, who locked his talons into Jack's flesh. The Brigadier laughed at him. A horrible, maniacal laugh. His moustache flickered like a TV effect. There one moment, gone the next.

That woke him up during the night. Like it was important, as much as it creeped him out.

All morning, Ollie egged him to sign up to the cadets. Jack kept saying he'd do it, but he had to talk to his father first. They had maths class before the lunch break, and Ollie spoke to the Brigadier all hush-hush, but when the toe rag bounced towards him he guessed what they'd agreed. Sure enough, at the end of the lesson, the Brigadier told Jack to stay behind.

'Glad to hear you're volunteering to join the Corps, Armstrong. Floyd-Jones says you need to speak to your father to tell him. What time will your father get home? I'll make sure someone is in the office who can let you call him with some privacy.'

'Sir, I think he gets in at six. My family normally have tea at half six.'

'Excellent, Armstrong. Quarter past six this evening is when you go up to the office, unless you hear different from Floyd-Jones.'

'Yes, sir.'

For the rest of the day Jack feigned enthusiasm about it, just to keep Ollie from poking and teasing. Ollie only left his side a few times, and never for long. The toe rag didn't pass on any messages contrary to the Brigadier's instructions.

At ten past six, Jack trudged up the stairs to the offices. Miss Nugent waited for him. His father answered as though he expected the call. Jack told him what he had to, and his father greeted the news joyfully.

'Of course, son. We'll organise what you need. We are very proud of you, my boy.'

Jack spoke for a few moments with his mother. He didn't even ask about Jacquie. He said his goodbyes and hung up.

'Thanks, Miss Nugent.'

'Do they agree?'

'Yes, miss.'

Miss Nugent nodded, her lips tight.

A crash reverberated from downstairs at the front of the building. Footsteps echoed, as did a woman's voice. 'Oi. Who's in charge here?'

'What now?' Miss Nugent glanced at Jack. 'You'd better go.'

Jack nodded, his eyes wide as a tall, thin woman stormed up the stairs towards them. She pointed a finger with bright red nail polish on long, sharp nails straight at Miss Nugent.

'You, love. You look important. I want to lodge a complaint.'

Jack froze in place. Miss Nugent sighed.

'What about, miss?'

'One of your teachers left me standing at the cinema on Sunday, without so much of a by your leave. I waited two days for a call. Two blinking days, and nuffin. Disgraceful.'

'I see, miss. Which teacher would that be?'

'Alastair Lethbridge-Stewart. That's with the *a*, not an *i*. He's very particular about that.'

CHAPTER FIFTEEN
Switched to Overload

JACK SAID nothing to anyone about what he witnessed. He told Ollie his father approved of him joining the blasted cadets, and he bore Ollie's delight stoically.

In a spare moment when Ollie left the dorm room, Alfie sidled up to him. 'What's going on?'

Jack considered telling him, his best mate, but Ollie returned. 'I'm good.' He smiled, but even Alfie would have spotted he didn't mean it. Dear Alfie. Not the smartest, but he demonstrated the wherewithal to ingratiate himself with Ollie, too. Jack vowed that he would do nothing to harm dear old Alfie, even if Ollie-the-oik demanded it of him.

All through Tuesday he kept his secret to himself. He mulled it over, though, what it might mean for the Brigadier. His way-too-young-for-him girlfriend coming into the school and making a scene like that. Good thing it was after classes and after most of the staff who didn't live in had gone for the day. Poor Miss Nugent having to cop that ire, and clearly she had no idea about the ex-soldier's philandering. After the woman left, he promised Miss Nugent solemnly and truthfully that he wouldn't gossip about it. He dropped the hint that him keeping mum cleared any debt he might have with her in the favours department, and she indicated her acceptance.

On Wednesday morning at breakfast, he received a letter from his fake pen pal, Behzad. Jack glared at Ollie before he opened it, but Ollie grinned and told him to open it and read it out aloud.

Jack ripped it open. It looked the same as all the others. Neatly typed in double-space. No, not as neatly typed as the previous letters. On three lines words were crossed out and replacements made in handwriting. He glanced up at Ollie, who egged him on to read it out. He shrugged and did so. It went through the usual guff of responding to his own overt letter; he was well, he was glad all was well at the school, et cetera, et cetera. Behzad had news. He was moving on.

'I am eternally grateful for your correspondence while I am in London. I am only sorry we never met in person. Perhaps one day we can if you come to visit me in the Kingdom of Arabia.'

'Blimey.' Alfie stared at Jack, open-mouthed.

Ollie sniggered. Jack scowled at him, but said nothing. He itched to read the hidden message, even though Jacquie had told him that what she wrote would be fake. He guessed the corrections made in pen provided a hint to the real message. He couldn't investigate it now, so he folded it up and put it in his inner jacket pocket.

Ollie stuck with him the whole day, and so did Alfie. They had cadets after lessons finished, which meant using the lunch period to do their homework. Jack decided to make Ollie wait until after they finished playing soldiers for the second time that day.

Every time the Brigadier yelled at him for his sloppy stance or about turns, he recalled the sight of his teacher's girl and her fury at him, and Miss Nugent's surprise about the woman's existence. Jack didn't quite manage to keep the smirk from his face, but no one pulled him up on it.

Dismissed, he and his two shadows swarmed up the stairs to their dormitories along with everyone else. They readied themselves for bed and then headed for the television room.

Jack figured that since Ollie said he knew about the secret message Jacquie hid in the letters, he didn't need to hide his deciphering. He grabbed his pencil case and took it and the latest letter with him. There, he studiously revealed the invisible ink of Jacquie's encoded message. He noticed the handwriting she used and whoever wrote the 'corrections' were different.

Clever.

Jack pretended to ignore Ollie as the oik leaned over to watch. He put on a little show about working out Jacquie's cipher from the key in the number one song that week. Dr

Hook and the Medicine Show's *When You're in Love with a Beautiful Woman*. He resisted sniggering at the aptness of it given the Brigadier's bint and her show earlier in the week. He skimmed ahead of his painstaking deciphering for Ollie's benefit. There wasn't much, but it looked convincing for a nice bit of deception. She kept close to the truth. This method of communication had to change because of postal reasons. The references to events and games from their childhood, and their favourite sayings, revealed to him the double layer of cipher hidden in plain sight in the corrections made to the main letter.

Very clever.

In the doubly deciphered text he read through her plans to break into the school on Thursday night.

Wind and rain lashed the gardens of the clinic with a ferocity that didn't let up all afternoon. The Brigadier breathed a sigh of relief when the nurse told him to go to Dr Pelham-Rose's office for their therapy session. He enjoyed being outside, and the summer house by the pond relaxed him into sharing more than he would normally. But, it also distracted him and Dr Pelham-Rose.

Yesterday's appointment proved that point. He apologised to her about the misunderstanding from the night before, which she waved off and they both let it go. Only, he needed to address the complexity of his feelings about it.

The matron knocked on his door and stuck her head around it. 'Doctor's ready for you, Brigadier.'

He smiled and thanked her, then strolled down the corridor to her office. Dr Pelham-Rose held her phone to her ear, but waved him in and mouthed how sorry she was. He sat on the sofa and gazed around her room while she made polite noises. After a minute, she cut in.

'I don't have the time to discuss this right now. It's best if you send a copy of the advertising material to the clinic and we can make a decision as a practice. Goodbye.' She hung up. She put the electronic 'do not disturb' sign on, gathered up her files and swept in to sit opposite him.

'Sorry about that. Those salesmen never seem to understand we actually work in between listening to their sales pitches.' She put the folder on the coffee table.

The Brigadier smiled at her.

They went through their usual greeting ritual, but before she launched into her plan for the session, he said, 'Doctor, if I may...?'

'Yes, of course. I prefer these sessions to be patient-led.' She leaned forward.

'I know we spoke about it yesterday, and I don't believe any harm's been done, but I haven't been able to stop thinking about our little misunderstanding from Monday night.'

'Go on.' Her voice sounded neutral.

'I've been married before, and engaged more than once. I've enjoyed the company of several women outside of both, and I have been called a "lady's man" in my time.' He frowned for a moment as he struggled to remember who by. He shrugged it off. It didn't matter. 'I do find you attractive.' He held up his hand as she looked like she was about to speak. 'However, I am well aware that anything more would upset the doctor-patient relationship.' He cleared his throat. 'I didn't realise it fully at the time, but I behaved disgracefully with a young woman during my army days.' His breath caught in his throat. He coughed. 'There were rules we disregarded, but I held a superior rank to her and I believed I knew better than those rule-setters.'

Tears prickled. He reached for a tissue from the box Dr Pelham-Rose kept on the coffee table and used it to blow his nose.

'Her name was Sally, and I've only just remembered her.' He blew his nose once more. He couldn't bring himself to look at Dr Pelham-Rose. She kept quiet, as she often did. He knew it was to encourage his talking by giving him space. He shook his head, and then told the therapist everything he remembered about Sally.

'She sounds like a lovely woman.'

He nodded and finally looked at her. 'She was, yes. She's been dead some years now...' He frowned. 'There doesn't seem to be any rhyme or reason to the gaps in my memory.' He tapped the side of his head. 'I wish there was.'

'How does it feel to remember her?'

The Brigadier glanced away from the therapist once more. He gazed at a print on her wall of a generic English pasture.

'Good,' he said. 'Relieved that I can recall parts of my past and not feel frightened or angry. I feel sad at what could have been, but we can't change the past.'

At eleven o'clock on Thursday night Jacquie crept out of her house. Even though most Sundays she went with her olds to church, she didn't really believe. Despite that, she whispered a prayer that night that her brother Jack had worked out the double-cipher and his nemesis failed to. Better yet, that Jack managed to do something about his nemesis.

The cold bit through her coat, gloves and scarf. At least the rain held off. The icy air hurt her throat and lungs, and as she breathed out the steam added to a swirling mist.

She arrived outside Brendon School and found the gap in the wall that hadn't been repaired. The ivy shrank back from the steady march into winter, but the overgrown nature of the gardens belied the school's drive to discipline. She squeezed through the gap and paused to listen out for any sound she'd been spotted.

Nothing.

She crept towards the main buildings of the school. No lights glowed from any of the windows. She glanced around at what she could see of the other buildings and saw nothing from there, either. She settled into a waiting spot and wished the clouds and mist would clear to let the half-moon give her some light.

'Hey, hey.'

Jacquie jumped at her brother's voice, loud in the stillness. 'Whatcha,' she returned. They hugged, fiercely. Jacquie felt the tremor in Jack's body and she broke their embrace. 'Are we safe here?'

Jack nodded. 'I slipped the little oik a Micky Finn. He's out for the night.'

'Where'd you get it from?'

'Ms Peters.'

'For serious?'

'She takes sleeping powders when she's not on night duty. She's always the best bet. The nurse locks her stash up.'

'What?'

'Boarding is horrible, especially if you have to stay all the time. The Toad worked out that imbibing a bit of the sleeping stuff takes the edge off. He was the one who discovered Ms Peters' stash. He takes from both her and the nurse, and he's got a bunch of first formers play-acting to confuse the nurse as to how much she's administered for legit purposes.'

'Blimey.'

He shrugged. 'Having said that, I'm not sure how long I can stay out.'

'Yeah. Me neither.' She shivered. She told her brother everything she could think of that she needed to.

Then he told her everything, and she listened with mounting horror. It was worse than she'd imagined, and she imagined some pretty bad stuff. He described the Brigadier ranting and raving about the state of the country, and how slow the government was in making the changes they promised.

'He goes on and on and on about the dangers of socialism and communism, and hints at seeing the horrors of that first-hand,' said Jack. 'So, yeah, my maths teacher has gone full-on fash. Like, for serious. And the rest of the teachers are nodding along and letting it happen. I mean, Newton's helping. So is our father.'

Jacquie swore. 'I didn't know. I don't think mother does, either. Not the full extent of it.'

'You think she might do something if she did?'

She heard the incredulity in his voice, and felt it herself. Their mother's complicity in keeping the two of them apart, and sending her to that horrid Scottish island during the summer, spoke to her siding with their father. 'No, not really.' She shuddered into her coat. 'But I think the newspapers might.'

'What do you mean?'

'The right-wing papers love their precious prime minister. She can do no wrong in their eyes. I think it's weird because they're hardly feminists.'

'I know that.'

'Sorry. You're the only one who listens to me on this stuff. Don't you read the papers?'

Jack laughed. 'Firstly, they're boring. I mean, I did look at the headlines, mostly, just to keep up. But the school has stopped letting us see most of them. The Brigadier says they rot our minds with their lies.'

'They're not perfect. None of them are, even the broadsheets, but they don't usually out and out lie. No one's kicked up a fuss?'

'Most of the lads reckon they're boring. The teachers still get them, and Mr Grey shares articles about history.'

Jacquie blinked at her brother. She shook herself. 'Well, what I was getting at is that the lefty papers might be interested in these changes. We'd need some kind of proof, though.'

Jack shrugged again. 'Man, it's cold. Yeah. I see that. Um, the Brigadier may have mentioned a group he's working with that's got the ear of the prime minister, so he says.'

She rubbed her hands together. 'There'd be paperwork, then, wouldn't there? Maybe you could see if you can get a copy?'

'I don't know, Jac. It's not like it was before, with the little oik hanging around me bad-smell-like.'

'You could always slip him another Mickey, or otherwise cause his incapacitation.'

She heard him smack a fist into his other, open hand. 'Nothing I'd like better.'

'We also need to consider how to remove his nasty little hold on you. He has no proof it's your *In Other Words* the kid nicked?'

'He's got your letter asking me about how I liked the mag.'

'Yours can't be the only copy of it in this school. I won't believe it.'

Jack made another audible shrug. 'Not everyone's got an understanding and switched-on sibling, have they.'

Jacquie play-punched his upper arm. 'I'd better scarper. Unless there's anything else?'

'Nah. Thanks for coming out. Miss you.'

'Look, focus on getting through the year, and getting those O-levels. Then we can both leave this rubbish behind.'

'Yeah, I hear you, but I want to bring the toe rag down, and the Brigadier. Oh, hell, yeah… Old Stewpot's bit on the side came to the school complaining about being stood up.'

'Huh. Now that is interesting.'

*

Friday morning after a long, long week saw Rebecca trying and failing to stifle her yawns during the weekly practice meeting. Dr Kent looked concerned, and Gloria frowned through another apology spoken through Rebecca's hand. 'The nights drawing in always catch me by surprise. It takes my body a wee while to get used to it. I'll be fine again in a few weeks.'

They sped through the lists of out-patients and slowed down over the in-patients. Kent talked through the file on a new patient, a medically discharged flight lieutenant named Turner. 'The Ministry's been forthcoming on this one, but Turner's signed all sorts of legal documents to keep his story hush-hush beyond us.'

'UFOs?' Gloria snorted a short laugh.

Kent looked over his glasses at her. 'It only means the flying object has yet to be identified. Our patient served in dangerous places and at great risk to his physical health. Unfortunately, it affected his mental well-being, and that is what we need to treat. He's younger than the majority of our patients, and likely to need quite some time in our care.'

Gloria apologised and Kent accepted it. 'Right. Lethbridge-Stewart. I've left him until last. He's much better in group therapy than he was when he first arrived. Thoughts, Dr Pelham-Rose?'

Rebecca cleared her throat. 'He has made progress, yes, especially during the last couple of weeks. Earlier this week he remembered a former fiancée of his, but when we tried to open up his memories from her he retreated again. Nowhere nearly as far back as even when he first returned to the clinic as an out-patient this year.' She took a deep breath. 'However, I think he's also learned how to present the impression that he is further along the path to recovery than he, in fact, is. I've seen it with a few other patients similar to his age and background.'

'So, not yet ready for discharging?'

Rebecca shook her head. 'Maybe in a fortnight, but I suspect a month. Depending on whether he continues to push forward and he recovers more memories, or if he regresses. I would be pushing for his discharge sooner, along with a programme of in-house sessions that reduces over time, but he took himself away from in-person sessions far too soon before the summer.'

'As you've mentioned before, yes. That is a concern.' He paused.

Rebecca nodded. 'There is also the way in which this memory manifests that is highly unusual, in my experience. He can tell me her name, certain details about their courtship, and also a painful description of when they called off their engagement, and the fact she died a few years ago. He recalls all that with remarkable clarity, and with intense emotional resonance.'

'That is an extraordinary breakthrough.' Kent tapped a pencil against the folder on his lap.

'Yes, Dr Kent. It is.'

'But...?'

'He cannot recall exactly where she worked, or how they met, or any mutual friends.'

'Ah, I see. Like his mind has released part of the story, but is still fiercely protecting whatever it is that caused his collapse two years ago and his relapse this year.'

'Yes, and the partial regression I mentioned came about when I suggested she might have served directly with him. He denied it quickly at first, but looked troubled as he worked through the potential. Then he shuttered up, and I guided his thoughts elsewhere. I noticed then that he seemed cagier than he was during our first session, but he hid it. Or tried to. That was what tipped me off that we brushed up against a raw nerve.'

'I understand what you mean about him being good at disguising his problems from us as well as himself. Let's review in a week, but I agree with you about your concerns. His amnesia is unusual, and clearly the result of self-preservation. From what, we still don't know, because he doesn't. That means anything can be a risk of triggering another relapse. Do we know yet what caused either of the two relapses this year?'

Rebecca shook her head. 'The nightmares came from nowhere that made any sense to him, or me, to be honest, and the incident at the school he admits might have been his imagination. It's likely he knew the man who met him in Whitehall, but his amnesia caused him embarrassment.'

'I see. Yes. Look, just a thought, but what do you think about him being a mentor to young Turner?'

Rebecca paused to consider. 'I think that would be good for him, actually. The Brigadier is a natural leader and that's one thing he misses here. Being from different arms of the Forces might prove a salve, too. The RAF is quite different in culture from the Army.'

Friday morning and Ollie complained to Jack and anyone else in hearing range about his headache. Jack struggled not to grin, but when the little oik disappeared for a while to the bathroom, Jack and Alfie high-fived each other.

'What did you do?'

Jack slouched. 'Nothing. Weren't me. Wish it was, mind.'

'He's back.'

'Who's back?' Ollie strolled back to Jack and Alfie, his usual swagger all but gone.

'Sting.'

'You what, Jack my lad?'

'Sting and The Police are back in the charts, or so I heard. Should be number one tomorrow, or maybe next week.'

'Now, now. Popular music isn't the sort of thing we should pay much attention to. It ruins your ears and rots your brain. Socialists and commies like it. Real men don't.'

Jack buried his hands in his trouser pockets to stop from burying his fists in Ollie's face. He swallowed back the temptation to say something he would regret. Revenge would come tonight when he dosed the toe rag with as much of the sleeping powders as he could safely lay his hands on. Maybe he could lace it with some of that vodka that Mr Wade kept in his classroom desk drawer. Ollie would taste the gin that Ms Peters stocked, but he wouldn't taste the vodka.

'Well, Jack my lad. You understand my point about popular music?'

Jack nodded. 'Yes, Oliver. I understand your point about popular music.'

'Good. You can save your money from buying that rubbish and spend it on your uniform for Cadets. Speaking of which, your da's being a bit slow on coughing up the cash for your basic kit.'

'Yeah, yeah. I'll ask him on Sunday when I call them.'

'All right then.'

The rest of the day crawled as though each and every one of their lessons slowed the very nature of time itself. They got through Cadets, Jack zoning out the bilge shouted by the Brigadier concerning unemployed layabouts. He groaned inwardly when he tuned in to hear a tirade about pop and rock music that sounded suspiciously like Ollie from the morning. Only the Brigadier lambasted disco music as 'music for deviants and sub-humans masquerading as men'. Jack didn't want to know what he meant, but the vehemence in which he spat his message out turned Jack's stomach.

Jack ran through the same procedure as he had the night before, only he added a measure of vodka to Ollie's chocolate drink. The little oik drank it down, oblivious. He dropped off almost as soon as his head hit his pillow, and then the soft snores rumbled forth. Jack shushed the others up and grumpily told them all to hit the sack, too. He sank gratefully into his bed.

Lights out, and he struggled to stay awake while pretending to slumber. Finally, the night's calm descended over the entire school. Not even the distant foxes screaming caused anyone to stir.

Except for Jack.

Carefully, he stole out from under his covers and put his pillows in place to fool a casual observer. He wrapped his dressing gown around him, and set off out.

He arrived, unseen and unheard, in the administration offices. He made fast work of finding the folder about the think-tank the Brigadier and Ollie mentioned a few times. It was out on the secretary's desk with a note on top to the Brigadier saying his last dictated letter had been typed and sent, and the copy filed.

Heart thudding, Jack opened the folder. He copied out the relevant information, and once done he retraced his steps to his bed. He settled back and fell into a deep sleep. Mission accomplished.

CHAPTER SIXTEEN
Oliver's Army

JACQUIE PACED outside the public lending library despite the drizzle and cold. She worried about Jack and his ability to escape Brendon that day but, earlier on the telephone, he seemed confident. He had phoned the shop where she now worked on Saturday mornings. They spoke quickly, and he assured her he could meet her at the library at three that afternoon. He used a variation of a code they used when much younger, so she assumed Ollie-the-oik listened in.

At five minutes to three, the bus she expected him to be on had been and gone.

As a church bell tolled the hour, a sleek silver Mercedes sedan rolled up. Jack and Alfie emerged from the back. Alfie told the driver they would be about an hour. Jacquie's eyebrows danced as she stood, hands on hips, waiting for an explanation from her brother.

'You remember Alfie?'

She nodded.

'We told the school that we needed a bit of study time away from the grounds. Mr Grey's an amiable sort if you get him in the right mood. We told him that this library has a good collection of local history resources, which we need for a project we're doing. Alfie's pa swung the rest for us.'

Jacquie looked at Alfie and gave him a smile, which he returned. The three of them trooped into the library and Jacquie led them to her and Jack's usual table. A middle-aged man reading a paper got up and shifted when he saw them. Alfie gave a quiet whistle.

'We really do have a history project we need to do.' Jack yawned.

'Yeah,' said Alfie. 'Jack mentioned you could help.' He busied himself with taking out an exercise book and pens from his satchel.

'He did, did he?'

Jack shrugged and rubbed his nose. Jacquie burst into a wide grin. 'Yeah, of course. Anything to help a helper.'

Alfie smiled back. 'Has Jack told you about the nightmare that Floyd-Jones has become?'

Jacquie glanced at Jack. 'A bit. And the Brigadier.'

'Oh, for sure. Him, too.' Alfie opened his book. 'Jack told me about the funny turn he had up at the obelisk a few weeks ago, and then after that he's been all cadets all the way. I don't mind. Not really. Although drilling every morning and most afternoons is a bit much.'

Jacquie asked what the project was, and Alfie told her. She sent him off to the stacks where she knew there was a good run of books that would answer the set questions. While Alfie disappeared, she thought for a moment just how lucky she was with Miss Starr as a history teacher. She shrugged to herself and turned her attention to Jack when he explained further.

'I found out the name of the Brigadier's government contact. It's a bloke named Woolton. The outfit he's in charge of is called... uh.' Jack pulled a crumpled piece of paper out from his shirt pocket. 'The Cranbourne Institute for Education Reform. The Brigadier's been meeting with them and they've agreed all sorts of mental stuff. Getting us all to join the cadets is the first part. They want us to train with real guns so we can defend against the Irish bombers, and, if it works at Brendon, then they'll push the government to get every school with a CCF to do the same.'

Jacquie sat back. 'That's monumentally stupid.'

Jack shrugged. He gave her the paper with his notes from the files he saw the night before. 'According to a letter the Brigadier's sent them just yesterday, he reckons we're ready to start the next phase, whatever that is. I'm scared, Jac. The stuff that Ollie comes out with is horrible, and the Brig copies it, and vice versa.' He glanced up and leaned forward. 'Talk to the First Form kid who got expelled. I told you about him before.'

Alfie returned with an armful of books. He dumped them

on the table and sat back down with a heavy sigh. He slumped on the chair and looked up at Jack and Jacquie. 'Sorry.'

'It's all right.'

'He telling you about all the changes?'

'A bit, yeah.' She shook her head at Jack, and he nodded. Both quick, small movements they used to do when they were much younger and lived together at home. Their olds never noticed, and now neither did Alfie.

Alfie shook his head. 'It's intense. Pa is happy with it all, of course, but also doesn't like it when it inconveniences me.'

'Handily for us.'

Alfie sighed again. 'Not that we can abuse it, and I doubt Floyd-Jones will let us out of his sight again.'

This time Jack shook his head in the tight movement. Jacquie smirked. He didn't need to tell her he'd knocked the kid out for a second night in a row, but any more would raise too many questions.

The Brigadier strolled into the sun lounge and sank into his usual seat. He rested his head back and let his mind drift over his last conversation with his doctor.

Remembering Sally meant realising he had forgotten about her.

Previously, he used the analogy of a brick wall keeping his memories safe from recollection. A brick wall the therapy sessions wore away at, and after several weeks, one part crumbled and revealed Sally.

Only his memory was not complete, even as his mind strove to provide a narrative to paper over the stubborn gaps. He recalled calling off their engagement, but he couldn't remember the details about meeting her beyond them both working together. Let alone their courtship, aside from flashes of convivial drinks and the occasional restaurant meal.

Archie Turner, former flight lieutenant, shuffled into the room. 'Good morning, sir.'

The Brigadier nodded at him and returned his greeting. The airman looked twenty years older than his true age, and he presented himself as someone who did not want to be wherever he was. Dr Pelham-Rose had asked the Brigadier to look out for the lad, which he agreed to do. She asked him to see if he could get the younger man to open up and talk about what happened to him.

Turner perched himself on one of the other seats in the room. He clutched a newspaper, folded up. He licked his lips as though they were parched. He cleared his throat.

'Uh, sir. Am I correct in recalling that you teach at a public school for boys?'

'I do, yes. Mathematics, rugger, as well as commanding a small contingent of the CCF.'

'What's the school called, sir, if you don't mind me asking?' The former RAF man tightened his grip on the newspaper.

'Brendon. Why?'

Turner sank back into his chair and his hands relaxed. 'I thought so. Only, my memory's not as good as it was. That's why I'm here. I have black outs, when I just can't recall anything. No idea why, but it makes flying a plane impossible. Flying was all I ever wanted to do. Have you ever flown?'

'As a pilot?' The Brigadier's eyebrow quirked upwards. 'No, I can't say I have.' He took a breath. 'I also have gaps in my memory. Like you, that's why I'm here. The doctors know what they're doing.' He smiled at Turner. 'But why the question about my teaching?'

'Oh, yes.' Turner held out the newspaper to give it to the Brigadier. 'There's an article about your school. Like I said, I can't trust my memory. I thought Dr Pelham-Rose said you taught there, but then I wasn't sure she had.'

The Brigadier accepted the paper and unfolded it. It was *Education Weekly*, and he wondered why Turner had it. But, sure enough, a picture of the old buildings that housed the main part of his school took up most of a page. The headline read, *Public Boys' School an Exemplar of Government Education Policy*. He read the article, full of quotations from the staff and the think-tank he promised to liaise with before his admission to the clinic. It highlighted the CCF as a strong influence on the way the entire school ran. It noted the new Discipline Code, too, in a positive light. In fact, the entire piece seemed too good to be true.

Monday's history lesson proved to be actually interesting. Jack and Alfie basked in rare praise from Mr Grey about their project. Of course, they'd never have been able to do it without Jacquie's help at the library on the weekend. Alfie understood the need to keep Jacquie's involvement out of it, and Jack trusted him enough to not let it slip.

Jack expected a reaction from Ollie about Mr Grey's praise and his mention of their visit to the public lending library, but the little oik said nothing. He made not a twitch, not even when Alfie pressed their luck in asking Mr Grey if he would approve another visit.

'Not immediately, sir, but as and when.'

'We'll see, Mr Granger.'

Jack told Alfie to quit talking about it, and reluctantly the other boy agreed. For the rest of the day, Alfie resisted the urge to babble about their trip out of the school.

In the afternoon, Jack's cadet uniform arrived. Both Alfie and Ollie excitedly helped him with it while they all prepared for that afternoon's drilling. Jack felt self-conscious as he clattered down the stairs with Alfie and Ollie. That feeling vanished as he got in line and they began their usual activity. The Brigadier said nothing about Jack's new uniform, but at least it meant he didn't get singled out for not having one. The former soldier directed his ire at the new set of boys who signed up and their slovenly attire. His words.

Sixty boys now stood in the ranks of the school's CCF, when at the start of the school year only twenty formed the contingent. After the Brigadier berated everyone for laziness and sloppiness, he ranted about sixty being an improvement. But he would not rest until all the boys enrolled at the school joined up.

They went through their usual marching practice, and a second inspection as they stood ram-rod straight at attention. 'Better.'

Jack expected the Brigadier to dismiss them with an earful about how they needed to improve. Instead, the Brigadier strode to the place on the stairs he liked to use to address them all. Jack's heart sank. It was cold and he was hungry.

'Mr Newton has approved a new rule that allows you all to wear your cadet uniform at all times. I shall lead by example, and I expect to see everyone suitably attired in future. This country's enemies would like to see you cower in disguise, pretending to be civilians in case they target you, when you should wear your uniform with pride. It is a show of strength against the real cowards who bomb innocent people from a distance.'

The Brigadier paused and cast his eye over them all. No one moved or made a sound.

'Mr Newton has also extended the amount of time each week we can spend on CCF duties, as well as the range of our operations.'

Jack flinched at that news. The next phase, he guessed. The Brigadier's thin smile made him shiver.

'Finally, I appoint Corporal Floyd-Jones to the rank of sergeant. He will be my second-in-command. Dismissed.'

Two days later, the Brigadier opened up a copy of *The Sentinel* after he finished his breakfast. One of the nurses brought him that paper instead of his usual copy of *The Echo*. He didn't mind too much, variety being the spice of life or some such.

He recoiled at the picture of Brendon School and the lurid headline about bullying and excessive use of corporal punishment. The contrast between this article and the one in *Education Weekly* couldn't be more stark. If they didn't have the picture and omitted the name of the school, he could be forgiven for thinking the two newspapers published exposés about two different schools. If he was brutally honest, he recognised neither establishment beyond the name and picture.

He read the new article closely. Charles Redfern, the journalist responsible for the story, referred to the other article, but used a different statement from Mr Woolton. They quoted the government's education policies and explained how the changes made to the school so far during the new academic year fell within the extreme end of the government's reform proposals.

Damningly, an unnamed First Form student spoke out about a climate of fear permeating throughout the school. According to the quotations, students and teachers bullied those who didn't fit the military mould. The anonymous boy described how his hair had been shaved into a short-back-and-sides style.

Redfern wrote about the growth of the Combined Cadets

Force contingent, both in student members and the amount of time each week devoted to its activities. The *Education Weekly* article also noted that, and included quotations from the local community about how helpful and impressive the contingent was. The Brigadier's pride had stirred about that, but now he sensed something not quite right. He frowned as he considered who might have taken on his role during his prolonged absence. Perhaps a supply teacher, and maybe Mr Newton saw the point at last about the cadets and encouraged it. Odd, though.

The Brigadier shook his head. Neither article mentioned him by name.

The report about searches for anything among the students' belongings deemed unsuitable raised the Brigadier's hackles. All the teachers kept an eye out for questionable items, of course, but the school policy was quite lenient. Even punk rock records were allowed, so long as the boys who owned them played them at an acceptable level. Likewise, the standards expected in the boys' dress and overall presentation was fairly relaxed for a school of Brendon's calibre. The quoted boy must surely be exaggerating his experiences under cover of anonymity.

'Ah, there it is.' The Brigadier rattled the paper as he turned the pages to continue reading the lengthy article.

The boy had been expelled because the school's headmaster determined he lied about a magazine found among his belongings. A quotation from Mr Newton established the boy was questioned about the magazine, an unnamed adult publication, and maintained it belonged to another student he refused to name. No other boy came forward to claim it. The school exercised its right to expel the miscreant, and evidently the boy's parents decided to make a defensive meal of it.

When he finished reading the article, the Brigadier put the paper down on the table next to his breakfast things. He crossed his arms and frowned.

The publicity about the school, both good and dubious, rattled him. The clinic's matron had reassured him the school called after him regularly and affirmed the priority was for him to work on getting better. His job was assured, and while they missed his presence they survived without him.

Better than surviving, as far as the CCF was concerned. Both articles agreed on that, which generated mixed feelings in him. He took the teaching job to make as clean a break as possible from his army life. He remembered that decision, although not the place where he made it, or the people who might have been nearby. Mr Newton asked him if he would take on the additional role of commanding the cadets when they discussed him joining the teaching staff. He lied back then about it being an honour. The job market being the way it was those years ago, he felt he needed to lie, and it wasn't a total fabrication. He took the job, and the extra task cushioned him from the change. He recalled that, too. The feeling of familiarity comforted him against the strangeness of teaching mathematics to boys from the First Form to the Upper Sixth. Lots of people scoffed at the idea of him doing such a thing, only he couldn't remember who they were. The best he could conjure up from his mind was a hazy sea of dusky khaki and forest camouflage uniforms impossible to distinguish as individual human beings.

A tentative knock at the door rescued him. He glanced up. Smiled. 'Archie. Come in, come in.'

The week plodded on for Jack at the school. He wore his cadet uniform all the time, as did more and more of the boys. While there was a certain amount of peer group comfort, the whole thing unnerved him. He hated the compulsory hair cut on Wednesday during the morning whole-school marching practice.

Having the Brigadier's second-in-command as a 'friend' who stuck close didn't help, either. Ollie press-ganged Jack and Alfie into extra cadet duties, only without the rank or privileges that came with it. The Brigadier excused Ollie-the-little-oik from doing his rostered kitchen and cleaning duties in order for the new sergeant to perform his additional CCF tasks, but was the same courtesy extended to Jack and Alfie or anyone else who did Ollie's work for him? Ha, ha, bloody ha.

Jack no longer missed his records or comics. He didn't have the time to enjoy them between lessons, rostered chores, and all of the CCF duties. Morning with the whole school, and evening with the signed-up members of the contingent. The latter involved more and more physical training – running, exercises, wrestling.

Ollie-the-oik spent time with the Brigadier, just never at a time suitable for Jack to be able to relax and never long enough. Jack tried to wheedle what was up from Ollie, but the toe rag kept quiet.

During a spare minute, Jack whispered his suspicions to Alfie. 'Those two are planning something.'

'How to make our lives more miserable. I mean, I like games. But not outside in the middle of blinking winter, and not when we're supposed to be studying for our blasted O-levels.'

The mystery was solved at the Thursday evening CCF training session.

It began the same as every other evening, with drilling practice and inspections. The Brigadier dismissed half of the group, leaving thirty boys standing at attention in the cold, misty darkness. Jack was one of them. Without turning his head, he nonetheless gazed with longing as the thirty lucky sods clattered up the stairs and into the relative warmth.

'All right, you lot,' the Brigadier bellowed, and Jack's attention swivelled fully to his front. 'We are going to do a spot of community outreach. We are going to march to the estate and help the lazy layabouts sort themselves out.'

Once there was a time the assembled boys would have groaned. Not now. They all stood rock solid, and deathly quiet. Jack didn't even risk a quick glance at Alfie. Alfie had been with the cadets back in April and May when they'd volunteered to help the estate clear up the detritus after that fire. They'd even helped with the building of the new community centre. Jack recalled Alfie's grumbles at spending his Saturdays thus employed, although he also tried to convince Jack that the work felt good to do. It had been a while since Jack's own last visit to the estate and he wondered what on earth the Brigadier wanted to volunteer them for this time.

The Brigadier continued. 'Once we arrive, you will form two groups. Sergeant Floyd-Jones will command one group, and I will command the other. Sergeant Floyd-Jones already has the battle plan. You will obey our instructions without hesitation and without question. Any cadet caught not pulling their weight will be punished immediately upon return to the school.' The Brigadier sneered. 'Remember that you are doing valuable work to build this country back to something of which it can be proud.'

Battle plan sounded ominous, thought Jack, but then everything in the cadets used militarised-speak instead of ordinary language. And there was the weird way in which the Brigadier referred to the UK. He never said 'our country'. It was like he didn't quite belong.

Jack expected the order to fall out, but instead the Brigadier thundered at them to form marching columns and then to forward march out of the school grounds. His body obeyed, thanks to the relentless drill practice morning and evening, but in his mind, he protested.

They marched in the dark along the road towards the estate. When they reached a house with enthusiastic guard dogs, both Ollie and the Brigadier shouted the command to move to double-time. As one, all thirty of them sped up to a jog, which at least got them quickly past the baying animals.

The cadets crashed into the main part of the estate, lit up by the street lights. Jack glimpsed the kids playing in the playground, their parents or older siblings looking out for them. Other people grouped by the community centre, smoking and chatting. A cold evening, misty, but not raining. Christmas lights already blinked in their greens and reds. Jack sensed a hint of spices in the air, along with a strange hush like that before a nasty storm.

He marched in the group commanded by the Brigadier, and it was like his body responded automatically to the man's orders. Like he couldn't resist. The barked commands compelled him to obey. Even if he wanted to stop, he couldn't withstand the chaos he helped cause. In the thick of it, he didn't understand the bigger picture. He couldn't see it, or even make sense of the overall plan. It all blurred into shouts and screams, of fists and boots. Bits of civilian clothing flung about. Hair. Blood.

Later, on their march back to the school, Jack pieced it together and his eyes stung with tears.

Ollie's group blocked off the exits. All those in the outside space couldn't run inside. Couldn't call the police or anyone else.

The Brigadier's group grabbed the estate people and shoved them into groups separated by gender. They forced the little kids to watch as they shaved the heads of the boys and men, and tore the veils from the women and girls who wore them. From out of nowhere, a gang of skinheads joined in.

All the while, the Brigadier screamed and ranted about Britain's destiny as a nation that would make the world quake.

At Friday morning recess, the administration office called Jacquie over the tannoy system to come to them. She turned up, dreading she would be told off even though she'd done nothing wrong. Not for a while at her school, at any rate. The woman who greeted her handed her a telephone receiver and told her not to take too long. They didn't say who it was who called her.

'Hello?'

'Oh, thank God. Jac.' Jack spoke in a rush.

'What's happened?' Jacquie cupped her hand over the mouthpiece and turned away from the office.

'The Brigadier's gone stark raving mad. He marched us to the estate last night and made us fight them. It was horrible. He was spewing all this racist and sexist bilge. We've got to do something.' He choked off.

'The news said it was skinheads.'

'We started it. They joined in, and we...' He broke off and swore. She heard footsteps and a mumbled conversation. 'I've got to go.'

The line went dead.

On automatic, Jacquie handed the telephone handset to the secretary. She nodded while the woman lectured her about personal calls, but otherwise ignored her. When the woman finished just as the bell rang, Jacquie headed to her next class in a daze.

The melee made the local news section on the radio that morning, but only mentioned neo-Nazi skinheads attacking the multi-ethnic estate and the damage they caused to the property rebuilt after the fire. To learn that her own brother had taken part because he'd been forced to...

Jacquie shuddered, and thought desperately about what to do.

CHAPTER SEVENTEEN
Going Home

REBECCA FILED into Dr Kent's office behind Gloria for their Friday meeting. As usual, they ran through the patient lists and discussed each individual's ongoing needs. Rebecca appreciated how efficiently her colleagues dealt with each patient, only spending extra time on those who required it. While the practice had more out-patients than those lying-in, that section of the meeting took very little time to work through. The entire meeting usually only took about half an hour, leaving them all to get back to what they did best, which was look after their patients.

Kent summarised his observations of the in-patients who attended the group therapy sessions. 'Turner seems to have settled down and is responding well to his medication. Lethbridge-Stewart has helped him, too.'

Rebecca nodded. 'It's been mutually beneficial even in this relatively short time. I believe the Brigadier is ready to leave us, although we have a lot more work to do. Our breakthrough on a memory of his has stalled, but we are reaching an agreement that perhaps it's better for him to concentrate on living with his amnesia rather than trying so hard to recover all his memories. I'm recommending he remains on our out-patient list to monitor his progress, and that his return to teaching be staged. Assuming the school can handle that, but they seem to be financially healthy if the article about them in *Education Weekly* is to be believed.'

Kent chuckled. 'Indeed. They have been getting a bit of press attention. Last time we talked about his tendency to have sudden relapses of instability. Have you thought about how to manage the risk of more flare-ups?'

Rebecca smiled. 'Yes. I am going to insist that our therapy sessions are here at the clinic. We need to negotiate it, but I'd like two long sessions during the week initially, and taper it as he becomes more able to identify when those flare-ups are beginning and therefore manage them so they do not overwhelm him.'

'That sounds like a fair proposal from our perspective. When did you want to start?'

'I've agreed with the Brigadier that he can return to the school on Sunday when it's quieter than normal, to check on his living quarters. All being well, he'll return to the clinic for Monday and on Tuesday we'll start work on his phased return to the school. He plans to talk with the school administrators on Monday morning, which is when they have fewer distractions usually.'

Kent smiled. 'I have no objections. Matron?'

Gloria shook her head. 'I've no objections either, although I will miss him when he leaves.'

Jack's telephone call played on Jacquie's mind during each of her lessons. His abrupt ending must just have meant that little oik turned up like the apocryphal bad penny. What he managed to say before hanging up scared her.

Jacquie's gut twisted and turned all over the message, and she felt ill enough to consider asking to see the school nurse. She stuck it out until lunchtime.

Mr Devereux would be able to help. He had before.

A sign on the library door reminded her what he told her that morning. He had a dentist appointment at lunchtime and would have to close the library. She stood and stared at the sign, chewing a thumbnail as though the sign would vanish and the librarian appear in its stead.

With a grunt, she turned and left.

As she strode through the school grounds avoiding the other kids, a solution offered itself. *The Sentinel*'s article about Brendon Public School proved to be an excellent counterpoint to the glowing sales job in *Education Weekly*. She remembered the telephone number of Charles Redfern and figured he would love to hear about this latest outrage.

She swivelled and headed to a payphone in the

administration offices. She called the number and asked for the journalist.

Charles answered and listened to her. 'I'm very interested. I've a nasty feeling about a rise in politically motivated violence, especially if so-called respectable institutions are involved. But my bosses are wary about legal action. The paper got a letter from that school's solicitors telling us we're on notice and with all the industrial strife no one wants a court case landing, even if we'd win it. I know a chap at *The Examiner* that may be interested. He's also looking for something with edge. They've got more balls than us. The red tops always do. Wish I could do more.'

She thanked him and dialled the new number. The reporter answered almost immediately and sounded like he spoke through a cigarette jammed in his mouth.

'Harold Chorley, what can I do you for?'

She asked him if he was interested in knowing more about the fight in the estate.

'Depends on how hot it is. We could eke out a bit more from the story if there's something that will give another angle.'

'A bunch of cadets from the posh boys' school down the road from it kicked it all off.'

'What? How do you know that?'

She could hear him sit up and take notice. 'I was there and saw them. Everything was all normal before they showed up. Kids in the playground, you know.' She painted a picture based on the times she and Jack used to hang out there. 'I scarpered when the fists started flying so I didn't see it all. The skins are getting blamed for all of it, and I don't know about how much is their fault, but they didn't start that fight last night. The posh school kids did, and you know they'll get away with it if no one makes a fuss. It's not right.'

'Do you know why they started it?'

'No idea. Maybe for a laugh. Maybe to teach the poors and foreigners a lesson. I don't know. But there'll be people at the school who will talk.' She hung up, leaned back against the wall and blew out a long sigh.

She found herself muttering a prayer that the reporter would take her call seriously, and that whatever happened her brother Jack would be safe.

A couple of the secretaries emerged from the office, and Jacquie took it as a hint and departed before they said anything.

No one at the school mentioned the estate on Friday morning, and that carried through until that afternoon. Jack joined in with that silence because he didn't know what to say or who to trust.

On the Thursday night when they returned to the school, the Brigadier ordered them to clean their uniforms ready for a full inspection the next morning. He left his sergeant in charge, and headed off into the night.

Next morning, he was all chipper, but any hope of an easy time during the morning's full school drilling practice disappeared quickly. If anything, he bellowed louder and his keen eye picked up on the tiniest of infractions.

Jack stumbled through the day of lessons like a zombie. The droning lectures and rote recitations a balm to the chaos of his mind as he tried to work out what they did and why. He managed a quick telephone call to Jacquie's school. Waited an age for them to find her, and then had to cut it short because two cadets strolled past and had a natter with him.

Jack saw the exhaustion he felt all around him. Every boy looked wan, with dark circles around their eyes. Their eyes dulled. Everyone obedient. No one laughed or mucked around. Even Ollie-the-flipping-full-on-fascist looked tired, although he had a glow about him. Smug or self-satisfied, or something. Like he'd done a Good Job, and more was in the works.

Every time Jack closed his eyes he saw the scared faces of the little kids, and the women. The fear in the men's eyes, the blood, the shorn hair, and the torn clothing. He wasn't a stranger to violence. He'd used his fists often enough to warn people off. But this... This was something else. He needed to talk to Jacquie about it. She'd understand. Maybe she could find the Brigadier's girlfriend and convince her to talk to him and call him off.

Jack dragged his feet to what they now called the parade ground for their afternoon session of marching and who knew what else the Brigadier and his sergeant cooked up for the cadets.

The Brigadier told the sixty boys standing at attention how proud he was of the actions of the thirty. He didn't elaborate, but did say he and Ollie planned more such operations.

Jack swallowed back bile and bit the inside of his cheek to stop from keeling over in a dead faint. He blinked. Saw the set of Alfie's jaw, the subtle shift in the boys around him as they stood taller. No, no, no, no, no. He made fists of his hands at his sides.

As the Brigadier waxed lyrical about future conquests, two men dressed in civvies sauntered up the driveway towards them. One snapped pictures of them and the other held a microphone in his hand.

'Hello, lads. We're from *The Examiner* and wanted to have a word with you about a disturbance up the road that happened last night.'

The Brigadier turned slowly to face them. 'Gentlemen of the press. No one invited you here. This is private property.'

Jack swallowed. No one broke ranks. Everyone tensed. Even him. He blinked. Jacquie must have called them in after he spoke to her.

'Easy, Alistair.' The man with the microphone held up his other hand, palm out. 'We just want your side of the story.'

The photographer kept snapping.

'Sergeant. Corporals. You know what to do.'

Jack froze in place as Ollie stepped forward, along with the six corporals. They turned towards the reporters. They stomped forward. The reporter fell back, the photographer kept taking pictures.

'All right, now. Is this any way to treat an old friend?'

The Brigadier glared at the reporter, as if the very idea of them being friends was beneath him.

The reporter frowned, then shook his head. 'Fine, Alistair, have it your way. We're leaving. No need for this.'

Jack stared ahead, not wanting to see. He heard them turn and run.

Saturday dawned a clear day. The Brigadier took advantage of it and strolled around the gardens. Once upon a time he wouldn't have appreciated the work put in to create a design that would enable a subtle colour palette during an English winter. Reggie's explanations during the weeks of his recovery enlightened him. He would miss all this, but perhaps he could influence Brendon to invest in their gardens.

Archie Turner called his name. The young former airman stood by the door to the clinic. He waved a rolled-up paper in one hand. He wore his pyjamas and dressing gown, neither appropriate attire for outside in December. The Brigadier waved back and ruefully turned away from the garden bed he examined to return to the building.

'Good morning, sir. Sorry to disturb you, but your school is in the papers once more.' Archie held the paper out for him. The Brigadier accepted it. 'Not for good reasons again. Apparently, they were involved in that big fight on Thursday night.'

'What fight?'

Turner told him all about the assault on the estate near Brendon School that occurred on Thursday evening. 'The police said it was a gang of skinheads who stormed in without warning. They shouted the usual sort of racial slurs, and beat up the men.'

The Brigadier opened the tabloid to a two-page spread with lots of photographs and a lurid headline. He recognised the school buildings in the background of most of the photos, but the pictures of the boys in army uniforms didn't capture their faces with any clarity. He saw their anger, though. One photo showed a man dressed in the same uniform, only he wore an officer's cap rather than the beret. He squinted, but the photo was too indistinct and he failed to recognise the teacher. He shuddered at the pure rage in the man's body language. He skimmed the text in a box as Turner kept talking.

'They say that witnesses claim a group of twenty or more boys from Brendon's CCF turned up before the skinheads did. That they started it, and it was totally unprovoked.'

The Brigadier's mouth went dry and he nodded. He folded the paper up and gave it back to Turner. He cleared his throat. 'I don't want to believe it. We helped them tidy up and rebuild after a fire destroyed two of the buildings. To do this.' He shook his head slowly.

'They hint that the commanding officer went with them.

168

That he incited it. They don't name names, but you've got your work cut out to salvage their reputation.'

'If it's true. Those papers do like to sensationalise things, especially men like Harold Chorley. Fan the flames. They don't like the Conservatives and I can see them trying to discredit the school because the government has indicated their support.' The Brigadier smiled at Turner, who nodded, but he couldn't shake those images of hatred and rage.

On a cold but clear Saturday morning, Jacquie loved being in the Patel's shop rather than out on her bicycle throwing newspapers into front gardens. Another kid took that job on. The shelf stacking bored her, but being on the till kept her interest up. She enjoyed being treated like an adult as she ran up the prices and handled the money. Best was the money they paid her.

Her new job gave her the opportunity to skim through the papers. She shivered as she read Chorley's article in *The Examiner* all about the fight in the nearby estate and she peered at the pictures. She didn't recognise any of the boys because of how blurred the photographs were. They did give the impression of action, of the boys in soldier uniforms charging to attack the photographer.

The article didn't pull any of its punches. If only the police would get involved, but the bland statement from the local station gave the impression they were content to plod along with their investigation.

At one o'clock she returned home. As she entered, she heard raised voices from the kitchen. Both her olds were engaged in a heated conversation, so she closed the door quietly behind her and crept forward to earwig.

'I think they've gone too far with their playing at soldiers. They're boys, not men.' Her mother didn't sound quite as pleading as she normally did when she argued that point.

'Can't deny the good it's done them. All his teachers say that Jack's no longer playing the class clown, but is buckling down.'

'But to do what they did on Thursday night?'

Jacquie raised her eyebrows. They didn't read *The Examiner.* She wondered if other outlets picked up their story.

'We don't know how true those stories are. They might be exaggerations or misunderstandings.'

'Those interviews with the poor people from that estate didn't sound like they misunderstood what happened, or who did it. I won't have my son involved in violence like that.'

Jacquie hugged herself to stop from clapping. It seemed other outlets had picked up the story and were doing their own investigative journalism. She felt a bit sorry for Charles turning her down.

'We don't know if he was.'

'Well, I'm going to phone the school and find out.'

Jacquie backed up to the front door and managed to open and shut it again just as her mother emerged from the kitchen to go to the telephone in the hallway.

Later that Saturday afternoon, the Brigadier greeted Dr Pelham-Rose when she came by to visit him. She told him the welcome news that Dr Kent approved their plan that began the process to discharge him, starting with a trip home on the next day to get things ready. She asked him if he wanted anyone to come with him, and he said no. He would take a taxi and return to the clinic on Monday afternoon like they arranged. That would give him the time to see the headmaster and administrative staff to organise the formalities of his return in person.

He didn't mention his concerns about the two newspaper articles, which she seemed to notice. She asked a couple of times if he had anything to share with her, but he demurred. He wanted to see for himself what occurred at the school. She didn't press for a third time.

On Sunday after lunch, he climbed into the waiting taxi and leaned back to enjoy the ride to the school. He thought back to the reverse journey, which he could only recall in patches. So much had changed within himself since he scurried away from the school in a confused state.

Those documents he found in the obelisk. He would have to do something about them. No one had come looking for him, so perhaps it would be safe to destroy them without raising the alarm. He could ask a few discreet questions just to be sure. The Armstrong boy spent time up there on that hill so he'd be a good student to question first.

The taxi driver pulled up outside the school. 'It's been in the news, this place. Not all good, either.'

'You know what the papers can be like.' The Brigadier paid his fare and gave the driver a little extra for keeping his own counsel during most of the journey.

'Right enough.' The driver tipped his hat and drove off.

The Brigadier walked up the driveway. He saw no one about, and figured that the fine drizzle and low temperature kept everyone else inside. As he reached his quarters, he saw a boy on the far side of the nearest sports ground. He appeared to be running laps. The Brigadier shook his head and headed to his digs.

Inside, he leaned against his closed door for a few moments. He smelled a sharp cologne over a lingering scent of fried bacon and eggs. Odd.

It spurred him to move. He wandered into the main room and gazed around with a deepening frown. His few pieces of furniture now sat in different places. He scratched his head and turned slowly around. Someone had also moved his photographs. Worse, they'd removed four of his favourites and replaced them with strange emblems. He peered at them.

One stirred something in his memory, like he should know it, but it remained stubbornly behind the mental wall built by his subconscious mind. The letters, SRS, resembled Nordic runes. Nordic runes were a theme of all the four emblems he realised as he stepped back from them. The designs themselves were all angular and harsh. All of them were in stark black, white and red. The Brigadier stepped away.

He wandered into his bedroom to see if he could find any clues as to who had moved in during his absence. His bed was dressed to army standard. His parade ground uniform hung from the door of his wardrobe. His frown deepened.

Back out in the main part of his quarters, he crossed over to his desk. His typewriter sat on it and held a piece of paper. He looked at it, his brow furrowing even deeper.

The paper in the machine spelled out proposals to make the revised Discipline Code harsher than that which he had pulled back from the edge. It hovered over genuinely obscene territory. Next to the typewriter a few folders were piled up.

They bore the name of the think-tank Mr Newton had asked him to liaise with back before his latest breakdown. He backed away from the desk, and turned around.

A headache thumped in his temples and nausea roiled in his stomach. He needed to get away.

'Official Secrets.'

He crossed over to where he'd hidden the file he found in the obelisk. That part of his bookshelf looked undisturbed, judging from the order of his books and a thin layer of dust. He pulled out the box where he put the file and opened it up on his desk. His other precious documents remained, but the file wasn't there.

He put his hand to his temple. He had seen them, and put them away. Now they were gone.

He closed his eyes against a rush of dizziness as the world lurched.

Things were very, very wrong, and he had to leave before the wrongness dragged him down.

Jack hadn't hopped-to quickly enough that morning, so the Brigadier ordered him to run laps during the lunch hour. The Brigadier watched him as he started, then turned and marched into the school buildings. Jack knew better than to slack off in the teacher's absence. The man had spies everywhere now.

The cold, damp air burned through his nose and mouth into his lungs even as his exertions warmed his body. Mud from recent rain splashed up his legs as he crashed through puddles. He settled into an easy rhythm, pacing it out, and trying not to think about the meal he missed. To stave off boredom, he counted his laps and kept an eye out for the Brigadier and his watchers. All he saw for the first two laps was a curtain twitcher on the second floor.

Half-way around his third lap a black cab arrived at the gates. Jack slowed and peered through the trees, but as he passed the best spot to spy on the road he picked up his pace again to keep warm. He glanced behind him at the sound of someone walking up the driveway and he stumbled as he saw the Brigadier. He recovered quickly and powered on to avoid more punishment.

But the Brigadier had gone into the main building earlier.

He'd been wearing the blasted sixty-eight pattern fatigues he favoured on weekends, not the tweed suit he now wore.

Jack risked another glance in the Brigadier's direction, but the man's attention was on his quarters and he disappeared inside.

Jack huffed, shook his head, and kept going.

Three laps later and Jack's muscles protested at the abuse. Hunger growled in his stomach. A stitch stabbed at his side. He blinked and swallowed and told himself off for slacking. He'd fallen twice, but picked himself up and kept stumbling on. This might be hell, but he preferred it to a beating and the risk of expulsion. He didn't share Jacquie's enthusiasm for her plan for them both to collect as many O-levels as they could before they left school and gained their independence, but he saw the point of it. He was sixteen now. Could leave, but then what? Seven months into the new government and all its promises to get Britain working, and it wasn't. Even he worked out that a kid like him expelled from a model school wouldn't be able to land on his feet.

The Brigadier emerged from his quarters. Jack had a direct line of sight as the man in the tweed suit blundered towards his car. He fumbled for the door, climbed in and started the engine. Smoke billowed from its exhaust pipe as the motor roared into life.

Jack staggered to a halt as he clutched his side and leaned over. He looked up as the car puttered down the driveway and left the school grounds.

A shout from the main school building dragged Jack's attention away from the departing Brigadier and his vintage car. Jack swore and spurred himself into a bumbling jog once more.

The Brigadier in his sixty-eight pattern fatigues ran out to the driveway, his fist in the air as he shouted invectives after the man who stole his car.

The Brigadier.

Two Brigadiers.

Twins.

Jack giggled. They *had* to be twins.

CHAPTER EIGHTEEN
Off the Wall

REBECCA PUT her feet up on her sofa and leaned back to listen to a concert being played on Radio 3. Good food and company over a relaxed lunch at a friend's house eased her into a doze. The gentleness of the classical pieces chosen by the orchestra calmed her mind and she drifted as though carried on warm eddies over a tropical island.

The telephone's discordant clang startled her awake. In the gloom of the December evening, she stumbled for the handset and fumbled picking it up. 'Hello?'

A duty nurse at the clinic introduced herself and told her a patient had returned, distraught and asking for his treating doctor.

She changed into more suitable attire, grabbed her car keys, and headed to the clinic. She half-expected the Brigadier's chaotic return and questioned her own competence at misjudging his wellness. After she parked, she paused for a moment. She'd seen cases before when patients appeared to settle into better health within the safety of an institution, only to have their defences crumble on contact with the outside world. She'd hoped the Brigadier would have been more resilient, but evidently the underlying trauma was far more dangerous. Not his fault.

She clapped her hands on the steering wheel. 'Not going to fix him, me idling here.' She left her car and strode into the clinic.

Inside, the Brigadier sat half-curled over on a chair.

Rebecca approached him. 'Come on, Brigadier. Let's take you back to your room so you can tell me what happened.'

She glanced over at the nurse who shrugged. 'It was left

as you and Dr Kent instructed.'

Rebecca mouthed a thank you to the nurse.

The Brigadier stood and looked sheepish as he joined Rebecca. They walked through the corridors to his room. 'I thought I would stay at the school tonight, but someone else has moved in.'

'I see.' She frowned. The contact from the school had not mentioned a replacement. 'Have you eaten?'

'I'm not hungry.' He sat on his bed, head bowed, hands on his knees.

Rebecca shut the door and sat down. 'Did you meet anyone there?'

'No, no. As we discussed, it was quiet. I was supposed to talk to the office tomorrow morning. No one told me someone else moved into my quarters. They'd moved things around. My pictures. My furniture. They were wearing my clothes. My uniform.' He stopped. His hands gripped his knees. He turned to look directly at her. 'They moved my medals. It's only just come to me. How dare they?' His face splotched with red. His hands tightened their grip on his knees.

Rebecca's eyes widened. She kept quiet to give him the room to talk. To share. To calm down.

'They changed the order of them.' He looked away. 'There was more.'

He told her about the strange, brutal designs that looked to him like stylised Nordic runes. She shivered. They sounded like neo-Nazi symbols. She fought a frown as she thought about the newspapers claiming a link between the school and skinheads causing violence in an estate where people from all sorts of backgrounds lived.

He told her about a set of important, secret papers he'd hidden, but someone had taken them. That chimed with what he said when he arrived weeks before and they admitted him as an in-patient. He wrapped his arms around his body and rocked gently back and forth. He muttered about the papers. About someone breaking in and making all those changes. About someone using his typewriter to knock out horrific ideas to inflict on the boys in their care.

Rebecca moved closer to him. She laid a hand on his shoulder. He gazed up at her. 'I'll get you a mild sedative so you can sleep tonight. In the morning, we'll work out what to do.'

He nodded, and smiled, and lay down on the bed in a semi-foetal position.

The Brigadier didn't tell him to stop. Neither of them did.

Neither.

Two Brigadiers.

Jack collapsed to his knees. He stared at the Brigadier's living quarters.

The Brigadier in the fatigues was the one who yelled and lashed out. He was the one who ordered Jack to run around the sports ground instead of eating lunch. He had to run laps until the Brigadier or Sergeant Oliver Floyd-Jones told him to stop. Neither of them had told him to stop. They'd be looking. Ollie-the-oik from the warmth of the main school buildings, the Brigadier from his digs.

Jack looked up and lights danced from both buildings. Everything spun around. He groaned.

Jack told himself to get up. To keep running or he'd get a thrashing.

There were not two Brigadiers. There had to be only the one.

'Come on, Jack-my-lad.'

His legs refused to obey his order. He toppled over, and blanked out.

Later, warm hands grabbed his arms and legs. Jack stirred. Tried to run, but nothing moved. His muscles twitched and ached under the numbness. Too dark to see. Everything blurry and hazy. Voices he couldn't understand. Not shouting. A blanket wrapped around him. He faced up instead of down. Bright lights and murmured words of encouragement. Mr Grey. Mr Ellis. Ms Peters. Alfie.

Bed. The nurse. Warm pyjamas. The nurse's hand on his forehead. Thermometer stuck in his mouth. Bright lights. Soft noises. People talking through cotton wool. Thermometer removed.

'Can you sit up? Have some broth.'

He slurped a spoonful, but more dribbled out than went

in. A soft cloth wiped it away.

Must keep running. Must.

His father's voice spoke to the nurse, but Jack couldn't make out the words. His mother loomed in front of him, her face contorted in worry.

'We're taking him home. He needs proper looking after. I'll have words with Mr Newton tomorrow.'

The nurse and Mr Grey tried to placate his father. 'We didn't know. If we'd known, this would never have happened.' Jack couldn't distinguish who said what.

His mother helped him sit up. She put her arm around his shoulders. She said a whole lot of comforting words, but he drifted in a space where he couldn't understand.

They swaddled him in his dressing gown and half-carried him to their car. His mother sat with him in the back while his father drove. His mother hugged him and murmured to him. Kept him awake.

They arrived at home, and neither of his olds shooed Jacquie away. She helped their mother help him to his bedroom where he sank on to his bed.

'He'll be fine. He's exhausted. He was running laps and got cold. One of the teachers found him unconscious outside, poor lad. We'll take him to the doctors tomorrow, but right now he needs to rest. Best not disturb him, right, love?'

'All right.'

He heard the worry in Jacquie's voice as he drifted into slumber.

The Brigadier woke in his bed in the clinic. He sat up, grabbed his journal on the bedside table, and wrote about the most remarkable dream. He'd gone back to the school and found a neo-Nazi living in his digs. Furniture moved around, his favourite pictures replaced by Nazi symbols, and Top Secret papers missing.

Nightmare was a better word to describe it.

A knock at his door startled him. He checked the time. Six o'clock. At this time of year, the sun had a few more hours left before rising. 'Come in, come in.'

'Brigadier. Good morning.'

He shifted in his bed to sit up straighter. 'Doctor? You're

here early.'

Dr Pelham-Rose entered and shut the door quietly behind her. 'I stayed over. Did you sleep well?'

He slumped. 'It wasn't a dream, was it?'

Dr Pelham-Rose raised an eyebrow.

'My visit back to the school.'

She shook her head. 'Afraid not.'

He closed his journal and returned it to the table. 'Am I ever going to be free of this? Give me an enemy to aim at and I'm fine. Five rounds rapid...' He froze. He'd seen active service. He knew that. He had the medals and citations to prove it. Right now, he could recall none of it.

Dr Pelham-Rose sat.

'I saw the Armstrong boy running laps. I didn't think much of it. He's a middling long-distance runner. Could be better if he put his mind to it. Could be better at anything, if he applied himself. Thing is, back after the summer holidays he said something very strange to his pals about my moustache. I didn't really hear it all, and dismissed it at the time as a fanciful thing teenaged boys imagine. Something about how long it takes for moustaches to grow.' He ran a finger against his. 'Took me years to cultivate this and I haven't been without it, even when teased by some of the lovely ladies in my life.' He flashed her a smile that didn't reach his eyes. 'Thinking about it now, I think he saw someone who looked like me but who didn't sport a moustache. I think that person has been hanging around the school for a while and when I was here he took over.'

To her credit, she refrained from dismissing his claim immediately. Her brow puckered and a frown appeared, then vanished quickly. 'Do you have any proof?'

He sighed. 'Nothing substantive, and I know how this must sound. Like I'm paranoid.'

'I don't think you are paranoid, Alistair. I'd like to hear your concerns.'

He glanced at her and saw sincerity. He nodded. 'The main thing was the document about the new Discipline Code. I had every intention of sharing my ideas with the headmaster, but I ended up enjoying my summer vacation.' He smiled as he remembered Sandrine. He cleared his throat. 'I told you before about how the headmaster's secretary, Miss Nugent, showed me notes in my handwriting proposing much harsher ideas than I would ever entertain.'

Dr Pelham-Rose nodded.

'Well, in my digs yesterday I found more notes about even harsher punishments for the boys for minor infractions.'

'Why would someone impersonate you to instil such discipline?' She kept her voice even.

'Look, I know this all sounds preposterous. It's not like the safety of Earth is at stake.' He huffed. 'I know I forget things, but these examples are different to my amnesia. You've helped me work that out.'

'That sounds interesting.'

He rushed on, cutting her off. 'The thing is, the government is interested in a return to old fashioned values in school education. Before I ... uh ... had to return here, the headmaster asked me to liaise with a think-tank working closely with the government in forming details for their policies. The school stands to get an increase in funding and the government gets a poster-child for their plans.'

'I see. Yes.'

'It's more than that. Those papers I found before coming here, I put them away in a secure place. Only someone's taken them. I don't think it's the person who's taken over my life at the school, but whoever has them has discovered some highly secret things. Things my mind won't let me remember, but I must find and destroy those documents.'

'What about the authorities? Can they help?'

'I don't have proof, and I don't know how the papers got into the school. I need to find those things out first.'

'What do you propose to do?'

'I need to go back. Will you come with me?'

She smiled. Nodded. 'Today?'

'Please.'

'I can do that once I re-arrange my appointments.'

Jacquie stole into her brother's bedroom before dawn, before their olds stirred. She sat on his bed beside him and studied his face in the gloom. The room was lit only by a streetlight leaking in through a gap in the curtains. He looked so pale and thin. His short hair stuck out at all angles.

She didn't want to wake him, but despite their olds' behaviour the night before she didn't know how much time they would have together. Gently, she touched his shoulder. He stirred. Murmured something incoherent. His eyes opened and he blinked a few times.

'Hey, hey.'

'Whatcha.' He coughed. She grabbed the cup of water their mother left on his bedside table. He sat up and sipped from it. 'Thanks.' He tried a smile.

'What happened?'

Jack eased himself up to lean against his pillows. 'There's two Brigadiers.'

'What?'

'I saw them. I thought I must have dreamed it, but it's true. There's the nasty one in his army uniform that's made our lives hell, and I saw the old bumbly one in his tweed suit drive away in his car.'

'*Bumbly* isn't a word, silly.'

'It should be. Suits him. Bumbling about like a bumblebee.' He managed a grin, but stifled a grumbling cough.

She grinned back, and tilted her head to one side. 'You know, there being two Brigadiers might make sense of what's been going on. Do you reckon he's got a long-lost identical twin who's turned up out of the blue?'

'That's straight out of *Corrie*.' Jack's chuckle turned into a cough that made him flop back into his pillows once done.

Jacquie picked up his hand. 'You rest, yeah. I'll talk to the olds about it. Well, not everything. I've got to go to school today, but I'll see if I can find out anything more. Get some proof and see if we can do something.'

Jack nodded. 'The tweedy one might be dull-as and a bore, but he's all right, really. Not like the fashy one.' He squeezed Jacquie's hand and smiled.

She crept back to her own room to get ready for her day. Their olds had to be tired from their long night to not have stirred with Jack's coughing. She heard their alarm clock ring and their father stumble about. He plodded past her door, then paused, retraced his steps to Jack's room. He said nothing, and she guessed Jack must have returned to sleep. Their father's footsteps resumed and he knocked twice on her door.

'I'm up.'

'Don't disturb your brother. He needs his rest.'

She smiled. 'I know, and I won't.'

Their father went to the bathroom. Jacquie followed when he clomped down the stairs to the kitchen. When she emerged, she saw their mother standing at Jack's door. Her head rested against the frame. She started, turned. Jacquie saw the worry in their mother's face. For the first time in a long time, Jacquie wanted to hug their mother, but she refrained. She went downstairs.

When both their olds sat at the table nursing their cups of coffee, their father said, 'I think you need to tell us what you know.'

Their mother said, 'How has our boy become so sick?'

Jacquie steeled herself. 'All I know is that during the last half-term break, Jack saw his maths teacher, Brigadier Lethbridge-Stewart, take a funny turn. Since then, the whole school's been subject to escalating abuse, which the Brigadier is behind. And he took his sick views out on the estate.'

Their father shook his head. 'I can't believe what the red tops said about that.'

'Jack saw it. What the Brigadier made them do there is just plain wrong.'

A little later that morning, the Brigadier drove alone to Brendon School. An emergency involving young Archie Turner prevented Dr Pelham-Rose from accompanying him, and he couldn't ask anyone else. She had given him a brief note from the clinic explaining his status. 'To be safe.'

If he was wrong, he would deal with it. He knew he'd dealt with worse in his past, even if he couldn't remember much of it.

The fact that Dr Pelham-Rose didn't dismiss or downplay his worries and theories bolstered him. She told him to resist over-thinking, and to take heed of his instincts. She believed in him, and that gave him strength.

He arrived before breakfast was scheduled to be served at the school and before the sun peeked weakly over the horizon. He reversed a few yards up the driveway so he could make a quick getaway if needed. He felt silly and self-conscious, and shook his head.

He left his car and strode towards the main buildings. He had no plan, no support, and no real idea about what was going on. Only, something was. He felt that in his bones.

In the misty light from the streetlights, he made his way to his digs. He slowed to a creep, all his senses alert. A light glowed from within. His bathroom. It clicked off. A few moments later a softer light came from the direction of his bedroom. Whoever had moved in was up and about. He set his shoulders and cleared his throat. He knocked on the door to his own home.

More lights came on. A shape loomed behind the frosted glass in the door. The latch released and the door opened.

The Brigadier stared at himself.

'Well.' The version of himself dressed in an army shirt and pattern sixty-eight combat trousers stroked his chin.

The single word unlocked the Brigadier and he barrelled into his home, pushing his doppelgänger back into the biggest room in the pokey little cottage. Surprise robbed his double of strength and the Brigadier succeeded in pushing him into the chair by the desk.

His double held his hands up. A smirk twisted his face. 'I was about to ask you in, old chap.'

'What the devil are you doing here?'

'Not asking me who I am? Do you know?' His double lowered his hands to rest on his knees. He shook his head. 'I doubt you do, from what I understand of your life. On that, I have you at the disadvantage.'

'Quiet.' The Brigadier narrowed his eyes while his double feigned relaxation. They weren't identical. They had the same moustache, more or less – his double's was thinner, more clipped – and over the left side of his face, there appeared to be some minor, but clearly permanent bruising. His opponent also looked fitter, but the Brigadier wasn't ready to be put out to pasture just yet. He backed into his kitchenette, his gaze locked onto the stranger who seemed to know him. Without taking his eyes off him, the Brigadier squatted to open the drawer where he kept a roll of duct tape and other items for emergency repairs. He quickly slid it on his lower arm and grabbed the box cutting knife.

His double laughed. 'If you think I'll let you do what you think you're going to do...' Like his legs were coiled springs, he launched at the Brigadier.

The Brigadier sprang up and met him with a left hook that connected. The knife dropped to the ground, got kicked under a table. The two men wrestled, and grappled, landed blows where they could. Different men who looked the same. The Brigadier forced his mind to go blank and fight the man who'd moved in. Muscle memory kicked in from his training, his soldiering, and luck saw his fist land a blow that knocked his opponent senseless.

The Brigadier stood for a few moments over the man who stole his place. He hoisted him up and sat him back on the chair. And noticed something roll across the floor. The Brigadier reached down and picked it up, and screwed his face in disgust. It was a glass eye – an easy copy of his own eyes. After placing the eye on a small table, he secured his double with the tape, not wanting a second round. His luck couldn't hold.

He ran cold water over his bruised and bleeding knuckles and dried them off. He filled a tumbler of water and splashed it over the interloper's face.

The man spluttered, shook his head, and looked up with a twisted grin. For a moment he looked around, as if testing his field of vision. 'Damn,' he said, his left eyebrow twitching above the now empty socket. He tested the restraints. 'What a way to treat a guest.'

'Thief, more like.' The Brigadier retrieved the box cutter. 'Now, who are you?'

'Guess.'

The Brigadier tossed the box cutter to his left hand and with his right hand punched the man's face. 'I don't like Nazis much.'

'Who says I'm a Nazi?'

The Brigadier pointed at the Nordic designs on the wall.

'Oh, that. I just wanted a little bit of my home here, but I'm no Nazi. I admire them, despite their ignominious defeat.'

The Brigadier narrowed his eyes. Part of a memory pushed a brick from its wall inside his mind. 'You're from an alternative Earth.' Sweat pooled in his lower back and across his brow. His head pounded.

'Oh, well done, old chap. I would clap, but.' The doppelgänger shrugged. 'Before you ask, I have no idea how I got here. I woke up in an erupting volcano and got out. I trust in fate, which has served me quite well. Your old military chums helped me. They thought I was you. Turns out that for a teacher you have some fascinating secrets. I'm meant to be here. To show the way for your England to regain its glory.'

'Quiet.' The Brigadier clenched his jaw. Too many memories swarmed his mind and he couldn't make sense of any of them. He tightened his grip on the box cutter.

'What are you going to do, old chap?'

The Brigadier swallowed. He checked the restraints, placed tape over the man's mouth. Without a plan, he left.

CHAPTER NINETEEN

In the Flesh

JACQUIE SNUCK from her school at nine thirty and spotted Jack's teacher driving through town in his old car. She made her way to Brendon as fast as her legs could carry her, intent on finally confronting the man. She found Alfie Granger lounging about on the driveway. No one else hung around near him. He wore his cadets' uniform and for a moment she thought he looked like a sloppy sentry. Remaining vigilant, she strolled up the driveway and waved at him.

'Hey. Hi. Have you seen Jack?'

'He's at home. He's sick with flu or something.'

Hollering and whistle blows erupted from further inside the school grounds. She guessed a rugby game occupied the others.

'Do you know what happened?'

Jacquie nodded. 'The Brigadier got him running laps for not doing something, and then didn't tell him when to stop. Fortunately, one of the other teachers saw him and called our olds. He's really not well.'

'The Brig's gone weird. For serious.' He shook his head and scuffed his boots on the asphalt. He glanced up at Jacquie. 'He's vanished. The Brig. He didn't lead the whole school parade this morning. His car's here, but not where it should be. It wasn't here yesterday, but he was.'

Jacquie stared at him, weighing her options. 'Jack says there are two Brigadiers.'

Before Alfie could react, their attention was drawn to the Brigadier's quarters as he emerged and climbed into his car.

'What's got into him now?' Alfie straightened up and scratched the back of his neck.

'No idea. It might be his girlfriend. Jack told me she turned up here and raised a bit of a stink.'

Jacquie agreed with Alfie's sheer look of scepticism, but she kept quiet. She hugged herself. She should get back to her school before they missed her. Their olds' magnanimity would not tolerate her truancy.

A crash came from the Brigadier's quarters.

'What the...?'

Seconds later, another Brigadier emerged. He wore army fatigues and a pair of sunglasses, and looked about him wildly. With a snarl, he ran to the cars in the carpark and tested the doors. He clambered into one, and its engine revved. It spun back and out, then accelerated forth.

'Blimey.' Alfie turned to Jacquie when the second Brigadier sped past in the stolen car. 'You and Jack are right. There are two of them.'

Brigade Leader Alastair Lethbridge-Stewart changed the gears and the car juddered up the hill. It got over the peak and he caught sight of his quarry. As ridiculous as the vintage car was, it had more pep than the thing he drove. At least on the downward side it picked up speed. He saw the lights of emergency vehicles blocking the route to the motorway and he grinned. His double took the diversion the Brigade Leader would have chosen. Interesting. He plotted out a way to catch up, or head him off. Not hard to guess where he aimed for: Whitehall and his chums.

Barely ten o'clock in the morning, and the skies glowered, dark enough to make him think night fell. Symbolic. He shrugged it off. Province of Mrs Young the daft English teacher, not him.

Rain smattered against the windscreen, and the wipers brushed uselessly against it. What was he doing here risking his life in the driving rain?

Short answer, saving his new life from a senile version of himself.

Long answer, no idea.

He hadn't lied; he didn't know exactly how he'd crossed from one Earth to another, but he had an idea.

One minute he'd been lying on the floor of that hut on the

grounds of Project Inferno, shot by Section Leader Shaw, and the next minute he was on the floor of a cavern as the volcano exploded around him. Gasping to breathe in the toxic air, taunted by a waking dream of inordinate boredom. Cool air, boys chanting their times table, and a memory full of holes. Rescue, thankfully, from the sulphur hell-hole. Later learning he was in a hospital in Jamaica where the doctors kindly repaired an old injury they mistook for a new one – an injury that, if he believed what James had once told him, was the result of a previous crossing between alternative worlds. Not only had they fixed the scar, they had given him a nice glass eye. It left a little bruising, and although his depth of vision remained the same, it felt nice to have two eyes to move again.

Embassy men had fussed about him, thinking he was someone else. Sorry. His mistake. Men from the British *High Commission*, not Embassy. Jamaica was a former colony-turned-Commonwealth member. MI6, Ministry of Defence, and Foreign Office types. None of them knew him for sure, but he played along from his hospital bed.

Pretended he was the Brigadier – even the rank was similar to his own; that of Brigade Leader.

Slight difference in the spelling of his first name, though. He corrected the *i* to a second *a* in Alastair only once, and obscured it every other time he signed all the paperwork bureaucracy demanded. It seemed a man who looked like him, and carried a nearly identical name, had a reputation that excited all these officials who enjoyed the cushy Caribbean island life a bit too much.

One of the men dressed in a safari suit asked him what he'd been doing on St Vincent to be caught in the Soufriere volcano as it erupted. He'd coughed half a lung up in reply, and the man answered himself. 'Secret mission, eh.' The man tapped the side of his nose and nodded. 'Understood, Brigadier. We'll keep mum about your presence here, what.'

Idiots with no idea about security.

He swerved around a lorry that nudged out from a side street. The lorry driver slammed on his brakes and, despite the skid, narrowly missed hitting Alastair's car. More amazingly, the car didn't stall. It revved and whined, but it responded to his sheer force of will. He followed his quarry who led them away from the outskirts of Greater London and into the villages and towns around it.

The heavy rain and thundery skies kept pace with them. He fought the steering wheel to keep from skidding on the rain-slicked road.

The damage in his throat from the volcanic fumes meant he'd had to shut up and listen to the idiots. He learned a lot about this other man who shared his looks and name from their prattling. He got away with initial slip-ups by claiming a knock on the head. Turned out, his doppelgänger suffered from a weird amnesia far worse than he pretended of his own affliction.

They ferried him to the UK during the northern summer. The Brigadier was away enjoying a bit of a sexy fling, cheeky sod. The waking dreams let him see little glimpses into his doppelgänger's life. He laid low, scoped out the possibilities, and made a few plans. He borrowed the vintage car a few times, and liked how it handled. Picked up a few ladies for exciting nights of passion. He tried out new lines and looks on them before dumping them.

He went out with a bird named Cindy Parton a few times. She got what he was about. Well, as much as he let on. Agreed with him that the Conservative Government could make a real show for the country he found himself in. He refrained from telling her about how there were different versions of Earth (just like that Doctor had claimed – indeed, Alastair had a feeling it was the Doctor who had brought him to this Earth, albeit unintentionally). She was a game bird, was Cindy, but that truth might just flip her over the edge.

Mild-mannered teacher of mathematics and rugger and soldiering in a modest public school for boys on the outer edge of London proved to be the perfect cover for a life of derring-do. Running secret missions against the communists and anarchists, and who knew what else that threatened this version of Earth. Doing what the Leader, his father, had taught him to do.

Alastair shifted his grip on the steering wheel, and changed the gears. He stamped down on the accelerator and yelled at the car to go faster than it could.

Best plans are those that adapt. It didn't take much to send his doppelgänger back to the funny farm. A few notes on those papers left by those meddlesome twins.

More notes to nudge the school in the right direction in terms of discipline.

Right. He chuckled. *Right.*

He peered through the rain-blurred windscreen. His quarry's brake lights blinked on and off, like he slowed. Right. He stamped down harder on the accelerator and changed gears. The whole car shook and shuddered. 'Come *on!*'

Luck favoured him. Right place, right time. He'd called the clinic, pretending to be another teacher, to keep his doppelgänger away from the school as he took over. He expected a bit of resistance, but none came. It seemed allies came from all corners, and the headmaster enjoyed the praise from the government and the locals as they commemorated their war dead.

He shook the steering wheel as he urged the car forward. He felt the clang as bumper bar crashed into bumper bar.

The Brigadier swore when the car behind him rammed into his. He clamped his hands on the wheel to keep control of his car as she wavered left and right on the narrow road. He pulled away once they crossed the single lane bridge.

Lightning flashed all around him as the rain redoubled its efforts to dump all the water it could. Thunder crashed.

He glanced at the fuel gauge. The needle flickered. Under half a tank left, and she consumed petrol to the mile faster than the modern car that chased him would.

The headlights from behind dazzled him as they caught his rear vision mirror and reflected back into his eyes. He pressed his foot down on the accelerator and avoided another ramming. He apologised to his car for all this, and shook his head against his foolishness.

He sped through a four-way junction and missed reading the signs. He had little idea as to where they drove. When he saw his doppelgänger in Mr Wade's car raging after him, he followed his instinct to take the maniac away from built-up areas. It didn't mean either of them would avoid other vehicles, but it did reduce the risk of civilian casualties.

'Civilians?' He snorted.

He and his pursuer were both civilians, and one of them would be a casualty in a road traffic collision the way this all headed. He prayed it would only be either him and/or his pursuer and no one else.

He'd already castigated himself for not securing the man better. Or not taking him with him. He shook his head at that. He couldn't have taken him. He'd won their fight through luck rather than prowess, and certainly not brute strength. The other man was fitter than him. That would have to change.

If he survived this.

The other man also held the advantage over him in terms of knowing what the blazes was going on. All the Brigadier knew was that somehow his double slipped over from another version of Earth.

Another version of Earth. What in the name of all that is good does that mean? And why in hell did he accept it as somehow normal?

His unconscious mind refused to give up anything else about such things, and part of him railed at the very idea as utterly preposterous. Yet, here they were, racing through a terrible storm on a wintry late morning in the English countryside. Him and his doppelgänger.

He'd be laughing if he wasn't the quarry in the chase. And if he didn't hear that blasted double-beat. His heartbeat, doubled up and slightly out of sync.

'Think, man.'

He heard his butterfly, Dr Pelham-Rose, advise against over-thinking. 'Trust your instincts. There are reasons why your soldiering career was so revered.'

The roar of the car behind him shook him out of any complacency. The asphalt stretched out ahead in a straight line, as if it followed an ancient Roman road. Hedgerows lined it, boxing them both in. His car was slightly wider in the body than Mr Wade's. Heavier, too, but more powerful. He gunned her engine, and apologised once more.

The double heartbeat thumped in his head. He recalled his nightmares from months ago of being trapped in a burning cave in an erupting volcano. His pursuer mentioned waking up in an erupting volcano…

He barked a laugh. Hunched over and willed his car to

190

keep going. Then what? His only hope was to out-run his pursuer. Get to London and tell people who understood this sort of thing. He knew they existed. That man who recognised him on the school outing. If he could find him again.

Lightning flashed and thunder cracked. The rain refused to let up, and the unnatural darkness from the low, angry clouds meant he couldn't see too far ahead. The twist and turn rushed him, then another narrow bridge. Naked trees lurched from the road sides in place of the stalwart hedges. He hit a pothole that knocked the car, but he wrestled her back. He overcompensated, and everything exploded.

After Jacquie left him that morning, Jack fell back into a deep sleep. The next time he woke it was to their mother's gentle shake of his shoulder. He blinked against the bedside light she'd switched on. His curtains were drawn, and rain lashed against the window. Thunder bellowed and lightning flashed. A storm.

'I've got you something to eat. Scrambled eggs and beans on toast. Your favourite.'

Jack struggled to sit up. His lungs growled and he doubled over in a spasm of coughing.

'Poor pet. That school. That Brigadier.' He heard the contempt in her voice.

When he could, Jack looked up at his mother.

'Your sister told us about him. I don't know why or how you two persist in defying your father, but it seems you were only looking out for each other.'

He nodded, and wished he hadn't. He closed his eyes against the dizzy spell. 'Where's Jac?'

'School. Your father's gone to work. He didn't want to, but I told him I'd stay and look after you.'

He gave her a weak smile. Over his legs, she put the little table she used to eat breakfast in bed when she had one of her heads. Things must have been bad if she used it for him. His favourite, no less.

His lungs rattled and his stomach rumbled. He ate, which settled his stomach.

Their mother sat on his desk chair. She watched him eat. 'The doctor's coming to see you in the afternoon. You did give us all a terrible scare.'

'It's been horrible. Any excuse and they give us a thrashing. Like they enjoy it.' He coughed again. Not as bad as before, but it hurt. 'All I did was be a bit slow in the morning drill and I had to run laps until they told me to stop instead of having my lunch.'

'Your father believed that a bit of discipline would do you good, but I said to him that too much is the opposite. He was surprised when you asked to join the cadets. We both were. The expense of the kit, but then the school said not to worry about that. It would replace the normal school uniform and even out. That should have sounded the alarm that something wasn't right.'

'I didn't want to join, but everyone was being pressured.' He stopped himself from confessing about the magazine and Ollie-the-oik's blackmail. He didn't want to put Jacquie in it.

'One of the men at my office told me about the glowing story about the school in the *Education Weekly*. I asked for a copy, and he said he'd see if he could get us one. We were so proud of you all at the Remembrance Sunday ceremony. We took a few pictures, but they're not very good. Then the red tops ran those other stories.' His mother shook her head. 'I don't know what's happening to this country, it's been awful for so long. All those strikes, and I'm not sure about the prime minister. Not like your father. He admires her and wants to give her a chance. I don't know why people from far away want to come here, but they shouldn't be subjected to violence like that attack in the estate. Those boys with the shaved heads and big boots scare me, I'm not afraid to say.'

'They're Nazis. Literal Nazis.'

She folded her arms and frowned. 'Your sister says the red top stories are true.'

His mouth went dry. Truth or lie? He nodded. The truth won. 'The Brigadier led us into that attack. I was there, but I didn't want to be. I can't go back to that school.'

The Brigadier couldn't dislodge the weirdly out of sync double heartbeat from his head. One beat sounded strong and steady, the other faded in and out. He couldn't tell which one of them belonged to him, or whether he hallucinated both.

He couldn't see. He couldn't open his eyes.

He could barely move. He thought he sat upright. That the car hadn't rolled because of the way her weight was distributed. He guessed the car that chased him hadn't been so lucky.

He heard the rain ease off and rolls of thunder sound further away. He'd evidently lost consciousness for a while for the storm to pass over.

He tried to open his eyes, and managed to get one open a bit. His head pounded and he closed his eye again. He groaned and tasted blood.

Sirens sounded in the distance, discordant against the drumming of his headache and the double heartbeat. The weak heartbeat faded, strengthened, then faded completely away.

He must have lost consciousness again for a few moments, maybe longer. Men bustled around him. Gloved hands touched his head and he wanted to bat them away, but his arms refused to obey. He moaned.

'We've got to get him out before that blaze reaches here.'

'Wait just a moment. Check his legs. Is he trapped?'

'No, he's bloody lucky. Looks like he banged his head. More blood than anything, although I'm worried about his eye. Looks like it snagged on something and has torn. Yet this beast of a car is barely dented. Lucky sod probably won't even need to spend that much on repairing it. Not like that other car.'

'Exploded like it was in the movies.'

A needle pricked the Brigadier's hand and he flinched.

'Get me that neck brace, just to be sure.'

Everything hurt and he swam in and out of consciousness. He tried to tell them he was okay. No need to fuss.

They lifted him on to a stretcher. Rolled him into an ambulance. Carried him to a hospital. They fussed around his eyes. Removed his clothes. Stuck needles in his arms. Bright lights blinded him.

Someone wiped the blood from his face. They opened his good eye and he made out a concerned face he didn't recognise. A narrow torch beam stabbed into his brain as they flashed it to check his pupil responses. The owner of the concerned face asked him to press his legs down, his feet, and his arms and hands.

'Doesn't appear to have spinal damage. Get theatre ready for his eye. We might be able to save it. When can we expect the other casualty?'

'Oh, didn't they tell you? He'll be going straight to the morgue. Car exploded into a fireball no one could survive.'

He struggled to sit up, or thought he did, but the darkness descended and pushed him down.

The police arrived at the clinic late the next morning. DI Hayes and her sergeant, an older man named Fraser, telephoned ahead so Rebecca could reorganise her list of patients. She'd already spoken to the hospital that morning, so she knew the Brigadier's surgery had been successful and he was in recovery. He had family and some old colleagues with him.

Hayes was all business and Fraser took notes. They danced around patient confidentiality, and then around the Official Secrets Act. Hayes wanted to know all about the Brigadier's demeanour, and Rebecca summarised her impression of him without providing the details of her professional opinion. Hayes asked about the longer-term problems and Rebecca explained about his amnesia.

'Do you think he's a risk to national security?'

Rebecca shook her head. 'Absolutely not. This clinic is unique in its patients and their backgrounds. All of the staff are vetted in case any of the patients let slip about things they ought not and we know to steer them away from further disclosures. I work closely with Alistair, and his amnesia affects his recollection of what I imagine to be his secretive past.'

Fraser scratched away in his notebook.

'Can you think of anyone who would want to hurt him?'

Rebecca leaned back in her chair. This was the key question. The hospital had let slip the accident involved a car chase. 'I have no personal knowledge of anyone who would want that, but I suspect his past was such that he may well have enemies. You think the accident was deliberate?'

Hayes glanced at Fraser. Fraser shifted in his seat. Hayes didn't answer immediately. 'We are not having much joy in being able to piece together exactly what happened. We know the Brigadier arrived at Brendon early in the morning and then left in his car. We know someone stole another teacher's car at Brendon and gave chase. Identifying the pursuer has proved… difficult.'

'I'd say impossible, ma'am.' Fraser glanced up, his face grim. 'Unless he confided in the doctor here.'

Hayes uncrossed her legs and leaned forward. 'Can I speak in confidence?'

Rebecca nodded. 'Of course.'

'The pursuing vehicle impacted the Brigadier's car at speed, which caused the Brigadier's car to go off the road. The pursuing vehicle looks like it spun and swerved away, and then it exploded. The resulting fire was so intense that anyone in it was destroyed completely. The car itself is a total write-off.'

'There's no clue about the driver's identity.' Fraser cleared his throat. 'None at all. Not even any trace that forensics can do anything with.'

Hayes fixed Rebecca in her gaze. 'Witnesses at the school have not been wholly forthcoming. They seemed unaware that the Brigadier was here as an in-patient.'

'That's odd.' Rebecca frowned. 'I know they've been in regular contact with our matron, and I was led to believe they organised a replacement. Alistair was put out to find someone living in his rooms at the school.'

They finished up and the two detectives left. Late the next afternoon, as Rebecca ended her working day, Detective Sergeant Fraser telephoned.

'The DI asked me to let you know that we're wrapping up the investigation, pending the coroner's inquest.'

'I see. Was the other driver identified?'

'That is one of the mysteries to be left unsolved. Pressure from Whitehall, is what I've been told, and no doubt I've told you too much.'

Rebecca paused. 'I understand.' Not that she did, but she could guess.

CHAPTER TWENTY
Comfortably Numb

THE BRIGADIER listened to the hospital radio's barrage of Christmas songs and smiled at the memory of his son, Mariama, who had paid a visit alongside a few old friends, including Anne and Bill Bishop and Harry Sullivan. At least some memories stayed. Unlike the accident...

He still wasn't sure what had happened. He remembered the car ramming into his. He remembered the driver of that car being his doppelgänger, his double from another version of Earth. The mysterious man stole his home and job like a cuckoo barging into the nest, and caused just as much chaos.

And that was where his memory stuttered and stammered to a halt. The idea of different versions of Earth from which doppelgängers came and went was ridiculous. Preposterous. The stuff of science fiction, and not the type of thing a man with his career would ever entertain.

He'd mentioned it to Anne, once he'd had a moment alone with her.

'We had some experiences, Alistair,' she'd told him with a gentle smile. 'I know your memory is foggy, but I think it's probably true. That other Earth... The Schizoid Earth, that's what we used to call it. We thought it was all over, but... You should ring Dylan, when you're well enough. Trust me, he'll understand.'

His nephew. They hadn't spoken for a while. The Brigadier decided he would do just that, give Dylan a call. Maybe even a visit, when he was strong enough. Yes, it would be nice to visit Bledoe again.

A doctor entered with a nurse in tow. The Brigadier didn't recognise either of the two women. The nurse elevated his bed so he sat up rather than lay down, while the doctor fussed over the clipboard. The doctor plonked the clipboard back in the slot and beamed at the Brigadier in that way consultant doctors did.

'How are we feeling?'

'Like I've been trampled by a herd of elephants.'

The doctor nodded. 'What do you remember?'

'Losing control of my car and being trapped in her.' He glanced at the doctor and quickly looked away again. 'It.' He harrumphed quietly. 'Lots of flashing lights. I'm not sure of anything following that.' He touched the bandages that wrapped the side of his head and covered an eye. He recalled the phantom injuries he'd experienced at odd times throughout the summer.

'You were lucky. If you'd been driving a different car you may not have survived. As it is, you knocked your head and it resulted in serious lacerations into your eye socket.'

'I'm not...' The Brigadier coughed. 'I'm not going to lose it, am I? I mean, I do have a spare if the need arises...' His attempted humour left a sour taste in his mouth.

'Your eye sustained some damage, but we saved it and it ought to heal with rest. It was a tricky bit of surgery, if I say so myself, and we also ensured you'll have minimal scarring. Apart from that, there's bruising across your body, arms and legs, but no bones broken. There are signs of concussion, so we'll keep you in for at least another twenty-four hours. We've notified the clinic in which you've been a patient, and the police want to have a word. Although I understand they're already wrapping up their enquiries.' She shook her head as though she didn't approve. 'I passed on your blood-alcohol level, which was nil.'

'The school?'

She arched an eyebrow.

'Brendon Public School. It's where I teach and live. Normally.'

The nurse cleared her throat. 'The flowers are from there, and a Miss Nugent has telephoned asking after him. There does appear to be a bit of confusion about where the Brigadier has been prior to the accident.'

'A matter for the police, I would say. Our job is to patch

people up, not investigate such things.' The doctor nodded primly, turned on her heels and left the room.

The nurse remained. 'Are you comfortable, Brigadier?'

He started to nod, and stopped. His head hurt to move too much. He cleared his throat. 'Comfortable enough, yes. Thank you.'

The nurse checked a jug of water sat on a table to the side. She seemed satisfied with it.

'Someone was impersonating me at the school while I was away.'

The nurse smiled softly at him. 'Doctor's right. That is a matter for the police.' She turned to leave as well.

'Do you know what happened to the other driver?'

She paused and chewed her lip. She turned back. 'I believe he died, Brigadier. His car exploded leaving very little trace.'

The Brigadier laid back and blinked with his good eye. He recalled extracts from conversations he overheard from the men who crowded around him at the time of the collision. They expressed surprise about the explosion.

Something else teased at his memory. A doubled-up heartbeat. Something else that was impossible but yet he took in his stride, even though he had no idea as to why.

The squeak of the nurse's shoe on the linoleum floor made him turn towards her again. 'Nurse?'

She stopped once more and turned towards him. She smiled. 'My heart.'

'Is there a problem, Brigadier?'

He heard the alarm in her voice and saw her half twist as though to summon help. He put up his hand. 'It's fine, but I just wanted to know if anyone expressed any worry about it since I arrived, or during surgery.'

She clopped over to the foot of his bed and withdrew the clipboard that held his notes. She flicked through the pages and frowned. Shaking her head, she looked up at him. 'According to your notes, you have a good bill of health. Pulse and pressure are both in healthy ranges, and there's nothing about any concerns raised during theatre. Why do you ask?'

He half-smiled. 'No reason.'

She left and he settled back. He wanted to talk to Dr Pelham-Rose about what had happened, and how he felt about it all.

On Wednesday evening, the Armstrongs ate their tea as a complete family for the first time in over six years. It progressed through as strained an atmosphere as could be expected.

Their mother began the awkward conversation. 'Your father and I have talked about this, and as you're both sixteen now, you should have a say as well.'

Their father said nothing, but he glowered with a deep frown.

Their mother continued. 'Given what has happened at Brendon, we no longer feel that it is an appropriate school for our son.'

Jack grinned. 'It really isn't.'

Their father grunted. 'I will not hear of you wanting to quit school this year. I know you're legally able to leave, but a good education is essential in this job market. You're smart enough to pursue some A-levels, and you should.'

Jacquie noted that neither of their olds included her in their warning. She swallowed down her instinct to take umbrage when once she would have blurted it out.

Their mother nodded. 'Jacqueline's school might not have the same prestigious reputation as Brendon, but I am impressed by the way her grades have improved this year.'

Jacquie glanced at Jack. He winked at her and under the table used his fingers to spell out that he'd had words with their mother. 'Keep quiet. It'll come.'

Their mother glanced at their father, who nodded, his mouth pressed closed. 'We are open to the idea of Jack enrolling at Jacqueline's school.'

Jacquie gaped. 'For serious?' She looked at both their olds in turn.

Their father crossed his arms. He directed his gaze at her. 'Any sign of trouble, no matter how small, and you, young lady, will leave both the school and our house. Understand?'

Rage flared within her, but Jack's hand on her thigh stopped her. She nodded, sullen. Glanced at their mother. She saw the worry. She nodded once more. 'I understand, and I promise.' Even though it was all grossly unfair. She was the better student.

'Good.' Her father twitched a smile.

On Friday afternoon, shortly after lunchtime, Dr Pelham-Rose went to visit the Brigadier in the hospital. She found him easily enough, and tapped on his doorjamb with a knuckle.

'Dr Pelham-Rose? How good to see you.' He placed the book he was reading down on his lap and used his finger as a bookmark.

'Alistair.' Rebecca walked to the chair beside him and perched herself on it. 'Please call me Rebecca. This isn't a professional visit.' She smiled at him. 'You look quite dashing with that eyepatch. Like a Hollywood pirate.'

He touched it self-consciously. 'The doctors say they'll remove it in a few weeks when they're certain the eye's healed. I was lucky not to lose it, apparently.'

'You sound sceptical.'

'I don't mean to.' He huffed a long sigh. 'I was getting ready to return to normal life, and here I am back in hospital.'

'Indeed. But you're going to be all right? Physically, I mean.'

'Oh, yes. Nothing broken, except my pride. Even my car escaped with just a few scratches. Not like the other man's.' He stopped. Shook his head slowly, sadly. 'I shouldn't speak ill of the dead.'

'Did you find out who he was?'

He folded his arms and looked away. 'I'm not sure.'

'I see.' She slid back in the chair. 'The police have been quite strange about it all. The detective sergeant informed me that Whitehall took over the investigation and warned the local police off. Have they seen you?'

'Briefly. A constable, yesterday. I spoke to a few old colleagues, and they assured me things are being taken care of.'

'I told you this isn't a professional visit, and it's not, but do you need to discuss anything?'

He looked up at the ceiling. 'No, actually.' He brought his head down and glanced at her, then away. 'Which means I ought to tell you that I think my symptoms that began in April were connected somehow to this man. What I can't tell you is how I know this.'

'Do you mind me asking why you think this?' She shifted forward, her attention fully on him.

'The double heartbeat. I heard it along with the nightmares months ago. Heard isn't quite the right word. Experienced? Felt?' He thumped his chest near his heart with a fist. 'Two hearts, beating like one. That and he told me he arrived in an erupting volcano, which matches those nightmares of mine. All of these things I should regard as unlikely to be true, and yet, I am told, they're the sort of thing I'm used to dealing with.'

'Which would be the sort of thing Whitehall would want to keep quiet about.'

'Official secrets. Precisely.' He nodded forcefully.

They sat quietly for a few moments. Rebecca pondered over what Alistair told her. Any other patient, and she would be making her excuses and telephoning Dr Kent for an immediate hospitalisation in the clinic. It wasn't Alistair's sincerity – she'd worked with plenty of patients who excelled at putting on a sincere front. No, his explanations fit everything they'd spoken about over the months, as weird as that all was. She closed her eyes for a moment, and sighed softly.

'Alistair, there was another reason why I came to visit you today.'

He turned to face her.

'I was never going to stay in England for ever. It's where I was born, but I like to travel and see the world.'

'And cure it of its ills?'

She blushed. 'One can but try. A hospital in Ecuador has accepted me for a year.'

He reached a hand out and she clasped it. 'Thank you, Rebecca. For everything.'

Her heart ached at leaving, but she made her excuses and left.

EPILOGUE

JACK'S RECOVERY from the flu quickened once their olds confirmed his immediate transfer to Jacquie's school. They both solemnly promised to behave and concentrate on their O-levels.

Friday would be their first day walking through the school gates together. They didn't have all the same classes, and in the few they did they deliberately sat apart. At lunch, they both gravitated to the library. Jacquie introduced him to the girls she maintained an acquaintance with, and later the librarian.

Jacquie asked Jack about contacting his friends at Brendon. He screwed up his face about that. 'Not yet.' He folded his arms across his chest. 'I will, I mean, but I'm not sure I want to just yet.'

She nodded. 'I heard the Brigadier that lived is still in the hospital.'

His frown deepened. 'Anything about the other one?'

She shook her head. 'No one seems to be remotely interested in it, too, which is weird.'

'Maybe we should let it be.' He picked at a bit of skin flaking from his thumbnail.

'For serious?'

'I suppose it would be good to check the good one lived, and not the fashy one. I mean, for my old school. Alfie might want to know, to put Ollie-the-oik in his place.' He half-smiled, sheepishly. It felt so good to not be at Brendon any more.

'Let's go after school.'

They bumped fists with each other, ate their sandwiches, and when the bell rang headed to their afternoon lessons. After the final bell clanged, releasing them for the day, they met at the gates. Jacquie checked he was still okay with their plan, and he nodded.

'If it is the tweedy one, we can apologise to him.'

'And if it's the fashy one?'

'He should apologise to me.' Jack shoved his hands deep into his trouser pockets and walked faster.

They caught the bus and sat silently together. Jack followed his sister as she did the detective work to find the Brigadier. They strolled past a flower shop. He tapped her shoulder and nodded at them.

She frowned. 'Got the dosh for them?'

He shook his head.

'What if he's the wrong one?'

He shrugged, and twisted a grin. They rode up the lift. 'Smells bad.'

She tilted her head to one side. 'Disinfectant, body waste, and boiled cabbage.'

Their school shoes squeaked along the polished floor. Doctors and nurses gathered around a central area, talking in hushed tones. A few people in ordinary clothes shuffled at the same speed as the pyjama-clad patients they accompanied.

Jacquie counted the doors to the wards. 'Here he is.'

The door stood open to a small room with four beds. Only one was occupied. The Brigadier, wearing an eyepatch, sat up reading a book. Jack backed up a few steps, but the Brigadier looked up and caught him.

'Mr Armstrong?'

Jack glanced at Jacquie. 'Tweedy.' He grinned. She pushed him forward. 'Yes, sir. Do you remember my sister? Jacquie.'

The Brigadier rested his book in his lap. 'How could I forget you? Come in, come in.'

They shuffled in.

'What brings you two here?' His one eye gazed at them both.

Jacquie said, 'An uncle of ours is poorly. He's in another ward, asleep, so we, ah…'

'Went for a walk and found you here, sir.'

The Brigadier's forehead furrowed and he winced. 'That's not a Brendon uniform, Mr Armstrong.'

'No, sir. I left.'

'Expelled?'

Beside him, Jacquie huffed. She folded her arms.

'No, sir.' Jack took a breath. 'We know what happened.'

'The accident?'

'Before that, sir. Remember I was with you when you lost it at the obelisk?'

'I should have known you two would be behind those papers. Do you have them?' He leaned forward in his bed.

Jacquie took a step towards the Brigadier. 'The Ministry of Defence sent them to me. I was curious about you and your service record, but Jack says your twin brother turned up. We have the documents. They're safe, not that they say much.' She tilted her head to one side.

The Brigadier regarded her for a few moments with a stony silence. He turned his attention back to Jack. 'I don't have a twin brother.'

Jacquie said, 'Alfie Granger and I saw both of you, so if he's not your twin, who is he?'

The Brigadier turned back to stare with his one eye at Jacquie. 'A man who looked like me, yes, but we're not related. He's gone, anyway.'

'Arrested?' Jacquie glanced quickly at Jack.

'No.' The Brigadier's voice softened. 'He wasn't as lucky as I was in the accident that did this.' He waved one hand in front of his eyepatch.

The doctor on her rounds dropped a hint that the Brigadier might be able to leave the hospital over the weekend. She was pleased with his progress, but hammered home the point about his eye needing to be covered at all times until she gave him the all-clear. The Brigadier did his best impression of a compliant patient. She had done a good job, but her bedside manner left a lot to be desired. She was no butterfly.

He wasn't surprised at Dr Pelham-Rose's news. England's loss would be Ecuador's gain, in his humble opinion. Yet again, he appreciated her taking his ideas seriously. She even agreed to organise his formal discharge from the clinic.

Which left him to worry about the school. He felt guilty about Mr Wade's car, even though he hadn't stolen it. His doppelgänger had, and his doppelgänger died or disappeared. For now, at least. Fact remained, he had to shoulder some of the responsibility of what his doppelgänger had done while impersonating him. Duty, in a sense.

He felt the brick walls in his mind clunk around at that. Like there was something hidden away desperate to get out.

On Saturday morning, the weekend doctor bore the bad news that Monday would be the day for leaving, if his main doctor approved. The Brigadier grumbled quietly to himself about institutions failing to look after the human beings in their care. Raising hope, only to dash it because of bureaucracy.

At eleven o'clock, Mr Newton arrived. He wore his usual weekend outfit of casual trousers, an open-necked shirt, with a blazer and overcoat. He carried a brown paper bag stuffed full of grapes. The Brigadier thanked him and asked him to sit.

'You're not going to fire me, are you?'

'No, no. Certainly not, Brigadier. However, an explanation would be helpful.'

The Brigadier sat up straighter. He'd thought over what he would do should the headmaster ask the inevitable question. The man didn't dally over small talk, but then he did have a school's reputation to rescue. The Brigadier cleared his throat.

'As you know, I've suffered from amnesia from that incident two years ago. I've had a few moments this year when I needed the assistance of the clinic where I was admitted in '77. My absences have been due to that.'

'These incidents include you forgetting your own work?'

The Brigadier pressed his mouth shut. He nodded. 'Also my uncharacteristic behaviour on occasion.'

'Leading the boys to the estate? I'm not sure what to believe since one of the boys claims the tabloids reported correctly on that. It's one thing to extend the cadets, but quite another to deliberately provoke violence.'

The Brigadier narrowed his good eye. 'The Armstrong boy?'

'Of course. He's left, and good riddance.'

'I promise that I won't lead the cadets anywhere in future without your express permission.'

Newton stared at him for a few moments, then nodded.

Well, good. I don't mind your encouraging a greater involvement of the whole school, but perhaps we can reach a balance between that, school sports, and the academic stream.'

'Yes, of course.'

Newton nodded once more. 'Good, good.' He clapped his hands on his knees. 'The accident?'

'Ah, that I'm afraid I can't tell you much about.'

'No one can, not even the police.' Newton shook his head. 'It's quite unbelievable. Mr Wade is concerned about who stole his car, although replacing the car itself is less of a worry. He was adequately insured, and the police have given enough information to satisfy his insurance company. Your car needs a bit of work on it, but all things considered it's a miracle. For a vintage car, it's indestructible.'

'A bit like me.'

'Yes, Brigadier.' Newton sighed. 'A bit like you.'

And the Brigadier smiled.